D0409879

CANCELLED

CANCELLED

The Ninth Hour

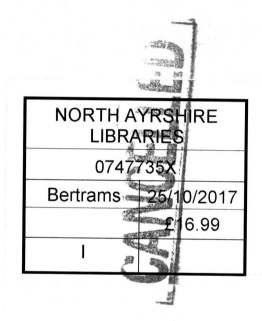

NORTH AYRSHIRE LIBRARIES	
0747735X	
Bertrams	25/10/2017
	£16.99
I	

The
Ninth Hour

Alice
McDermott

B L O O M S B U R Y

LONDON · OXFORD · NEW YORK · NEW DELHI · SYDNEY

Bloomsbury Publishing
An imprint of Bloomsbury Publishing Plc

50 Bedford Square
London
WC1B 3DP
UK

1385 Broadway
New York
NY 10018
USA

www.bloomsbury.com

BLOOMSBURY and the Diana logo are trademarks of Bloomsbury
Publishing Plc

First published in Great Britain 2017

© Alice McDermott, 2017

Alice McDermott has asserted her right under the Copyright, Designs and
Patents Act, 1988, to be identified as Author of this work.

An excerpt from *The Ninth Hour* originally appeared, in slightly different form,
in the *New Yorker*.

This is a work of fiction. Names and characters are the product of the author's
imagination and any resemblance to actual persons, living or dead,
is entirely coincidental.

All rights reserved. No part of this publication may be reproduced or transmitted
in any form or by any means, electronic or mechanical, including photocopying,
recording, or any information storage or retrieval system, without prior
permission in writing from the publishers.

No responsibility for loss caused to any individual or organization acting on or
refraining from action as a result of the material in this publication can be
accepted by Bloomsbury or the author.

British Library Cataloguing-in-Publication Data
A catalogue record for this book is available from the British Library.

ISBN: HB: 978-1-4088-5460-0
        TPB: 978-1-4088-5461-7
        ePub: 978-1-4088-5462-4

2 4 6 8 10 9 7 5 3 1

Designed by Abby Kagan
Printed and bound in Great Britain by CPI Group (UK) Ltd, Croydon CR0 4YY

MIX
Paper from
responsible sources
FSC® C020471

To find out more about our authors and books visit www.bloomsbury.com. Here
you will find extracts, author interviews, details of forthcoming events and the
option to sign up for our newsletters.

For Sister Mary Rose, C.I.J.

The
Ninth Hour

These Short Dark Days

FEBRUARY 3 WAS A DARK AND DANK DAY altogether: cold spitting rain in the morning and a low, steel-gray sky the rest of the afternoon.

At four, Jim convinced his wife to go out to do her shopping before full darkness fell. He closed the door on her with a gentle wave. His hair was thinning and he was missing a canine on the right side, but he was nevertheless a handsome man who, at thirty-two, might still have passed for twenty. Heavy brows and deep-set, dark-lashed eyes that had been making women catch their breath since he was sixteen. Even if he had grown bald and toothless, as he seemed fated to do, the eyes would have served him long into old age.

His overcoat was on the hall tree beside the door. He lifted it and rolled it lengthwise against his thighs. Then he fitted it over the threshold, tucking the cloth of the sleeves and the hem as well as he could into the space beneath the door. Theirs was a railroad flat: kitchen in the back, dining room, living room, bedroom in the front. He needed only to push the heavy couch a few feet farther along the wall to block his wife's return. He stood on the seat to check that the glass transom above the door was tightly closed. Then he stepped down. He straightened the lace on the back of the couch and brushed away the shallow impression his foot had made on the horsehair cushion.

In the kitchen, he pressed his cheek to the cold enamel of the stove and slid his hand into the tight space between it and the yellow wall. He groped a bit. They kept a baited mousetrap back there, or had in the past, and it made him careful. He found the rubber hose that connected the oven to the gas tap and pulled at it as vigorously as he could, given the confined space. There was a satisfying pop, and a hiss that quickly faded. He straightened up with the hose in his hand. The kitchen window looked into the gray courtyard where, on better days, there would be lines of clothes baking in the sun, although the floor of the deep courtyard, even in the prettiest weather, was a junkyard and a jungle. There were rats and bedsprings and broken crates. A tangle of city-bred vegetation: a sickly tree, black vines, a long-abandoned attempt at a garden. From rag-and-bone man to wayward drunk, any voice that ever rose out of its depths was the voice of someone up to no good. Once, Annie, sitting on the windowsill with a clothespin in her mouth and a basket of wet linen at her feet, saw a man drag a small child through the muck and tie him to the rough pole that held the line. She watched the man take off his belt, and, with the first crack of it against the child's bare calves, she began to yell. She threw the clothespins at him, a potted ivy plant, and then the metal washbasin still filled with soapy water. Leaning halfway out the window herself, she threatened to call the police, the fire department, the Gerrity Society. The man, as if pursued only by a change in the weather, a sudden rain, glanced up briefly, shrugged, and then untied the sobbing child and dragged him away. "I know who you are," Annie cried. Although she didn't. She was an easy liar. She paced the street for an hour that afternoon, waiting for the man and the boy to reappear.

When Jim ran into the kitchen at the sound of her shouting, she was from head to waist out the window, with only one toe on the kitchen floor. He'd had to put his hands on her hips to ease her out of danger. Just one more of what had turned out to be too many days he hadn't gone in to work or had arrived too late for his shift.

His trouble was with time. Bad luck for a trainman, even on the BRT. His trouble was, he liked to refuse time. He delighted in refusing it. He would come to the end of a long night, to the inevitability of 5 a.m.—that boundary, that abrupt wall toward which all the night's pleasures ran (drink, talk, sleep, or Annie's warm flesh)—and while other men, poor sheep, gave in every morning, turned like lambs in the chute from the pleasures of sleep or drink or talk or love to the duties of the day, he had been aware since his childhood that with the easiest refusal, eyes shut, he could continue as he willed. I'm not going, he'd only have to murmur. I won't be constrained. Of course, it didn't always require refusing the whole day. Sometimes just the pleasure of being an hour or two late was enough to remind him that he, at least, was his own man, that the hours of his life—and what more precious commodity did he own?—belonged to himself alone.

Two weeks ago they had discharged him for unreliability and

insubordination. Inside the shell of his flesh, the man he was—not the blushing, humiliated boy who stood ham-handed before them—simply shook off the blow and turned away, indifferent, free. But Annie wept when he told her, and then said angrily, through her tears, that there was a baby coming, knowing even as she said it that to break the news to him in this way was to condemn the child to a life of trouble.

He took the tea towels she had left to dry on the sink, wound them into ropes, and placed them along the sill of the kitchen window.

He carried the length of rubber tubing through the living room and into the bedroom. He slipped off his shoes, put the tube to his mouth, as if to pull smoke. He had seen this in a picture book back home: a fat sultan on a red pillow doing much the same. He sat on the edge of the bed. He bowed his head and prayed: *Now and at the hour of our death.* He lay back on the bed. The room had gotten dimmer still. *Hour of our. Our hour.* At home, his mother, the picture book spread out on her wide lap, would reach behind him to turn the clock face to the wall.

Within this very hour he would put his head on her shoulder once again. Or would he? There were moments when his faith fell out from under him like a trapdoor. He stood up. Found his nightshirt underneath his pillow and twisted it, too. Then placed it along the edge of the one window, again pushing the material into the narrow crevice where the frame met the sill, knowing all the while that the gesture was both ineffectual and unnecessary.

Down in the street, there was a good deal of movement—women mostly, because the shops were open late and the office workers had not yet begun to file home. Dark coats and hats. A baby buggy or two, the wheels turning up a pale spray. He watched two nuns in black cloaks and white wimples, their heads bent together, skim over the gray sidewalk. He watched until they were gone, his cheek now pressed to the cool window glass. When he turned back into the room, the light had failed in every corner and he had to put out his hand as he walked around the pale bed, back to his own side.

He stretched out once again. Playfully lifted the hose to one eye, as if he would see along its length the black corridor of a subway tunnel, lit gold at the farthest end by the station ahead. Then he placed the hose in his mouth and breathed deeply once more. He felt the nausea, the sudden vertigo, he had been expecting all along but had forgotten he was expecting. He closed his eyes and swallowed. Outside, a mother called to a child. There was the slow clopping of a horse-drawn cart. The feathered sound of wheels turning in street water. Something dropped to the floor in the apartment just above him—a sewing basket, perhaps— there was a thud and then a scratchy chorus of wooden spools spinning. Or maybe it was coins, spilled from a fallen purse.

AT SIX, the streetlamps against the wet dark gave a polish to the air. There was the polish of lamplight, too, on streetcar tracks and windowpanes and across the gleaming surface of the scattered black puddles in the street. Reflection of lamplight as well on the rump of the remaining fire truck and on the pale faces of the gathered crowd, with an extra gold sparkle and glint on anyone among them who wore glasses. Sister St. Saviour, for instance, a Little Nursing Sister of the Sick Poor, who had spent the afternoon in the vestibule of the Woolworth's at Borough Hall, her alms basket in her lap. She was now on her way back to the convent, her bladder full, her ankles swollen, her round glasses turned toward the lamplight and the terrible scent of doused fire on the winter air.

The pouch with the money she had collected today was tied to her belt; the small basket she used was tucked under her cloak and under her arm. The house where the fire had been looked startled: the windows of all four floors were wide open, shade cords and thin curtains flailing in the cold air. Although the rest of the building was dark, the vestibule at the top of the stone stoop was weirdly lit, crowded with policemen and firemen carrying lamps. The front door was open, as, it appeared, was the door to the apartment on the parlor floor. Sister St. Saviour wanted only to walk on, to get to her own convent, her own room, her own toilet—her fingers were cold and her ankles swollen and her thin basket was crushed awkwardly under her arm—but still she brushed through the crowd and climbed the steps. There was a limp fire hose running along the shadowy base of the stone banister. Two of the officers in the hallway, turning to see her, tipped their hats and then put out their hands as if she had been summoned. "Sister," one of them said. He was flushed and per-spiring, and even in the dull light, she could see that the cuffs of his jacket were singed. "Right in here."

The apartment was crowded with people, perhaps every ten-ant in the place. The smell of smoke and wet ash, burned wool, burned hair, was part and parcel of the thick pools of candlelight in the room, and of the heavy drone of whispered conversation. There were two groups: one was gathered around a middle-aged man in shirtsleeves and carpet slippers who was sitting in a chair by the window, his face in his hands. The other, across the room, hovered beside a woman stretched out on a dark couch, under a fringed lamp that was not lit. She had a cloth applied to her head, but she seemed to be speaking sensibly to the thin young man who leaned over her. When she saw the nun, the woman raised a limp hand and said, "She's in the bedroom, Sister." Her arm from wrist to elbow was glistening with a shiny salve—butter, perhaps.

"You might leave off with that grease," Sister said. "Unless you're determined to be basted." The young man turned at this, laughing. He wore a gray fedora and had a milk tooth in his grin. "Have the courtesy to doff your hat," she told him.

It was Sister St. Saviour's vocation to enter the homes of strangers, mostly the sick and the elderly, to breeze into their apartments and to sail comfortably through their rooms, to open their linen closets or china cabinets or bureau drawers—to peer into their toilets or the soiled handkerchiefs clutched in their hands—but the frequency with which she inserted herself into the homes of strangers had not diminished over the years, her initial impulse to stand back, to shade her eyes. She dipped her head as she passed through the parlor, into a narrow corridor, but she saw enough to conclude that a Jewish woman lived here—the woman on the couch, she was certain, a Jewish woman, she only guessed, because of the fringed lampshade, the upright piano against the far wall, the dark oil paintings in the narrow hallway that seemed to depict two ordinary peasants, not saints. A place unprepared for visitors, arrested, as things so often were by crisis and tragedy, in the midst of what should have been a private hour. She saw as she passed by that there was a plate on the small table in the tiny kitchen, that it contained a half piece of bread, well bitten and stained with a dark gravy. A glass of tea on the edge of a folded newspaper.

In the candlelit bedroom, where two more policemen were conferring in the far corner, there were black stockings hung over the back of a chair, a mess of hairbrushes and handkerchiefs on the low dresser, a gray corset on the threadbare carpet at the foot of the bed. There was a girl on the bed, sideways, her dark skirt spread around her, as if she had fallen there from some height. Her back was to the room and her face to the wall. Another woman leaned over her, a hand on the girl's shoulder.

The policemen nodded to see the nun, and the shorter one took off his cap as he moved toward her. He, too, was singed about the cuffs. He had a heavy face, stale breath, and bad dentures, but there was compassion in the way he gestured with his short arms toward the girl on the bed, toward the ceiling and the upstairs apartment where the fire had been, a compassion that seemed to weigh down his limbs. Softhearted, Sister thought, one of us. The girl, he said, had come in from her shopping and found the door to her place blocked from the inside. She went to her neighbors, the man next door and the woman who lived here. They helped her push the door open, and then the man lit a match to hold against the darkness. There was an explosion. Luckily, the policeman said, he himself was just at the corner and was able to put the fire out while neighbors carried the three of them down here. Inside, in the bedroom, he found a young man on the bed. Asphyxiated. The girl's husband.

Sister St. Saviour drew in her breath, blessed herself. "He fell asleep, poor man," she said softly. "The pilot light must have gone out."

The officer glanced over his shoulder, toward the bed, and then took the Sister's elbow. He walked her out to the narrow hall. Now they stood in the kitchen doorway; the arrested tableau: the bitten bread, the dark gravy, the glass of reddish tea on a small wooden table, the chair pushed back (there had been an urgent knock on the door), the newspaper with its crooked lines of black ink.

"He killed himself," the officer whispered, his breath sour, as if in reaction to the situation he was obliged to report. "Turned on the gas. Lucky he didn't take everyone else with him."

Accustomed as she was to breezing into the lives of strangers, Sister accepted the information with only a discreet nod, but in the space of it, in the time it took her merely to turn her cheek and bow her head, her eyes disappeared behind the stiff edge of her bonnet. When she looked up again—her eyes behind the glasses were small and brown and caught the little bit of light the way only a hard surface could, marble or black tin, nothing watery—the truth of the suicide was both acknowledged and put away. She had pried handkerchiefs from the tight fists of young women, opened them to see the blood mixed with phlegm, and then balled them up again, nodding in just such a way. She had breezed into the homes of strangers and seen the bottles in the bin, the poor contents of a cupboard, the bruise in a hidden place, seen as well, once, a pale, thumb-sized infant in a basin filled with blood and, saying nothing at all, had bowed her head and nodded in just such a way.

"What's the girl's name?" she asked.

The officer frowned. "Mc-something. Annie, they called her. Irish extraction," he added. "That's why I thought to call for you."

Sister smiled. Those button eyes had dark depths. "Is that so?" she said. They both knew no one had called for her. She had been on her way home, merely passing by. She dipped her head again, forgiving him his vanity—didn't he say, too, that he'd put out the fire himself? "I'll go to her, then," she said.

As she stepped away she saw the milk-toothed young man, still in his hat, approach the officer. "Hey, O'Neil," the man shouted. No courtesy in him.

Inside the shadowed bedroom, the neighbor woman who stood at the bedside had her eyes elsewhere, on the gloaming at the far side of the cluttered room. She was a stout woman, about forty. No doubt there were children waiting to be put to bed, a husband to be placated. A woman with a family of her own, with troubles of her own, could not be expected to attend to the sorrows of another indefinitely.

The nun only nodded as the two exchanged places. At the door of the room, the woman looked over her shoulder and whispered, "Can I do anything for you, Sister?"

Sister St. Saviour recalled a joke she had once made, when a young nun asked her the same, in the midst of a busy morning. "Yes. Can you go tinkle for me?"

But she said, "We'll be fine." It was what she wanted this Annie Mc-something to hear.

When the woman was gone, Sister reached inside her cloak and took the small basket from under her arm. It was a flimsy thing, woven of unblessed palms, and much worse the wear for being crushed against her body so long. She straightened and reshaped it a bit, catching as she did the green scent that the warmth of her own flesh and the work of her hands could sometimes coax from the dried reeds. She placed the basket on the table beside the bed and untied the money pouch from her belt. It was all coins today, mostly pennies. She placed the pouch in the basket and then sat carefully on the side of the bed, her kidneys aching, her feet throbbing inside her shoes. She looked at the girl's form, the length of her back and the curve of her young hip, her thin legs beneath the wide skirt. Suddenly the girl turned in the bed and threw herself into Sister's lap, weeping.

Sister St. Saviour put her hand to the girl's dark hair. It was thick, and soft as silk. A thing of luxurious beauty. Sister lifted the heavy knot of it that was coming undone at the nape of her neck and brushed a strand from her cheek.

This much the nun was certain of: the husband had cherished this girl with the beautiful hair. Love was not the trouble. Money, more likely. Alcohol. Madness. The day and time itself: late afternoon in early February, was there a moment of the year better suited for despair? Sister herself had had the very same thought earlier today, during her long hours of begging in the drafty vestibule. We're all feeling it, she'd thought—we being all who passed along the street and in and out of the store, wet-shouldered, stooped, all who saw her and pretended not to, all who scowled and all (though not very many on this dank day) who reached into a pocket or a purse as they approached—we're all feeling it, she'd thought, in this vale of tears: the weight of the low sky and the listless rain and the damp depths of this endless winter, the sour smell of the vestibule, the brimstone breath of the subway, of the copper coins, the cold that slips in behind your spine and hollows you out at the core. Six and a half hours she'd sat begging today, so weighted by the weather and the time of year that she'd been unable to stir herself from her perch to face the daily humiliation of making use of the store's public stalls. And so she had left her chair an hour earlier than usual.

"What we must do," she said at last, "is to put one foot in front of the other." It was her regular introductory phrase. "Have you had your dinner?" she said. The girl shook her head against the nun's thigh. "Are there relations we can call for you?" Again she shook her head. "No one," she whispered. "Just Jim and me." Sister had the impulse to lift the girl's shoulder a bit, take the pressure of it off her own aching bladder, but resisted. She could endure it a little longer. "You'll need a place to stay," she said. "For tonight, anyway."

Now the girl pulled away and raised her face to the dim light. She was neither as young nor as pretty as Sister had imagined. It was a plain, round face, swollen with tears, streaked with wet strands of the lovely hair. "Where will I bury him?" she asked. In her eyes the nun saw the determination—no result of the Sister's admonition, but rather what the woman herself was made of—to put one foot in front of the other. "We've got a plot in Calvary," she said. "We got it when we were married. But the Church will never allow it now."

"Have you got the deed?" she asked, and the girl nodded.

"Where?"

"Upstairs," she said. "In the sideboard."

Gently, Sister touched the girl's cheek. Not as young or as pretty as she had first imagined, but already the face was familiar: the arch of the heavy eyebrows, the slight protrusion of the upper lip, the line of beauty marks along the cheek. Despair had weighted the day. God Himself was helpless against it—Sister St. Saviour believed this. She believed that God held His head in His hands all the while a young man in the apartment above slipped off this gray life—collar and yoke—not for lack of love, but for the utter inability to go on, to climb, once again, out of the depths of a cold February day, a dark and waning afternoon. God wept, she believed this, even as she had gotten off her chair in the lobby of Woolworth's an hour before her usual time, had turned onto the street where there was a fire truck, a dispersing crowd, the lamplight caught in shallow puddles, even as she had climbed the stone steps—footsore and weary and needing a toilet, but going up anyway, although no one had sent for her.

There had been the shadow of the slackened fire hose along the balustrade, like the sloughed skin of a great snake, which should have told her then that the worst was already done.

Once, when she was a younger nun, she'd been sent to a squalid apartment filled with wretched children where a skeletal woman, made old, discolored, barely human, by pain, was in the last throes of her disease. "There's nothing to be done," Sister Miriam had advised before they opened the door. And then as they entered—there was the tremendous animal odor of decay, the woman's hoarse moans, the famished children's fraught silence—she added, "Do what you can."

"Your man fell asleep," Sister St. Saviour whispered now. "The flame went out. It was a wet and unfortunate day." She paused to make sure the girl had heard. "He belongs in Calvary," she said. "You paid for the plot, didn't you?" The girl nodded slowly. "Well, that's where he'll go."

In her thirty-seven years of living in this city, Sister had collected any number of acquaintances who could surmount the many rules and regulations—Church rules and city rules and what Sister Miriam called the rules of polite society—that complicated the lives of women: Catholic women in particular and poor women in general. Her own little Tammany, Sister Miriam called it.

She could get this woman's husband buried in Calvary. If it was all done quickly enough, she could manage it.

"How long were you and Jim married?" the nun asked her. She understood that there was some small resurrection in just speaking the man's name.

"Two years," the girl said to the ceiling. And then she brushed her fingertips over her belly. "I've got a baby coming in summer."

Sister nodded. All right. God had His head out of His hands

now, at least. He knew the future. "All right," she said out loud. There would be a baby to care for in the summer. For once, she would not foist the diapering and the spitting up onto one of the younger nuns. She nearly smiled. Out of the depths— the phrase came to her like a fresh scent on the air—the promise of a baby this summer. A green scent coaxed out of dried reeds.

The girl raised one hand from her stomach and clutched the crown of her hair. "He lost his job," she said. "They let him go. The BRT. He was at odd ends."

Gently, Sister moved Annie's hand from out of her hair—it was a mad, dramatic gesture that would lead to mad, dramatic speech—and placed her fingertips once again on her middle, where her thoughts should be. "It might be best," Sister said, "if you don't move tonight. I'll speak to the lady of the house. We'll get something arranged."

In the parlor, they all turned to Sister St. Saviour as if she had indeed been summoned to direct the proceedings. It was agreed that the lady of the house, Gertler was her name, would spend the night with her sister-in-law across the street. Since the gas had been turned off and would not be turned on again until tomorrow, most of the building's occupants were clearing out for the evening. In the vestibule, neighbors were coming down the dark staircase with bedding and small satchels in their arms. Sister sent word with one of them to the owner of a boarding-house nearby: the man in the carpet slippers would go there. The rude young man in the hat had already left, so she asked Officer O'Neil to knock on the door of one Dr. Hannigan. "Mention my name," she said. "He'll roll his eyes, but he'll come."

It wasn't until they'd all cleared out, and well before Dr. Hannigan arrived, that Sister allowed herself to use the toilet. She was sixty-four that year, but the stiffness in her back and her knees and the arthritis in her hands on these damp days, not to mention the more recent, arbitrary swelling of her ankles and her feet, had begun to limit her usefulness. More and more she was sent out with her basket to beg rather than to nurse. She kept her dissatisfaction with the arrangement to herself, which meant she complained only to God, who knew how she felt. Who had sent her here.

She helped Annie undress and get comfortable in Mrs. Gertler's bed. And held a candle over his shoulder while Dr. Hannigan examined the girl, put a stethoscope to her belly and her rising chest.

As he was leaving, she asked him to go by the convent to tell them where she was—"So they don't think I've been murdered." And to please, as well, go by the morgue to tell them Sheen and Sons Funeral Home would be making the arrangements. She bent her head back to see him better, to make sure her small black eyes were right on his own. There were some details, she added, she'd ask him to keep to himself.

Later, two Sisters from the convent arrived with more blankets and two hot water bottles wrapped in rags, and a dinner of biscuits and cheese and hot tea, which Sister St. Saviour ate in the chair she had pulled up to the side of the bed.

She dozed with her rosary in her gloved hands and dreamed, because of the cold, no doubt, and the familiar, icy ache of it in her toes, that she was on her stool in the vestibule of Woolworth's. She startled awake twice, because in her dream the woven basket, full of coins, was sliding off her lap.

When the darkness had lifted a bit—there was a whiteness to the dawn that made her believe the day would be something more promising than gray—she stood and walked into the parlor. The two Sisters who had brought the supplies, Sister Lucy and a young nun whose name she couldn't recall, were still there, sitting side by side on the couch, asleep, puffed into their black cloaks like gulls on a pier. Slowly, Sister climbed first one flight, then the second, until she found the apartment that had burned. In the growing light it was difficult to say what had been ignited in the blast, although the smell of smoke and burned wool was strong. And then she saw on the floor a man's overcoat and the sodden cushions of a high-backed couch and the black traces of a large burn across the waterlogged rug. In the kitchen, there were the charred remains of a pair of muslin curtains and an arc of soot all along the oven wall. She ran her finger through it, only to confirm that it would be easily removed. What would be difficult to remove, she knew, was this terrible odor, which she was certain the night air had sharpened. It was the smell of wet cinders. The smell of doused peat, of damp stone and swollen wood. Fire, shipwreck, the turned earth of graveyards. She went to the single window in the narrow kitchen. The courtyard below was full of deep shadow and the movements of some small gray birds, but looking down into it disheartened her in a way she had not been prepared for. She sat on the sill, lifted the twisted tea towel that had been left there.

Outside, most of the facing windows were still dark, only a small light here and there: an early worker, a mother with an infant, a bedside vigil. Reluctantly, she cast her eyes down into the courtyard again. The sun would have to be well up in the sky to light that dark tangle, but even at this hour there was a variation in the shadows that caught her attention. It was, no doubt, the movement of the birds, or of a stalking cat, or of a patch of puddled rainwater briefly reflecting the coming dawn, but for just a moment she thought it was a man, crawling, *cowering* was the word, beneath the black tangle of junk and dead leaves, the new, vague light just catching the perspiration on his wide brow, his shining forehead, the gleam of a tooth or an eye.

She shivered, flexed her stiff fingers. She smoothed the towel on her lap and then folded it neatly.

She could tell herself that the illusion was purposeful: God showing her an image of the young man, the suicide, trapped in his bitter purgatory, but she refused the notion. It was superstition. It was without mercy. It was the devil himself who drew her eyes into that tangle, who tempted her toward despair. That was the truth of it.

In the dining room, the sideboard was as big as a boat. She found the lease and the marriage license before she put her hand on the narrow blue folder on which someone had written— it was a man's severe script—*Deed for Calvary*. She slipped it into her pocket.

In the bedroom, the windows were wide open, the shades rolled up, and an ashen cord pull moved slowly in what must have been a dawn breeze. The bed was made, the blankets smoothed, no trace of fire in here, although there was more soot along the far wall. No trace, either, of where the husband might have lain on the bed. She knew immediately—it was the sympathy in his gestures, toward the girl on the bed, toward the apartment above—that it was the short officer who had come back after the body had been removed, to smooth and straighten the counterpane. One of us.

Sister lifted the two pillows, slipped off their covers, and shook them good—a few white feathers falling through the air—then piled the pillows in the open window. She pulled off the sheets and the blankets, pausing for a moment to remove her glasses and look closely at the bit of mending she felt beneath her hand— small stitches, she saw, neatly made—and said to God, "As You made us," at the familiar sight of the rusty stains here and there on the blue ticking of the mattress. She pushed the sheets into one of the pillowcases and wrapped the blanket around them.

As she stepped away with the linens in her arms, she kicked something with her toe and looked over her shoulder to see what it was. A man's shoe, broad brown leather, well worn. There were two of them at the foot of the bed. Gaping and forlorn, with the black laces wildly trailing. She nudged them with her toe until they were safely out of the way.

She carried the pile of bedding down the narrow stairs. Sister Lucy was still sunk into herself, breathing deeply. Sister St. Saviour dropped the linen on the couch beside her, and when that didn't get her to stir, she touched the Sister's black shoe with her own—and felt the keenness of the repeated motion, the man's empty shoe upstairs and Sister Lucy's here, still filled with its owner's mortal foot. "I'd like you to sit with the lady," she said.

In the bedroom, the young nun—Sister Jeanne was her name—had her rosary in her hand and her eyes on the pile of blankets and coats under which the girl slept. Sister St. Saviour signaled to her from the door, and she and Sister Lucy changed places. In the parlor, Sister St. Saviour told Sister Jeanne that she was to bring the bedclothes to the convent for washing and re-turn with a bucket and broom. The two of them were going to scrub the apartment upstairs from head to foot, roll up the wet rug, dry the floors, repair what they could, soften the blow of the woman's return to the place where the accident had occurred, the pilot gone out, because return she would, with nowhere else to go and a baby on the way come summer.

Sister Jeanne's eyes grew teary at this news. The tears suited her face, which was dewy with youth, moist-looking, the clay still wet. Obediently, the young nun gathered the linens from the couch. Sister St. Saviour went with her to the vestibule and then watched her walk delicately down the stone stairs, the bundle held to one side so she could see her tiny feet as she descended. The sky was colorless, as was the sidewalk and the street. The cold fresh air was still tinged with the smell of smoke, or maybe the smell of smoke only lingered in the nostrils. There were a few snowflakes in the air. Sister Jeanne was very small and slight, even in her black cloak, but there was a firmness about her, a buoyancy perhaps, as she hurried away, the bundle in her arms, so much to do. She was of an age, Sister St. Saviour understood, when tragedy was no less thrilling than romance.

Sister St. Saviour turned back into the apartment, peeked into the bedroom to whisper that she would return shortly, and then headed down the steps herself. Sheen's funeral parlor was only eight blocks over.

SISTER JEANNE FELT THE COLD on her hands—her gloves were in her pockets, too late to reach them now—but she felt as well the blood drumming in her wrists and in her temples. She felt her heart in her chest beating against the gathered bed linens as if she were running away with them. Last night's grief had made the new day profound, true, but for Sister Jeanne the first hour of any day, the hour of *Lauds*, was always the holiest. It was the hour she felt closest to God, saw Him in the gathering light, in the new air, in the stillness of the street—shades were drawn and the shops shuttered—but also in the first stirrings of life. There was the pleasant sound of a milk cart, tinkle of glass and clop of hooves, the sound of a few chirping songbirds, the call of distant gulls, of a streetcar down the avenue, a tugboat on the river, everything waking, beginning again. Deep night frightened her beyond reason; she knew herself to be a heretic of superstitions and weird imaginings, but knowing this didn't stop the terror she could brew for herself when she woke to pray at 3 a.m. And the busy, crowded sunlight hours, filled with casework, hardly gave her a moment to raise her eyes. Suppertime, ever since she'd come to the convent, was a calm that God need not enter, since the bread and the soup were always good and the company of the other women, tired from a long day of nursing, was sufficient to itself.

But it was at this hour, when the sun was a humming gold at the horizon, or a pale peach, or even just, as now, a gray pearl, that she felt the breath of God warm on her neck. It was at this hour that the whole city smelled to her like the inside of a cathedral—damp stone and cold water and candle wax—and the sound of her steps on the sidewalk and over the five cross streets made her think of a priest approaching the altar in shined shoes. Or of a bridegroom, perhaps, out of one of the romances she had read as a girl, all love and anticipation.

Sister Jeanne maneuvered her bundle through the wrought-iron gate at the front of the convent and climbed the steps to the front door. The other nuns were just coming out of the chapel, and their stillness as they walked through the dark corridor, which was untouched, as yet, by the outside light, made her feel even more buoyantly aware of the life in her veins. It was the feeling she'd had as a young child, coming from the sunshine into the solemn, shaded house and being warned, day after day, to keep her voice low because her mother, an invalid, was sleeping. She fell in line behind the other Sisters and then turned with her bundle as they passed the basement stairs. She went down. Sister Illuminata, the laundress, followed on her heels. The cellar was dark, full of shadows, although the pale morning was pressed against the small windows. The basement at this hour smelled only faintly of soap, more profoundly of dirt and brick, the cold underground. Somewhat breathlessly, Sister Jeanne told the story of the death and the fire and the baby coming, and the request Sister St. Saviour had made. Unsmiling, Sister Illuminata took the sheets and blanket and counterpane from her arms. She sent Sister Jeanne back up the stairs with the thrust of her chin. "Bring Sister her breakfast," she said. "And tell her it will be tomorrow, at best, before these things are dry. Even if I hang them by the furnace."

WHEN SISTER JEANNE RETURNED, the snow had become steady and the sidewalk was somewhat slick with it. She carried a broom and a bucket that contained both a scrub brush and the breakfast: a jar of tea, buttered bread, jam, all wrapped in a towel but rattling nevertheless inside the metal pail, a sound that added a quickness to her step and made some of the people she passed—the men mostly, who tipped their hats and said, "Sister"—smile to see her: a little nun with a pail and a broom and a determined walk. As she reached the building, Sister Lucy was just coming down the steps, wrapping her cloak around her hips and pulling down the corners of her mouth, as if the two motions were somehow connected—some necessary accommodation to what Sister Jeanne saw immediately was her ferocious anger.

"She's got the body coming back tonight," Sister Lucy said, and added for emphasis, "This evening. For the wake. And buried first thing tomorrow morning." She shook her jowls. She was a mannish, ugly woman, humorless, severe, but an excellent nurse.

Among the many helpful things she'd already taught Sister Jeanne was to notice the earlobes of the dying, first indication that the hour had come.

"Tomorrow!" Sister Lucy said again. "Calvary—she's got it all arranged." She shivered a bit, wrapped her cloak around her more tightly, and dropped her mouth into a longer frown. "And why is she rushing him into the ground?"

There was a yellow tint to her pupils, which were darting back and forth as they took in the rooftops and the icy snowflakes. "I'll say only this," Sister Lucy declared. "You can't pull strings with God." She leveled her gaze and pulled again at her cloak. Sister Jeanne thought of a painting she had seen, maybe in the courthouse or a post office, of a square-jawed general in the snow—was it George Washington?—his cloak drawn about him just so.

"You can't pull the wool over God's eyes," Sister Lucy said.

Sister Jeanne, the bucket in one hand and the broom in another, and the cold, for the first time this morning, whipping into her open cloak, turned somewhat gratefully to a woman who was passing on the sidewalk and saying, "Good morning, Sisters." She was a young woman bundled against the weather, a dark blue shawl wrapped around her broad hat, another thrown over her shoulders. She was pushing a baby carriage. A thin line of snow had gathered on the hood of the carriage, and there was a frosting of snow on the knuckles of her black gloves as well. She was pregnant under her man's overcoat. The nuns said, "Good morning," with a bow, and Sister Jeanne moved to peer into the carriage. She felt Sister Lucy, reluctantly, bending to look as well. The baby inside was so swaddled in plaid wool there were only two placid eyes and a tiny nose and the dash of a pursed, thoughtful mouth. "Oh, lovely!" Sister Jeanne cried. "Snug as a bug in a rug."

"He likes the snow," the mother replied. She was rosy-cheeked herself.

"He's watching it come down, isn't he?" Sister Jeanne said.

Sister Lucy also smiled. It was only a small, tight smile, but mighty, considering the weight of the anger it had worked itself out from under. She turned the smile toward the child and then the mother. Once more, the snowflakes began to gather in her yellow lashes, and she narrowed her eyes against them. "Is your husband good to you?" she asked.

Sister Jeanne briefly closed her eyes. Her cheeks grew warm. The young mother gave a short, startled laugh. "Yes, Sister," she said. "He is."

Sister Lucy raised her bare hand, one red finger in the air, and Sister Jeanne thought of General Washington again—or perhaps it was Napoleon. "Has he got a good job?"

"He does," the mother said. She straightened her spine. "He's a doorman at the St. Francis Hotel."

Sister nodded, barely placated. "Do you live nearby?" she asked.

"Yes, Sister," she said. She nodded over her shoulder. "Just at 314. Since last Saturday."

Now Sister Lucy turned the finger toward the woman's heart. "You come to see me," she said, "if ever he's not good to you."

"He's good to me," the girl said again, laughing.

"We're in the convent on Fourth. I'm Sister Lucy." She swung her hand. "This is Sister Jeanne. You come see us if need be."

The woman gave a little curtsy, but began to move the carriage nonetheless. "I will," she said. "Good morning, Sisters."

The woman was only a few feet away when Sister Lucy said,

"If he was good to her, he might let her catch her breath before starting another child." She blinked at the snowflakes that were trying to cover her eyes. "He might think of her health instead of his pleasure."

All joy was thin ice to Sister Lucy.

Sister Jeanne bowed her head and studied for a minute the tips of their identical shoes. Under the skim of cold on her cheeks she could still feel the rising heat.

"I'll go in, then," Sister Jeanne whispered, and turned to the steps.

"I'll try to get the word out," Sister Lucy called after her. "I'll talk to Mr. Hennessey, who knows all the motormen. But there's hardly time to gather a decent crowd, the way she's rushing things. And only one night for the wake."

Sister Jeanne nodded without turning, going up the steps. She had quite forgotten God was in the snow around her, in the cold and the wide sky; she had quite forgotten her pleasure in the day's work ahead. She was thinking instead that they were well rid of Sister Lucy.

A POLICEMAN AND A FIREMAN were conferring with another gentleman in the hallway by the stairs. They all turned and nodded to the young nun as she came through the vestibule. The door to the apartment was ajar and she let herself in. In full, if weak, daylight, the room seemed nicer than it had last night, if only because now, with the curtains in the big picture window opened, it had the view of the snow to make it cheerful. There was still the smell of smoke, but the smell of cleaning ammonia was now cut into it—the smell of the day going on. She crossed the living room and entered the narrow corridor that was lined with two portraits of dour peasants and found Sister St. Saviour in the tiny kitchen. Sister Jeanne placed the broom against the door and carried the bucket to the table where the old nun sat. The kitchen had been well scrubbed, the only trace of the lady's interrupted dinner was the newspaper that had been folded beside her plate. Sister St. Saviour now had it wide open before her.

Sister Jeanne poured the milky tea into a cup she borrowed from the cabinet and set it down. "It's still awfully cold in here, Sister," she said.

Sister St. Saviour moved the cup closer without raising it. "The men have just been in to turn on the gas," she said. "I asked them to carry out a few things that were damaged in the fire. They're going to wash the walls for me as well. So we've made some progress."

Sister Jeanne took a plate from the cupboard, set out the buttered bread and jam.

"Mr. Sheen will get the body from the morgue this morning," Sister St. Saviour went on. "First thing the lady wakes, she'll have to pick out his clothes. You can run them over for me. We've got a mass set for six tomorrow morning. Then the cemetery. The ground, praise God, isn't frozen. It'll all be finished before the new day's begun."

"That's quick," Sister Jeanne said. She hesitated and then added, "Sister Lucy wonders why it's such a rush."

Sister St. Saviour only raised her eyes to the top of the newspaper. "Sister Lucy," she said casually, "has a big mouth."

She turned the opened newspaper over, to the front page, straightening the edges. Then she touched her glasses. "Here's a story," she said, and put her fingertip to the page. "Mr. Sheen mentioned it to me this morning. A man over in Jersey, playing billiards in his home, accidentally opened the gas tap in the

27

room, with the pole they use, the cue, it says, and asphyxiated himself." She raised her chin. "His poor wife called him for dinner and found him gone." The glasses made her dark eyes sparkle. "Day before yesterday. Mr. Sheen mentioned it to me this morning. He was pointing out how common these things are. These accidents with the gas."

Sister St. Saviour moved her finger up the page. "And now here's a story of a suicide," she continued. "On the same page. Over on Wards Island. A man being treated at the hospital over there, for madness. It seems he was doing well enough, but then he threw himself into the water and disappeared. At Hell Gate. It says the water covered him up at Hell Gate." She clucked her tongue. "As if the devil needed to put a fine point on his work." She moved her arm once again. She might have been signing a blessing over the page. "And here's another story of a Wall Street man gone insane. Same day. Throwing bottles into the street, bellowing. Carted off to the hospital." She leaned forward, reading, her finger on the page, "'Where he demanded to see J. P. Morgan and Colonel Roosevelt.'"

Sister Jeanne leaned forward as well. "Is it true?" she asked.

Sister St. Saviour laughed. "True enough." Her smile was as smooth as paint. "The devil loves these short, dark days."

Sister Jeanne straightened her spine. She sometimes feared that Sister St. Saviour was wobbly in her ways. Hadn't she once said, on Sister Jeanne's first day in the convent, "Could you go tinkle for me?"

"Mr. Sheen told me," Sister St. Saviour went on, "that he could show the article about the billiard man to anyone in the Church, or at the cemetery, in case there was a question. To show how common these sorts of accidents are. And how easily they could be misinterpreted. This New Jersey man, after all, had come home early from work. And closed the door. Had he been a poor man, not a man with a billiard table at all, they might have made a different report out of it. The rich can get whatever they want put into the papers."

BY THE TIME MRS. GERTLER RETURNED to reclaim her apartment, Annie was up and dressed and sitting in a chair by the window with one of Sister Jeanne's handkerchiefs clutched in both hands.

The two nuns walked up the stairs with her, Sister Jeanne ahead and Sister St. Saviour just behind, her swollen ankles weighting each step with pain. At the apartment door, it was Sister St. Saviour who stepped back so the girl could enter with the young nun at her side.

At four o'clock, the black hearse pulled up. The three women watched from the bedroom window. Mr. Sheen, elegant in his long overcoat, left the cab first and was the first to appear upstairs. He was a tall man with the sharp nose and high cheekbones of an Indian chief, a pair of large, heavy-lidded eyes that couldn't have been better suited to his profession. He swept off his hat and took the widow's two hands into his own and, with a quick look around the sparsely furnished room, suggested the lady and the two nuns might want to wait in the bedroom while he made his preparations. Annie and Sister Jeanne sat together at the foot of the bed while Sister St. Saviour stood at the door. They could hear Mr. Sheen giving instructions. And then the unmistakable sound of the coffin being carried up the stairs, a bit of labored breathing, and the touch of the wooden casket against the doorframe. And then Mr. Sheen rapped on the bedroom door to say all was ready.

The husband's face was pale and waxen, but it was, neverthe-less, a lovely face. Boyish and solemn above the starched white collar, with a kind of youthful stubbornness about it as well. The look of a child, Sister St. Saviour thought, when met with the spoon of castor oil.

While Annie and Sister Jeanne knelt, Sister St. Saviour blessed herself and considered the sin of her deception, slipping a suicide into hallowed ground. A man who had rejected his life, the love of this brokenhearted girl, the child coming to them in the sum-mer. She said to God, who knew her thoughts, Hold it against me if You will. He could put this day on the side of the ledger where all her sins were listed: the hatred she felt for certain politicians, the money she stole from her own basket to give out as she pleased—to a girl with a raging clap, to the bruised wife of a drunk, to the mother of the thumb-sized infant she had wrapped in a clean handkerchief, baptized, and then buried in the convent garden. All the moments of how many days when her compassion failed, her patience failed, when her love for God's people could not outrun the girlish alacrity of her scorn for their stupidity, their petty sins.

She wanted him buried in Calvary to give comfort to his poor wife, true. To get the girl what she'd paid for. But she also wanted to prove herself something more than a beggar, to test the connections she'd forged in this neighborhood, forged over a lifetime. She wanted him buried in Calvary because the power of the Church wanted him kept out and she, who had spent her life in the Church's service, wanted him in.

Hold it against the good I've done, she prayed. We'll sort it out when I see You.

Only a few neighbors came to call, every one of them a little restrained in sympathy, given the unspoken notion that the son of a bitch could have taken them all with him. A trio of red-faced motormen stopped by, but stayed only a minute when no drink was offered. Later, the two nuns walked Mr. Sheen downstairs in order to give the girl some time alone with her husband. At the curb, he reached into the cab of the hearse and pulled out the day's newspaper. He folded back a page and tapped a narrow article. Sister St. Saviour leaned forward to read, Sister Jeanne at her elbow. In the descending light of the cold evening, the blur of a misting rain and a rising fog, the two could just make out the headline: SUICIDE ENDANGERS OTHERS. It was followed by the full report of the fire and the man's death by his own hand. "There's nothing to be done, Sister," Mr. Sheen whispered. "Now that it's in the paper, there's not a Catholic cemetery that will have him. I'll have my head handed to me on a plate if I try to bring him into the church."

To Sister Jeanne's eyes, the black newsprint, especially the bold headline that seemed to swell and blur under the blow of each raindrop, briefly transformed the world itself into a thing made of paper, pocked by tears.

But Sister St. Saviour pushed the undertaker's hand away. She thought of the rude young man with the milk tooth and the gray fedora. Her glasses flashed under the just-illuminated lamplight. "*The New York Times*," she said, "has a big mouth."

THE TWO NUNS climbed the stairs again. Sister St. Saviour was aware of how patiently little Sister Jeanne paused with her on each step, a hand raised to offer aid. Inside, they coaxed the sobbing girl up off her knees and into the bed. It was Sister Jeanne who took over then—no weariness in her narrow shoulders, no indication at all that she felt the tedium of too much sympathy for a stranger. With Annie settled, Sister Jeanne told Sister St. Saviour to go back to the convent to rest. She whispered that she would keep vigil through the long night and have the lady ready first thing in the morning.

"Ready for what?" Sister St. Saviour asked her, attempting to gauge how much the young nun understood—suspecting not much. "There will be no mass." Her pain, her bone-through fatigue, made her voice sharper than she knew.

Young Sister Jeanne looked up at the nun, moisture once more gathering in her pretty eyes. She said, with childish determination, "I'll have her ready for whatever's to come."

Sister St. Saviour left the two of them murmuring in the bedroom. At the casket, she paused again to look at the young man's still face. She went to the window in the kitchen and looked down into that purgatory of the backyards. At this hour, there was nothing to be seen. All movement, all life, was in the lighted windows above: a man at a table, a child with a bedside lamp, a young woman walking an infant to and fro.

Of course, it was Sister Jeanne who would be here when the baby arrived come summer.

It was Sister Jeanne who had been sent for.

The old nun felt a beggar's envy rise to her throat. She envied little Jeanne, true enough—a new sin for her side of the ledger—envied her faith and her determination and her easy tears. But she envied as well the coming dawn, *Lauds*, still so many hours away. She envied the very daylight, envied every woman who would walk out into it, bustling, bustling, one foot in front of the other, no pain weighting her steps, so much to do.

Confident of heaven—God knew her failings—Sister St. Saviour was, nevertheless, even now, jealous of life.

She turned from the cold glass, turned as well a cold shoulder to the God who had brought her here so that Jeanne would follow. It was the way a bitter old wife might turn her back on a faithless husband.

THE BABY, a daughter, was born in August, just three weeks after the old nun died. She was called Sally, but baptized St. Saviour in honor of the Sister's kindness that sad afternoon. That damp and gray afternoon when the pilot went out. When our young grandfather, a motorman for the BRT whose grave we have never found, sent his wife to do her shopping while he had himself a little nap.

And Then

OUR FATHER RODE sitting upright in the high baby carriage, like a boy in a small boat. It was his first memory. Displaced as he'd been from the shade under the perambulator's hood, occupied now by yet another bundled infant, he spread out his arms and clutched the sides of the carriage: a boy in a storm-tossed rowboat. His mother, pushing the thing, was behind him. She navigated the broken sidewalks, the curbs, and the street crossings with a banging determination that caused the whole contraption—high wheels and springs and the hard black body of the carriage itself—to shudder and quake, rearing at the curbs, bucking at the cobblestones, swinging left or right around poky pedestrians, dog droppings, the spilled contents of fruit markets, dry-goods stores, garbage cans. He rode every undulation, every swerve, with his spine straight, his arms outspread, and his hands fixed tightly around the gunwales of the carriage bed. He looked straight on. There were trees and cars, dustbins and lampposts on the left; on the right, buildings, gray stone and brick, with stoops and children and speared fence tops, but he kept his eyes glued to the horizon that began just above the arc of the black hood, focusing on the world ahead like a sea captain navigating an ice storm. He was petrified.

At his back, his mother out for a stroll. Although the word hardly accommodated her perpetual haste, her determined plowing-through. Beside her, his brother trotted along, holding on to her skirt. She leaned her weight against the handlebar and brought the front of the carriage up in the air—he was tipped backward and the horizon became treed—and then she lifted the back wheels—tipping him forward, a hint of gray sidewalk aiming for his skull—as they mounted another curb. Now shade covered them all, as if there had been a lowering of clouds, and she slowed her pace. Smoothly, shadowy, another baby carriage, the silent black ghost galleon he knew somehow had been following them all the while, pulled alongside. He heard his mother's voice, and the answering voice of another woman, as they passed into the smooth stream of the park. The conversation itself, an ongoing exchange, rippled with laughter, another smooth stream. It did not soothe him. He kept his back straight, his fingers locked on the edges of the carriage bed. He looked ahead, aware only peripherally of the other strollers, the passing trees and shade, the shadows of the perambulators and of the two women pushing them. He remained vigilant.

There was the duet of the women's voices, some birdsong, the faint cawing of a crow or a cat. Every once in a while, despite the curbless paths, the carriage beneath him shuddered abruptly—

a jiggling, a pause, a jiggling again. He tightened his grip, braced his arms. He peered down a tarred lane of dappled sunlight, a busy sidewalk at the far end. And then the slowing of the wheels. The sound of cat or crow was not distant at all but rose from beneath the black hoods of the two carriages. In tandem, the women, his mother and her silhouetted friend, paused. His mother walked past him, his older brother still attached to her skirt. She leaned down to reach beneath the hood and lifted out a swaddled infant no bigger than a loaf of bread. The other woman did the same. Recently, his mother had been delivered of twins. And then, as she rocked this new scrap of child on her shoulder, and her friend did the same, he turned his head just a few inches more and was met, as if in mirror reflection, with the face of another child, sitting up just as he was, her small hands, as his were, gripping the sides of the black carriage, holding on, holding on. Vigilant like himself, he saw. Erect and terrified, like himself.

She was dressed in white wool: bonnet, coat, and leggings, which was a flaw in the memory, since it must have been high summer. He stared at her, she stared back with wide eyes. He said to himself, There's the girl I'll marry.

IT WAS THE NUNS who got the two mothers walking together. Or Sister Lucy did, anyway. Sister Lucy, who could insist.

She had finagled a lovely baby carriage from a well-to-do couple on President Street, an older couple whose first and only child hadn't lived past infancy. Then she went with Sister Jeanne to 314, to the doorman's wife, to say there's a widow down the street with a new baby. "Put on your hat and go pay her a call." Still standing at the threshold, Sister Lucy cast an assessing eye around Mrs. Tierney, to the cluttered apartment behind her, then to the chapped cheeks of the baby on her hip, then over the woman herself, who was dressed in a bungalow apron of pale percale, a damp stain, mother's milk perhaps, on her chest. There was a baby bawling in another room. "Fix yourself up," Sister Lucy added, "and have a nice visit."

Mrs. Tierney smiled. She asked for the lady's name and address. Said she would be certain to visit her sometime soon.

Sister Lucy said, "Why not now? We'll watch the children while you go."

At the nun's side, Sister Jeanne blushed apologetically, shrugged, and then held out her hands to the little boy in Mrs. Tierney's arms. Mrs. Tierney felt his body, the weight of him, tilt toward the nun as if a magnet drew him.

And then she laughed. Invited the Sisters in.

GOING TO AND FROM THE PARK—hot weather or cold, snow or stifling humidity, only a hard rain ever kept them indoors—the two young mothers negotiated the crowded streets like impatient empresses. Together, they returned Elizabeth Tierney's boys and the twin girls to her apartment and then together carried both unwieldy carriages up the steep stone steps. Let other mothers park their baby carriages in alleyways and courtyards, beside garbage cans and under stairs. Not these two.

Compared to Annie's sparse rooms, Mrs. Tierney's place was a carnival of cribs and trundle beds, clothes and washbins and dirty plates. Each morning, the dining room table was filled with sticky glasses and piled saucers and ashtrays crowded with cigarette butts and cigar stubs, because Michael, her husband, liked a gathering of men in the evening. "His cronies," Mrs. Tierney called them—his coworkers mostly, doormen and bellhops and waiters who hailed, she said, from "all corners of the earth." "The more the merrier," she said. Despite the mess of glasses and plates, the lingering smell of cigar smoke that competed with the odors of wet laundry and dirty diapers, she said it with the same amused, eye-rolling fondness that she applied to everything that had to do with her husband, who was no immigrant himself but the well-spoken son of a schoolteacher from up near Pough-keepsie. Whose family had disowned him, she said, for "coming down in the world" to marry her.

With the two big black carriages secured in the narrow hall-way of Elizabeth Tierney's apartment and her babies settled into them once more, Annie and her daughter left the jumbled household each morning for the peace and the order of the Little Nursing Sisters' convent, where she had been given work in the basement laundry.

Sister St. Saviour had arranged it. Before her last illness, the old nun had slipped a note beneath the feet of the Virgin—via her statue in the convent's front garden—requesting that suffi-cient funds be found to pay the girl's salary. "Somehow, dear Mother." The women of the convent's Ladies Auxiliary found the note—they checked the statue daily—and presented the pe-tition to their members. The Ladies Auxiliary of the convent of the Little Nursing Sisters of the Sick Poor, Congregation of Mary Before the Cross, consisted mostly of idle Catholic women married to successful men. As Sister St. Saviour well under-stood, they felt a particular there-but-for-the-grace-of-God af-finity for impoverished young widows.

Out of the funds the Ladies Auxiliary provided, the nuns paid Annie eighteen dollars a week, and fed her, and her daughter when she was weaned, a breakfast and a lunch. It was, all agreed, a fine situation for a widow with an infant. A wicker basket was fitted with towels and a pillowslip, and the baby slept at her mother's feet while she washed and sewed and helped Sister Illuminata with the ironing.

As the child grew, the nuns added a donated crib, and then a small Persian rug, another donation, to cover a bit of the damp basement floor. There were scraps of cloth and empty spools for the child to play with, and the ducks and dogs Sister Illuminata carved from Ivory soap—an annoyance for Annie, since she had to remain vigilant in order to keep the girl from putting them into her mouth or her eyes, but nothing she could refuse, given Sister Illuminata's pride in her own whittling and the child's delight each time the nun produced a new figure from her robes.

The work itself was endless. Every day, donated clothing arrived at the convent, clothing for the poor, which had to be sorted and washed and mended. There were as well the stained bedclothes of the sick: sheets and blankets and pillowcases, diapers, towels, handkerchiefs, all brought home from the households where the Sisters were nursing. In any idle moment, there were bandages to make, worn bed sheets to be sterilized and rolled and placed neatly into the satchels each Sister carried to her casework.

There was also, every week, the routine washing and ironing of the convent linen and the Sisters' habits, the black serge tunics and short capes—the application of thick starch and the heated iron to their bibs and their bonnets. Whatever troubles the Sisters encountered in their daily work were illustrated by the stains on an apron or a sleeve—the odor of vomit on wool, a spattering of blood across a white bib. What troubles the Sisters' mortal bodies produced of their own accord were evident in the unending menstrual rags and long johns stained yellow at underarm or crotch. When Annie arrived in the morning, her first task was to empty the overnight soaking bin—the water pink with blood. And then the trip upstairs to the convent kitchen, to boil some water for the first wash, and while she waited, a cup of tea and a bun and a pleasant time of day with Mrs. Odette, the convent's cook, another widow from the neighborhood, or, if she'd arrived early enough, a laugh or two with Mr. Costello, the milkman.

In the basement, the low-hanging light was dim, the dark brick walls clammy to the touch. All day long there was the sound of agitated wash water, of the wringer's torturous crank and squeak, the hiss and thud of Sister Illuminata's black iron. In winter there was as well the bump and moan of the convent's fiery furnace. In summer, through the high opened windows, the chants of jump-rope songs, the organ grinder, the cries of boys playing ball in the street.

In every season, the changing daylight found its way into all corners of the cellar. Sometimes it was a discouraging gray in the morning, but a buoyant display of yellow and gold by the time the chapel bell was rung at three. Sometimes only the earliest hours illuminated the place, and when evening came a muffled darkness pressed against the electric lights.

At various times there was the smell of wet wool, bleach, vinegar, turpentine, pine soap, and starch.

On damp days, they hung the clothes and the linens from lines strung between the basement's iron support beams. When the weather was fine, they brought the wash out to the convent yard.

There was, each day, the clear and certain restoration of order: fresh linens folded, stains gone, tears mended.

Sister Illuminata was a wizard with a hot iron and starch, with scrub brush and bleach. On four dark shelves in a corner of her basement domain, she kept a laboratory's worth of vital ingredients: not merely the store-bought Borax and Ivory and bluing agents, but the potions she mixed herself: bran water to stiffen curtains and wimples, alum water to make muslin curtains and nightwear resist fire, brewed coffee to darken the Sisters' stockings and black tunics, Fels-Naptha water for general washing, Javelle water (washing soda, chloride of lime, boiling water) for restoring limp fabric. She had an encyclopedic understanding of how to treat stains. Tea: Borax and cold water. Ink: milk, salt, and lemon juice. Iodine: chloroform. Iron rust: hydrochloric acid. Mucus: ammonia and soap. Mucus tinged with blood (which she always greeted with a sign of the cross): salt and cold water.

In Sister Illuminata's unyielding routine, each item received two washings: inside out and then right side out, then a pass through the mangle, then another soaping, a boiling, another rinse, another wringing. If the garments were to be blued, then a rinse again in cold water to avoid rust stains. Wrung again, then starched, then hung to dry. Sister Illuminata would not allow the courtyard clothesline to be left out in the weather; she tied it up each morning and took it down again at the end of every bright day. She washed the clothespins themselves once a month. With sacred solemnity, Sister Illuminata demonstrated for Annie how a garment should be properly shaken and hung (chemises and shirts by the hem, pillowslips inside out and by the seam, with the wind, never against it). She demonstrated the precise way to sprinkle and roll what was newly dried, and how to pound the rolled fabric in order to distribute the moisture. The ironing was Sister Illuminata's special domain. She had four different irons of various sizes, which she washed on occasion in soap and water, then rubbed with sandstone and polished, lovingly, with beeswax.

Sister Illuminata was shrill in her demands, unbending in her routine; any washing Annie attempted during her first few weeks in the nuns' employ was dismissed as a mere "lick and a promise." Sister Illuminata had never asked them to send her an assistant.

She was a solid, plain, wide-bottomed woman. The pale skin of her cheeks and her forehead and her chin was crepe-thin; it hung like crepe over the edge of her white coif. Her hands were always a raw, bright red, her right index finger marked with the shining oval of a testing-the-iron scar. Except for the time she spent in the chapel, Sister Illuminata was always moving, her sleeves rolled up, her veil tied back. She was bending over the washbasin or feeding wet clothes into the cranking wringer, or ironing, ironing—this was the area of her greatest expertise—throwing her whole body into it, elbows and back and hips.

SISTER ILLUMINATA flicked her wet fingers over the cloth as if to douse a sinner. She thumped the black iron against the wooden board, thumped and lifted and thumped and shook—the steam rising—as if each piece she pressed involved some feat of determination and strength, a mortal struggle. Her elbows flared in the wide sleeves, her nostrils flared in her beaked nose. She called sharply to Annie to say, "Come here and learn something. This is a trick my mother had . . ." She ran the point of the iron—"See, like this"—along a perfect seam. "My mother," she said, "was a marvel."

Her mother, she said, had been a laundress in Dublin. A profession the Sisters of Mercy had found for her when she first came to the city as a young girl. She died of cancer when Sister Illuminata was just twenty. In her last suffering months, it was the nursing Sisters of the parish who offered comfort and care. Sister Illuminata entered their noviate a year later and emigrated to the States at thirty. But a bout of tuberculosis put an end to her own nursing days. She spent eight months at a sanatorium upstate, and when she returned, she was left to live out her vocation "down here."

Down here, in the basement of the convent, amid the dampness and the rising steam, the baby asleep in her crib, the sheets or long johns hung out on the line, Sister Illuminata called to Annie to say, Come and learn something. She said, My mother was a marvel at this . . . or, My mother had a trick. She told Annie, Here's how my mother turned a collar, mended a cuff, starched linen, sized, stretched, bleached . . . my mother did it this way . . . my mother taught me this.

The phrase giving way to the stories, as the weeks and months went by: and then my mother left the farm and made her way to the city, where the Sisters of Mercy took her under their wing . . . and then it was my mother they called on, his Lordship himself being the one whose britches were in need of repair . . .

And then my mother found herself a widow with a small child, just like you . . . and then she took me into the laundry with her, just like you do.

Down here, Annie knew, the words were a kind of contraband. None of the Sisters, in those days, spoke of their lives before the convent, in what they dismissively called the world. To take their vows was to leave all else behind: girlhoods and families and friends, all of love that was merely personal, all of life that required a backward glance. The white horse-blinder bonnets they wore did more than limit their peripheral vision. They reminded the Sisters to look only at the work at hand.

Annie imagined how silently the days must have passed for

Sister Illuminata during all the years she had labored down here in the convent basement alone, without an assistant, and, imagining this—recalling as well her own loneliness each silent, weary evening—she swallowed her anger at the nun's shrill demands. She swallowed as well the woman's insults—a lick and a promise—her implacable routines. Annie turned her face into her shoulder whenever Sister Illuminata was cross, when even a blessed saint would have been compelled to whisper, "Damn bitch."

And she lied, saying in all innocence, "No, I never heard it," when Sister Illuminata began again the story of how her mother repaired the britches of a magistrate or encountered a dray horse in the drying yard or saved the life of another laundress's child who had swallowed a fistful of alum—forty, fifty years ago this was, although as fresh in Sister Illuminata's telling, and retelling, as if it all had happened just this morning, just upstairs, in the world above their heads.

ON AN AFTERNOON IN EARLY SUMMER, when Sally was not yet two, Annie and the nun sat together in silence, the baby on the bit of rug between them. They were sorting through a collection of donated clothes, sorting, examining, determining what could be washed and mended and brought to the poor from what was bound for rags, or, if there was evidence of moths or lice, the incinerator. Because the nuns allowed Annie first choice in this— wasn't she the poor, after all?—most of her daughter's clothes came from these donation baskets, and not a few blouses and skirts for herself.

Which may well account for the white wool coat and leggings and bonnet our father so vividly recalled. A winter ensemble too fine to resist and too perfect a fit to save for cold weather.

Suddenly Sally let out a shriek and began to wail, a fist to her eye. Annie dropped the moth-eaten shawl she'd been holding up to the light and went to her knees beside the child. Sister Illuminata leaned forward. The girl was red-faced and screaming. "Something in her eye," Sister said, and Annie tried to move the child's fist away. Sally resisted. She was clutching something in her balled hand. "Let me see it, darling," she coaxed. But the girl wouldn't budge. She twisted her arm away from her mother, grew desperate, even as she screwed the balled fist against her face. It was a piece of white soap. Annie saw that the smallest of Sister's carved ducks was on the rug beside the child, decapitated. The girl was pressing the tiny severed head into her eye. "Give it to me, darling," Annie said. "You're hurting yourself." With some effort, she pulled the girl's fist away from her face, but she could not coax her to open her hand. Sister Illuminata, meanwhile, was fetching a wet cloth. She handed it to Annie. On her mother's lap, the child was still crying, but still clutching as well the offending piece of soap. Annie put the wet towel over the soap-stung eye. Gently, Sister Illuminata tried to take the soap from the girl's fist, and once again the child pulled away. She would not give it up.

"Oh, she's stubborn," Annie whispered. "She's not going to give in." And then she added, "She gets that from Jim."

Sister Illuminata leaned over them both, broad in her habit and her apron, which was slightly damp. She put a raw red hand to the child's fine hair. "Jim," the nun said firmly, "gets the credit, then. She'll never be a pushover."

Later that same day, when the smell of the Sisters' dinner wafted down the stairs, Annie heard herself say, "Jim would

45

never eat a turnip." Later still, when a heat wave struck the city, "Jim was never a drinker, thank God, but he'd take a beer on a day like today." When Sally, growing up, grew silent around strangers, "Jim had a shyness about him, too. The first time we met, I wondered if he was ever going to say a word."

In the dank basement laundry of the convent, Annie said, "Jim had a good voice, but he preferred a silly song to a ballad, which drove me mad." She said, "Jim had a friend who wore shoes like that." She said, "Jim couldn't abide a tight collar." She said, Jim was, Jim preferred, Jim told me once.

Mrs. Tierney was full of fond stories about her exasperating husband, but on their morning walks, decorum and superstition kept both women silent about Annie's loss. The people who had seen him in life, neighbors and friends, lowered their eyes whenever she passed them in the hallway or on the street. Sister St. Saviour was gone. And Sister Jeanne, who knew all, kept all in her heart.

His name, too, then, a kind of contraband. Jim was, Jim preferred, Jim told me once. But down here in the convent laundry, she spoke it as casually as she might have done if he still stirred about in the world upstairs. As if she were still a woman with an exasperating husband, no widow alone with a child. And Sister Illuminata listened, sympathetically, as any maiden friend of a married lady might do.

Sally was six years old when, looking up from a set of paper dolls that had arrived in the donation basket, she asked, "Who's Jim?"

She was nine when it occurred to her to wonder where her father was buried. Her mother only put her hand to her heart and said, "Here."

She was nearly eleven when she came home from school with

the delightful tale of a schoolmate's visit to a father's grave—a trolley ride, a lovely picnic on the green grass. Her mother threw back her head and said, laughing, "Let him come to us."

The sound of her mother's laughter always startled and thrilled the girl. She smiled, put her hand to her mother's broad cheek. Mistook the joke for a promise.

The Ninth Hour

I N THE HORARIUM OF THE CONVENT'S LIFE, afternoon prayers were said at three. Any Sisters who were not tied up with casework or alms-seeking returned to the convent then.

Much later, when the arthritis in her knees got the best of her and her days were spent in a chair behind the ironing board, Sister Illuminata would only raise her eyes to the ceiling and, blessing herself, silently pray, but in the years of Sally's childhood, she stopped what she was doing at the sound of the bell, dried her hands, rolled down her sleeves, and ponderously climbed the wooden stairs. Annie, finishing up some folding or mending, listened for the sound of the nuns' prayers, the psalms, the hymn, then for the sound of Sister Illuminata's return—breath short, beads clacking. And then, as Sister Illuminata settled back into her work, Annie would listen again, hopeful, for another, lighter step on the stairs. On the best days, she would look up to see Sister Jeanne bending over the banister, laughing like a child to find them there.

"Reprieved!" Sister Illuminata would declare whenever the young nun appeared. There was no keeping the resentment out of her voice. "Curfew will not ring tonight," she would add, pouting and jealous, but also, with the next thought, forgiving the two young women their clear delight in one another. Like is drawn to like, after all, and Sister Illuminata had been young once herself, arm and arm with one narrow, grimy, funny girl, Mary Pat Shea. She could recall the strong grip of Mary Pat's arm, the boggy smell of her, the freckles and dirty fingernails and shining green eyes, the muscular, lithe, little body beside her own. Sister Illuminata had, in another lifetime, known that same delight.

"Do you need a breath of fresh air?" Sister Jeanne might ask. Or, "Do you want to run out and get yourself a soda?" "Do you want to do some shopping?"

This routine, too, had begun at Sister Lucy's insistence. In the early days of Annie's work at the convent, when Sally was still an infant, Sister Lucy put her eyes on Sister Jeanne as they left the chapel after the Ninth Hour prayer. "If you're free this afternoon, go downstairs and take over with the baby," she told her. Sister Lucy could insist. "Let the mother go out and catch her breath."

"Do you mind?" Annie always asked, looking up at the little nun, laughing despite the way Sister Illuminata, jealous and pouting, was abruptly rolling back her sleeves or sucking her scarred fingertip.

And Sister Jeanne would skip down the stairs. "Do I mind?" as if the question couldn't be more absurd.

With her clasped hands to her heart, holding back her crucifix, Sister Jeanne peered into the wicker laundry basket where Sally slept or, as the child grew, hiked up her skirt to join her on the floor for whatever game she had devised out of soap animals and scraps of cloth and empty spools of thread.

The girl delighted her. In fact, every child delighted Sister Jeanne. She was a practical nurse without formal training, and what skills she had were sometimes limited by her size and her strength, but her way with children was astonishing. Perhaps because, even in full habit, she seemed to be one of them: small and soft-spoken and easily given to laughter or tears, but also with a kind of sly skepticism in her eyes whenever she raised her chin to attend to some tall adult. A skepticism it seemed only the children could perceive, and share. Sister Jeanne need only turn her face from some serious, long-winded grown-up, a parent, a priest, a doctor, even one of the other nuns, to the child in the room and some understanding was established. It's all silliness, isn't it?—her eyes alone could convey. Let's not let them know we know.

Didn't she do as much for us?

Because of her small size and her talent with little ones, more often than not the casework Sister Jeanne was given was very sad: sick children, failing newborns, toddlers neglected or abused or abandoned. Her expertise was in the eradication of scabies, ringworm, lice, the application of castor oil and poultices, the cleaning of ears and the soothing of tears. Sister Jeanne knew the route to the various Brooklyn orphanages, or to the Foundling Home in Manhattan, better than any of the others. It was often her task to accompany the children there, sometimes from the gate of a cemetery, sometimes from the court or the station house, sometimes from the very room where the poor mother, newly cold, still lay, the gamy odor of death already encroaching on the still air.

Out on the street with her charges, Sister Jeanne could make the trip an enchantment for the trembling little ones, pulling sugar cubes from her deep pockets or leaning down to point out something, or someone, that would make them laugh. She could negotiate the subway stairs and the crowded streets with a sleeping newborn tucked into the crook of her arm. And always—always, the Sister who accompanied her would report to the others—Sister Jeanne made the trip back to the convent in snuffling tears.

What Sister Jeanne struggled to keep in balance was the sorrow she felt at the suffering of the sick and her own perpetual wonder at the miracle of the healthy. Sally was healthy—nine pounds when she was born and strong-limbed and rosy-cheeked as a toddler and young girl—and Sister Jeanne looked forward to seeing her in the basement laundry after a sad day with a failing child or a grieving mother, if only to assure herself that God was, after all, as generous with good health as He was with bad.

She would hike up her skirt and join the girl on the small Persian rug, relishing her plump hands and bright eyes, her cleverness—by four she knew the name of every nun in the convent—her rapid growth; reassuring herself that the consumptive girl whose death she had recently attended was now restored in heaven with this same robust beauty. Telling herself that the poor mother's wailing sorrow would be transformed, not now, but soon—life was like the blink of an eye—into Annie's same joy as she took her healthy daughter into her arms here in the streaming afternoon light and said, "I'll be back in a jiff."

"Take your time," Sister Jeanne would say or, quoting Sister Lucy, "Go catch your breath," which made them both laugh.

When Annie had gone, Sister Jeanne and the child climbed the stairs. ("No, I'll be fine," Sister Illuminata might call after them. "Still so much to do. You'll have to send my supper down.") They stopped into the pretty chapel to kneel together and say their prayers. They went to the kitchen for some biscuits and a glass of milk, or—if it was far enough before dinner preparations were to begin—to mix up a pudding or a fool. When the weather was fine, they'd go out to the convent yard, where they'd dig in the garden with a spade and an old spoon. When it rained, they sat in the elegant parlor and said a rosary—Sister Jeanne making a fairy story of sorts out of each of the Mysteries—the girl counting the nun's beads and, more often than not, drifting to sleep beside her.

It was on these damp afternoons, in their brief and unaccustomed idleness, that Sister Jeanne considered Jim.

Sister Jeanne believed with the conviction of an eye witness that all human loss would be restored: the grieving child would have her mother again; the dead infant would find robust health; suffering, sorrow, accident, and loss would all be amended in heaven. She believed this because, because (and she only possessed the wherewithal to explain this to children—trying to say it to angry or grieving or bitter adults only left her tongue-tied), because fairness demanded it.

It was, to her mind, a simple proposition. The madness with which suffering was dispersed in the world defied logic. There was nothing else like it for unevenness. Bad luck, bad health, bad timing. Innocent children were afflicted as often as bad men. Young mothers were struck down even as old ones fretfully lingered. Good lives ended in confusion or despair or howling devastation. The fortunate went blissfully about their business until that moment when fortune vanished—a knock on the door, a cough, a knife flash, a brief bit of inattention. A much-longed-for baby slid into the world only to grow blue and limp in its mother's arms. Another arrived lame, or ill-formed, or simply too hungry for a frail woman already overwhelmed. There was a child in the next parish with a skull so twisted his mouth couldn't close, and every breath he took, every word he spoke, even his childish laughter, rattled through dry and swollen lips. Another with a birthmark like a purple caul. Blindness. Beatings. Broken or bent bones. Accident, decay. Cruelty of nature. Cruelty of bad men. Idiocy, madness.

There was no accounting for it.

No accounting for how general it was, how arbitrary.

Sister Jeanne believed that fairness demanded this chaos be righted. Fairness demanded that grief should find succor, that wounds should heal, insult and confusion find recompense and certainty, that every living person God had made should not, willy-nilly, be forever unmade.

"You know what's fair and what isn't, don't you?" Sister Jeanne would ask the sick child, the grieving orphan, Sally herself when she was old enough to understand the question. And us.

"And how do you know?"

Sister Jeanne would put a fingertip to the child's forehead, to the child's beating heart. "Because God put the knowledge in you before you were born. So you'd know fairness when you see it. So you'd know He intends to be fair."

"WHO'S THE DUMBEST BOY IN YOUR CLASS?" she once asked us. This was in the Hempstead house where we were young. "And if the teacher's dividing up sweets and gives him only one while everyone else gets two, what will he say? He'll say it's not fair, won't he? If you call him out playing ball when everyone can see he's safe by a mile, what will he say—dumb as he is in school? He'll say it's not fair, see? And how does he know? Did he learn what's fair from a book? Did he take a test? No, he did not."

ON THE NIGHT OF JIM'S WAKE, Sister Jeanne moved two chairs from the dining table to the side of his coffin. With Sister St. Saviour gone wearily back to the convent, she and Annie alone kept the long vigil. Sister Jeanne took out her beads, but she did not pray, and when Annie reached for her hand, Sister Jeanne found she could put no comfort in her grip. There was the newspaper article Mr. Sheen had held out for them to read, under the rain and the sad lamplight.

There was the logic of redemption, all undone.

Jim had not suffered the indignity of misfortune. He hadn't caught a flu or stepped off the wrong curb, hadn't had the pilot go out or the years wear him thin. He had endured no insult that God must amend. No accident. No illness. No unfortunate birth. He had been given his life and he had thrown his life away.

In Sister Jeanne's simple logic, the logic of her belief, fairness made no claim for him. His death was a whim of his own. His own choice. Who, in all fairness, could demand its restitution? The promise of the Redemption, the promise of everlasting life, of order restored in heaven, could hold no water, she believed, if it could not also be revoked by such willfulness, such arrogance. To gain heaven was no wonder if heaven could not also be lost.

Through the long night—Annie's hand in hers, her beads untold—Sister Jeanne studied his still and boyish face, cold stone. She could find no certainty in her heart, or in her imagination, that it would ever again know life.

Now his child, his living flesh and blood, was stretched across the couch in the convent parlor, her arms flung wide, her little hands open, palms up, her fingers flickering with her dreams. She was growing quickly. Sister Jeanne had to struggle to catch the infant still in the fair brows and the closed eyes, gently lashed, the little mouth, so solemn in sleep. She felt—it was a flood, a filling up—how delightful it was to love this child, to find her here, day after day after day, a tonic for every sorrow. A restorative. A joy.

She thought of Jim and what he had thrown away.

The quiet convent parlor, in the hush of the rain, was tinged a kind of sepia—by the hour, by the weather, by the brown velvet of the couch and the room's dark wainscoting. Mrs. Odette was murmuring to herself in the kitchen. The smell of cinnamon and apples was mixing with the convent's own scent of incense and old wood. There was some rumble of traffic outside, muffled by the weather.

And then a sudden sound—startling, like a bird hitting the window—and Sister Jeanne looked up to see the man himself, in his brown suit, watching her from the convent's dim hallway. She knew that suit. She had run a horsehair clothes brush down its length, flicked a bit of lint from its shoulder before she carried it to Sheen's funeral parlor. She knew the man. She knew that stubborn, solemn, lifeless face. It was lifeless still.

Sister Jeanne by then had sat vigil with any number of bodies, newly dead. She recognized the feral odor that filled the room.

What quickly followed, before Sister Jeanne could even raise her hand to her heart, before she could decide whether to shield the child or offer her to him—a balm, perhaps—was Sister Lucy's voice, just outside the convent door, unhappy with something, and another nun's, Sister Eugenia's, low and patient replies. There was a thump again, perhaps Sister's toe against the heavy door. It opened, letting a blue-gray, late-day light into the elegant foyer along with the sound of the rain. The two nuns stepped inside, bustling, bustling, shaking their umbrellas and their cloaks. They were arguing. Sister Jeanne, weak-legged, stood and went to them, indicating with one hand the sleeping child, the other placed over her lips. She saw that her fingers were trembling.

The gesture brought a brief pause to whatever the two nuns were fighting about, and in it, Sister Eugenia snatched the black satchel from Sister Lucy's hand and, shaking her head, went down the hallway, muttering Dr. Hannigan's name. Sister Lucy then drew her freed arm into her wet cloak and looked at Sister Jeanne with a raised eyebrow, an expression—quite familiar to all of them in the convent—that said, I am smarter than any of you. I am from better stock. That said, You women constitute my purgatory. That said, I will endure it, but not for your sake.

It was well known in the convent that Sister Lucy would have preferred a contemplative's life. Would have preferred to converse with God alone.

Sister Lucy moved her impatient eyes to the child on the couch. "Her mother's gone home?" she asked severely.

"Not home," Sister Jeanne replied. "Just out to the stores. Out to catch her breath."

Sister Lucy gave no indication that she knew she was being quoted. Her eyes, as was their wont, darted back and forth with her thoughts. "She's here too much," she said abruptly.

"Annie?" Sister Jeanne said.

Sister Lucy shook her jowls. "No, of course not. I mean the child." Her eyes moved again. "A convent child," she said, "is not the same as a convent cat. She isn't a pet." Looking down, she trained her eyes on Sister Jeanne. "She needs a proper home."

Sister Jeanne was still trembling with what she had seen. Had imagined. Had called forth. At the back of her tongue, something bitter lingered; not fear exactly—hopelessness, defeat.

She knew herself to be a pagan at heart—superstitious, fanciful. It was her most confessed sin. Yet what terrified her now was not imagination but faith. The logic of faith that told her she had seen a soul denied rest.

She touched Sister Lucy's cloak, guilty and afraid, as if the nun, so serious and sensible, so full of disdain, could right her.

"Her mother needs a proper home as well," Sister Lucy was saying. "A proper husband."

Sister Jeanne said, "I'll pray for it."

Sister Lucy gave a snort, and a kind of pity—although it was a cold, distant kind of pity, like a bit of cool shade offered by an outcropping of granite—swept across her yellow eyes. A kind of pain.

Her hands remained clasped under her cloak. Sister Jeanne would later learn that Sister Lucy's wrist had been broken that afternoon by a man with the DTs, that the argument she had been having with Sister Eugenia as they came in was about going straight to the hospital to get it set. Under her cloak, it was already swollen.

Which explained why Sister Lucy did not raise her red finger in the air as she was wont to do whenever she said "Make note." Sister Jeanne looked up at the nun to show she was making note anyway. "Next time you see Mr. Costello and our Annie in the kitchen," Sister Lucy said, "make note of what their faces give away."

Alone

M R. COSTELLO was a quiet, balding man with a ready grin. Polite and hush-voiced when he spoke to the Sisters, but loud and full of good humor when he called to people on the street. He was always offering the nuns extra pints of cream or discounts that he seemed to make up on the spot. Always admiring the "miraculous" cleanliness of the empty milk bottles they returned to him. At the invitation of the Sisters, he attended mass in the convent chapel every first Friday, sitting in the last row with his cap in his hands and his head bowed low.

When he was thirty-six, Mr. Costello had married a pretty, blue-eyed girl. Rheumatic fever as a child had left her with a weak heart. The case of Saint Vitus' Dance that followed left her isolated and strange. Not a year into their marriage, Mrs. Costello was bitten by a stray dog that was foraging in the tangled back-yard of one of the tenements. Infection set in. She lost her leg. There followed a nervous collapse, a touched brain, an invalid's cosseted routine. The Sisters called it a sad case.

Because they had been so often inside his home, the nuns knew there was no pretense in Mr. Costello. They knew he kept his place in manly order—few knickknacks, just a pair of Mrs. Costello's porcelain-faced dolls on the dresser in the bedroom, a statue of St. Joseph on the mantel—and that he did as much dusting as a man could be expected to do: the top of a bureau, but not the legs; the base of a lamp, but not the shade. They knew the apartment's one closet was arranged with military precision and the kitchen cupboards were neatly spare—one bottle of bootlegged whiskey, used only for toothaches or colds (the visiting Sisters checked it daily). He kept house, all the Sisters agreed, like a fastidious bachelor. No hint of anything unseemly to indicate otherwise. Or to tell them he was something less than the good, unfortunate man he appeared to be.

The intimacies of bathing and feminine hygiene Mr. Costello left to the nuns, but he cooked his wife a dinner every night and there was never a dish left in the sink or a crumb left on the table-cloth when the Sisters arrived every morning to wake her and give her breakfast. Caring for Mrs. Costello, who was childish, sometimes churlish, thin as a rail, light as a feather, was an easy enough bit of duty, easily dispensed. Because Mr. Costello was up and gone well before dawn, the Sisters could arrive as early as the day required, spend an hour, and then leave the poor woman, refreshed and well-fed, in her chair by the front window, a small sandwich and a glass of milk and a chamber pot all within easy reach. A Sister might stop in at lunchtime or, if Mr. Costello was going to be delayed—if he'd told the nuns that morning, sometimes via only a note left among their milk bottles, that he was driving up to the dairy that afternoon or attending a union meeting in the city—they might bring an early dinner as well, and then get her ready for bed, knowing that the clean linens and the soothed wife that would greet Mr. Costello at the end of his long working day was the Sisters' own way of telling him that he had their admiration.

ANNIE FIRST SPOKE to him in the convent kitchen early on a deeply gray morning with a rain so cold and steady it had kept him behind in his deliveries. He had paused in too many doorways, looking for a break in the low clouds. He had lingered in conversation with a complaining old woman he usually hoped to avoid. Against his preferred routine, he had smoked a morning cigarette in his cart, watching the steam rise from the flanks of the patient horse, reluctant to turn up his collar once more, to head out once more with his milk crate into the storm.

Annie, for her part, had come to the convent earlier than usual, just as the Sisters were going in to morning prayer. The rain had woken her before dawn—no walk with Mrs. Tierney today, and the lack of it made her wonder if she had the wherewithal to get herself out of bed. Sally was three years old, fast asleep beside her. Annie listened to the rain against the windows until the room had gathered enough light to see by, and then she got up carefully—the child was easily woken—and made her way into the kitchen. She meant to put the kettle on, to warm both herself and the room, but when she pressed her nose to the window to see if there would be any relief in the weather, the old smoky odor of the catastrophe arose again. She smelled it on the wet glass and the damp sill, on the twice-repainted kitchen walls, as if the odor of fire and sorrow was contained in the soaked brick of the building itself.

She glanced down into the backyard. Still too dark to see anything but her own reflection. She imagined opening the window to lean out into the rain. Imagined that if she did so, she would feel the sure pressure of Jim's hand on her waist, easing her away, whispering into her ear in the wordless way of ghosts. And what would he say? Would it be an apology? A pledge? A stumbling excuse, or the smiling, wheedling endearments he had spoken to her so often in the past, from this kitchen table, from their warm bed: "Oh, let me stay where I am a while longer."

On the day she buried him, they rode out to the cemetery in Mr. Sheen's hearse. Annie and the undertaker and Sister St. Saviour, wrapped in her black cloak. The nun was as monolithic, as sunken-eyed, as a defeated general.

Defeat was all about them as they passed through the dark streets. Early morning it was, rain and snow. Jim, the empty shell of him, riding behind them in the long car.

What had God been to her until that bitter morning? Father, guardian, comforter, king. All Annie seemed capable of remembering as they drove was a lifetime of negotiations, of pleas—so many of them, until that morning, about Jim. That he would smile at her, that he would come to call. Please God: that he would cross to New York in safety. Please God: that he'd be there to meet her when she followed him.

That he would get up out of bed.

It seemed the single prayer of her married life: that he would get up out of bed, go to work, come home—come home with something brighter on his face than that hooded scowl, please God. Please God, let him put an end to those long breaths through distended nostrils, to the sinking into himself, fists closing, for conversations she couldn't hear. Let him recount for her some-thing that had happened throughout his day that was not an insult, an affront. Let him lose his contempt. Let him keep his job. Let him get up out of bed and be on time for a change.

That cold morning, the cemetery trees were like black lines etched in window frost, the ground brittle with icy spears of grass. The casket was pulled from the hearse. When a plot was available, they would put him in it. She didn't ask where his body would stay until then. With Sister's help, she had money enough only for this. She was going to save the deed to Calvary for herself alone.

She touched the coffin, coated now with the fat drops of melted snow. Sister St. Saviour waved a vial of holy water and said a prayer. The three blessed themselves—Annie and Mr. Sheen and the nun—and then climbed back into the car with their clothes damp.

She didn't hold it against the Church: the miserable morn-ing, the cold, unconsecrated ground, the refused funeral mass, not even the money she'd lost on the double grave at Calvary. She well understood that there would be no rules at all if there were no punishment for the failure to follow them. Like any good mother, the Church had to cuff its children when they misbehaved. Make the punishment fit the crime.

He'd murdered himself and murdered something in her as well.

Who could argue for leniency? Who could expect absolution?

Sister St. Saviour did, of course. But the woman, childless, stubborn, coming to the close of her life, had a mad heart. Mad for mercy, perhaps, mad for her own authority in all things—a trait Annie had come to love and admire—but mad nonetheless.

Riding home from the cemetery, Sister St. Saviour had said, "It would be a different Church if I were running it."

And so lifted the burden of that terrible morning with some laughter.

But Annie never blamed the Church.

It was instead the recollection of her own unanswered prayers, simple as they had been, that made her grow cautious in her faith, wary of her own belief.

Let him get up, she had prayed—how often?—boiling an egg and making his tea and hurrying back into the silent bedroom to call him again. Hating her own desperation. Her own helplessness. Hating the way his gray moods and scarlet furies put himself between her and the simple happiness life was offering, a kind of paradise after the poor lives they'd left behind: this busy city, his good job, this tidy place of their own, a child coming in summer.

Let him get up and get going, she had prayed—avoiding his hand as he reached out from under the blankets he'd pulled over his head. Or, sometimes, giving in—she had done this, too— giving in to the luxury of what he wanted to believe: that their time belonged to themselves alone, that they could do as they pleased with it.

Now, at the kitchen window, looking into the black yard, tangled and wet, the tangle seeming to writhe in the sheen of falling rain, she stamped her foot and felt the old impatience that was as well her most vivid memory of her married life. *Jimmy, get up.*

Only her own pale face looked back at her in the gray glass.

Even his ghost was impossible to stir.

It was a cold hope at best to imagine otherwise.

The cold hope, nevertheless, that kept her in this apartment where he had died, where he had lived, when a smaller, cheaper place would do.

She woke Sally, and they both dressed and pulled on their rain boots. Annie carried the girl the five blocks to the convent, the big umbrella doing little good in the blowing rain, and arrived breathless and laughing, just as the nuns—their plain faces made plainer still by the lingering traces of sleep—filed silently into the chapel. In the bright convent kitchen, she shook the rain from her hair. Mrs. Odette had yet to arrive. Annie was rubbing a tea towel over Sally's wet head, the two of them singing softly together, "It's raining, it's pouring . . ." while the sound of the morning psalm floated from the chapel. She saw a black and bent figure through the glass of the back door, heard the rattle of the milk bottles. Impulsively, she pulled open the door. Mr. Costello looked up, startled. Rain dripped from the peak of his glistening cap and from his nose. "Poor man," she said. "Why don't you come in?"

He stepped inside with no other thought than that he wanted to. He stood, the two fresh bottles of milk in his hands, the two gleaming empties under his arm, his coat dripping on the mat at the threshold. The kitchen itself was not unfamiliar to him, but never before had he seen it like this, so well-ordered and warmly lit, with a pretty child seated on the high step stool the nuns kept at the counter, a child big-eyed and curious, and the woman who helped out in the laundry, a tea towel in her hand, smiling to welcome him. No beauty, perhaps, but with lovely dark hair that was wet and plastered in black ribbons here and there on her pale forehead and white throat. Despite the noise of the rain outside, he could hear the sweet voices of the nuns in the chapel.

They were singing "*O Salutaris Hostia*," a hymn he had known since his boyhood.

Annie stepped forward to take the two bottles of milk from his hands. He saw that one strand of hair ran in a jagged line across her flushed cheek, nearly reaching her mouth, which was crooked and prettily bowed.

It was only the long habit of caring for a sick wife that made him, still dripping, reach out to brush the wet strand away.

He heard the closing notes of the hymn, remembered the Latin from school, the words that touched his exile's heart. *O grant us endless length of days, in our true native land with thee.*

He was inspired to ask her, "Where are you from?"

THAT SAME AFTERNOON, Mr. Costello met her on the corner when she ran out to catch her breath. And then she saw him again on a brighter day as she left the butcher shop. He was, on occasion, paused in the doorways she passed. He greeted her, kept pace casually. He was as tall as she was, which was not tall for a man, and yet their shoulders never met. He did not offer to carry her bag. They walked to the park one bright day, and then as far as the promenade, where they sat, a good distance apart, on the bench. Even so, she could smell the stable on his clothes.

Their talk skimmed over everything. It was what made their hour together so delightful to her. He had a story to tell from the morning, or from only a few minutes before they met. He had a story to tell that was told to him just last Sunday after mass. She offered in exchange something Liz Tierney had said—a tale from the hotel, from her children. Since the first afternoon he had met her on the corner—out of the convent for an hour, thanks to

Sister Jeanne, out to catch her breath—they seemed to agree that nothing was worth saying, here in the middle of her busy working day and at the weary end of his own, if it did not make them both laugh.

No mournful tales, then, of her widowhood, of his frail wife. No indignant recounting of Sister Illuminata's demands during the endless hours in the laundry. No complaints from him about the cold weather or the milk trains or the vague and endless demands of customers and bosses. They sat apart as strangers might on a bench in the park, and their talk skimmed over all that preceded the time they were together and all that awaited them the rest of the day.

A year of this, and then she pressed the key to the downstairs door into his hand. "Come up" was all she said, and walked ahead of him in the street. At the corner, she glanced over her shoulder to see that he had already crossed to the other side. It pleased her that he knew enough to place some time between them.

She left the door ajar: she wouldn't have him knocking for all the neighbors to hear. She left the door ajar and sat in the living room, in the single chair, so she could hear his step or see his shadow as he approached.

She wondered how long he would keep her waiting. How much discretion she would have to endure.

She folded her hands, one over the other on her lap. They were not smooth. He would not, she was certain, expect them to be.

She thought of his own pale hands, big farmer's hands that belonged to a stouter man. His thick shoes, a piece of straw sometimes caught in a cuff or entangled in the frayed laces.

The door was ajar. The glass transom above it was closed. It was a cold bright afternoon in midwinter. The room was poor. The slipcover she'd made to hide the scorched couch was ill-fitting, the fabric dull, as if faded. The picture she'd hung above it was too small for the wide wall. It was a heavily framed oil of the Sacred Heart, the image darkened by time. It had arrived in the donation basket—the frame was chipped and there was a tear in the canvas. "Coals to Newcastle," Sister Illuminata had said when she saw it, but little Sally was enamored, and Annie herself had felt some piety when she hung it up—stood on the couch in her bare feet, drove the nail, Sally watching her from the floor. It seemed a pretension now. In her time at the convent, her eyes had grown accustomed to authentic elegance—the beautiful house itself, built for a wealthy man: the gleaming woods, the simple chandeliers, the plaster ceiling roses and graceful corbels. There was no denying that this bare room was a poor woman's room, an immigrant's small space. No denying that its spare cleanliness betrayed an immigrant's reserve. Twice since Jim died, she'd hung it with new paper—and now as she waited, she could see in the far corner that the latest attempt had already begun to curl. Twice she had repainted the kitchen walls, the bedroom walls.

He would find the place clean and well-ordered when he appeared.

She had a moment's doubt that he would indeed appear, a moment's fear that he had misunderstood her meaning, or disapproved of it, when she pressed the key into his hand. She dismissed both notions.

The Sisters said his own place was also neat as a pin. It was, she suspected, another kind of pretension, this immigrant reserve. A clean and well-ordered veneer over the trouble of a bedridden wife, a dead husband, over loneliness and worry.

The door was ajar. Through it, she heard what she knew was the sound of his footstep—although it might be the footstep of anyone—and then his shadow, hesitating. She stood. He was there. She opened the door just enough to admit him. Smell of the stable on his clothes, but also, now, the smell of alcohol and of pine soap, as if he had stopped before he came up. Stopped to take a drink. To wash his hands.

He took off his cap and smoothed back his hair, what there was of it. The bareness of his poor scalp moved her with pity, a sympathetic affection. It was an infant's delicate skull; it was a reminder that he was not young.

In this light his eyes were merely brown, although in the sun she sometimes saw green and black and gold.

He put his hand to her chin and she touched his cheek, knowing her fingertips were rough. A sound arose from the cluttered backyard and rattled the kitchen window. It was the familiar tapping of city grit, or wind-lifted leaves, or maybe a pigeon's wing against the glass. A sound that might once have filled her with fanciful notions: Jim's breath in her ear, his hand on her hip, something restored to her.

As they both turned toward the noise, she saw his eyes catch the painting on her wall, the familiar image of Christ, sorrowful, compassionate, barely visible in the darkening oils but for the pale hand that gestured toward a heart threaded with thorns.

And then they both turned their eyes away from it.

"Are we alone?" he whispered.

She said, "We are."

Rose

WE HAD ON OUR FATHER'S SIDE a great-great-aunt, Aunt Rose. A tiny woman, very old. We recall a velvet hat and a pale broadcloth suit, rose-colored perhaps, and maybe the smell of rosewater about her as she made her way into the house—one gloved hand steadying herself on the long server that had been our grandmother's, one skimming the backs of the chairs that lined the dining table, skimming our cheeks as well as she encountered us, one by one. Our father behind her, carrying her bags, saying, "Step aside," telling us, "Say 'Good afternoon,'" "Say 'Pardon me.'" Our father—the doorman's son—banging her two suitcases against the chair legs and setting the porcelain in the china cabinet ringing.

This was in the drafty house in Hempstead where we grew

up. It was an old house, red-shingled and white-trimmed, plagued with an endless series of tumble-down catastrophes that made our father in midlife a caricature of the hapless, city-bred, suburban homeowner. We recall him prowling through the rooms with a stepladder on his shoulder, with a hammer or a socket wrench in his hands, doing no good. Our mother, when she was well, always smiling indulgently, following him with her eyes.

The old Hempstead house. We recall the battered glass knob of the side door, our shoulders to its peeling paint. A nest of boots and shoes inside, no matter the season, a tattered rag rug, the dark basement-breath of heating oil and cinderblock and cold dirt. Then three steps up to the narrow kitchen—dark green countertops, black linoleum floor flecked with red, red cabinets, appliances of enamel and steel, scent of clove and cinnamon and sunlight and dust. The narrow passage to the dining room. Lace tablecloth, lace doilies, lace curtains at the window, and beyond it, a continuation of lace, the apple tree in full, wind-scattered bloom, or maybe a sudden shower of snow, as old Aunt Rose steadied herself, coming into the house, one gloved hand on the long server that had been our grandmother's, one running along our cheeks.

Just where she had come from and why she had appeared remained uncertain. "Upstate," we were told. "Because she is old," we were told. She was given the guest room, and directed by our father, we followed her halting journey up the stairs with our hands poised at her elbows or at her hips. She trembled, we recall, either because of her great age or because of her delight at our elaborate courtesies.

The guest room on the third floor of the old Hempstead house was narrow beneath the eaves, painted yellow, white curtains at the window.

Downstairs again, our father told the story of Great-aunt Rose and Red Whelan. Up in Poughkeepsie this was, he said. Just after the Civil War. A knock at the door when the family was at dinner. Rose only a small child. A man invited in: red hair, red skin, scarred red flesh from neck to ear as if a plow had scraped his face. One leg and one arm, so that he, too, Red Whelan, made a halting climb to the upstairs room—tap of crutch on each stair tread, on the attic's bare wood. Patrick, our great-grandfather, a young schoolteacher by then, standing silently in the room's narrow doorway as Red Whelan was shown the bed, the washstand, a small desk, and a wide wing chair, all the family had done to prepare the place for him. The room where he would live out his days.

And Great-aunt Rose, still a child, holding his dinner in a covered dish.

When we were teenagers, brooding in our bedrooms, brooding or hungover, or just sleeping through an afternoon, as our mother used to do, our father would complain, his voice annoyed, bordering on angry, but amused also, because he, too, had been a reader, a brooder, and the phrase had been his own father's refrain—"Hibernating up there like Red Whelan."

Any redheaded, fat-faced, freckled Irishman was a regular Red Whelan.

Any houseguest who stayed too long was threatening to become a Red Whelan.

Any mention of old Aunt Rose's long and lonely life included the forty-odd years she had devoted herself to Red Whelan, her brother's substitute in the Civil War. A widowed spinster, our father called her. A married nun.

We carried the tea things upstairs. We carried her sparse dinner, only small bowls of mush: soups and applesauce and

71

creamed farina. In the third-floor room, she blinked at us from her bed or from her chair, her face always dusted with powder, although it seemed to us then that she was dusted with dust.

And the Little Nursing Sisters of the Sick Poor standing by. "Aren't you good?" they told us when we brought in the old lady's tray or took it away. Sister Jeanne among them. Our favorite.

We knew them well, the Little Nursing Sisters. The order of nuns our mother had thought to join until—our father liked to say—she thought better of it.

We knew them from our own fevered mornings: waking to find their pale hands to our foreheads and to our cheeks, or seeing through our crusted eyes their serious faces within the white bonnets as they put a thermometer between our lips, commanded us not to bite it. We watched them float around our sickbeds, tugging and pulling with their short, clean hands until our night-tangled blankets and sheets were transformed into something clean again, and cool.

We knew them from all the long afternoons when we came home from school, hand to the glass knob of the battered side door, and found a nursing nun standing like a black-and-white beacon in the kitchen—her finger to her lips because our mother had once more taken to her shaded room to sleep off what they called her melancholy.

They arrived by taxi in those days, before their habits were amended to allow them enough peripheral vision to drive themselves. Our father scurried out to the curb to pay the fare.

For years we believed we were not unusual in this. For years we believed the Little Nursing Sisters of the Sick Poor, Congregation of Mary Before the Cross, appeared in every household whenever crisis or illness disrupted the routine, whenever a substitute was needed for She Who Could Not Be Replaced.

Sister Jeanne was our favorite.

She was an old woman then. Shorter than we were. Child-sized inside her habit. When she made us tea, she warmed the milk, and she carried in her black satchel a sleeve of biscuits we have never found since. Coated with chocolate, we recall, with a thin, summery taste of strawberry jam.

When she spoke to us—and not all the Little Sisters spoke to us so easily—her voice was always wry—"It's all silliness, isn't it?"—so that we never knew if we would be hushed into sacred silence by what she said or if her voice would suddenly curl up like a grin and we would see that inside her white bonnet and her dark veil she was shaking with laughter.

She said, "I knew your mother since before she was born. Same as I know all of youse."

She said, "youse," which delighted us. She said "pernt" for point, "erl" for oil. She was years out of Brooklyn by then, at the Old Age Home the Sisters ran out on Long Island, as an aide, not a patient. Although she must have been nearly as old as many of the women she cared for.

She asked us, "Who's the dumbest boy in your class?"

Reaching under her bonnet, she tapped her freckled forehead. She touched her white bib between the chain of her cross, as if her heart was centered there. She said, "Because God put the knowledge in you before you were born, see? So you'd know He intends to be fair."

She tagged her sentences with "see?" like a Hollywood gangster, and this delighted us, too.

Sister Jeanne told us that she had meant to join another order altogether, another order of nuns also called Little Sisters, but went to the wrong address. Where Sister St. Saviour simply shrugged and said, "God's will."

Sister Jeanne said, "I knew your mother before she was born because Sister St. Saviour introduced us."

She said, "No one called for her, but still she appeared. That was the miracle, see? God saw the need. There was an accident with the gas. God saw your mother and your grandmother's need, and so Sister St. Saviour appeared."

We were sitting at the dining room table in the long, hushed hours of those still afternoons when our mother slept off her sadness, or when Great-aunt Rose was in the upper room. It might have been any season: there were blossoms on the apple tree at the window behind her head. There was a squall of fat snowflakes.

She told us, "There was a lovely smell of roses when Sister St. Saviour died. She opened her eyes for just a moment, she hadn't opened them in days, and then she closed them again and sighed. It was a very deep sigh. But no weariness in it, see? No sadness. I would say it was a satisfied sigh. And after that, it was like a thousand roses had been brought, special delivery, into the room. It was just a glimpse of where her soul had gone. A whiff of it. As if a door had opened for a moment, just to let her in, and all of us still stuck here on earth got a glimpse. Because a glimpse is all the living can bear. All we can bear of heaven's beauty."

She said, her eyes to the ceiling, "It's not for me, you know. That beauty. But never mind. You'll see it, for truth. Your old aunty, too."

How long did Great-aunt Rose stay with us? A few weeks, a month, maybe two? On a warm afternoon, we came in from school to find the guest room empty. Our mother, up and about on that day, had opened the windows to let in the air. The white curtains stirred, the mattress was bare.

Our father said later that because our mother was delicate,

given to melancholy, it seemed best that old Rose go off to a nursing home for her final days. For expert care, he said. The nursing home was run by yet another order of nuns, not our own Little Nursing Sisters, whose numbers were diminishing even then. Whose Bishop had cast an acquisitive eye over their elegant convent, even then.

Great-aunt Rose, we were told, was gone to spend her last days in a nursing home run by the very order Sister Jeanne hadn't joined, an order that specialized in old people who had come to the end of their time. In a town called Valhalla.

"Of all things," our father said.

"If that's not a sure sign she's going to heaven," he said, well satisfied that his obligation to the old lady had been met, "I don't know what is."

The Convent Child

A FOX STOLE WITH A BROKEN CLASP found among the donated clothes, a lady's velvet chapeau, some elbow-length kid gloves, torn at the seams, and Sally transformed herself into Mrs. McShane, the elegant and imperious woman (Brooklyn hoi polloi, Annie said) who organized the Ladies Auxiliary's annual tea and Christmas Bazaar to raise funds for the convent. Sally brought the stole to her chin, extended a wavering arm to Sister Illuminata, and said in Mrs. McShane's studied, drawling way, "Our good Little Sisters." Said to her mother, the gloved fingers spread across her cheek, "But, Annie, my dear, where are the petits fours?"

She shimmied into a discarded housedress, slipped one of the nuns' bibbed aprons over her head, and pantomimed Mrs. Odette's kitchen dance—lifting imaginary pot lids, peeling imaginary apples held right before her squinting eyes, whispering "*Herregud*" under her breath until her mother and Sister Illuminata, laughing, were begging her to "Shush."

A babushka and a moth-eaten coat with a lambskin collar, an expression of peering curiosity, dawning disapproval, and there was Mrs. Gertler just as she looked every evening, watching the street from her parlor-floor window.

Once, when Annie was out at the shops, the organ grinder stopped on the street outside the convent, turning his squawking box and singing his off-key Italian. It was a hot day and the basement windows were open behind the grills. "For the love of God," Sister Illuminata muttered, "couldn't he play an Irish tune?" Sally—quick as a sprite—moved a coal box beneath the window, hopped onto it, and, grabbing the iron bars, shouted, in Sister Illuminata's own brogue, "Play us an Irish tune, for the love of God."

The poor man, searching the air for the source of the voice, cried out, "Yes, Sister," and attempted to sing some mangled, halfhearted version of "The Wearing of the Green."

"Good man," Sally cried when he had come to a halting finish. The child, Sister Illuminata said, was a born mimic.

THE DAYS IN THE LAUNDRY grew longer for the two women when Sally started school, but when she returned, she brought her mother and the nun tales from what they called the wider world. She could capture her classmates' broken English, or their solid Brooklynese, with perfection. She had the pastor's nasally Latin down to a T. She was a good and quiet child in the classroom, polite and shy on the street, but in the basement laundry of the convent, every impulse toward silliness, every outlandish pantomime or adolescent misfiring of elbows and feet, not to mention wickedness and wildness, was set free, and utterly indulged by her mother and the nun, provided—they were always reminding her—that she kept her voice low.

Provided, it was understood, that proper decorum was reestablished whenever she went "upstairs," which meant into the whole of the universe above the convent laundry.

Perhaps because of this indulgence, the girl, as she grew, chose to linger with Sister Illuminata whenever her mother went out in the afternoons—to do her shopping, to catch her breath—rather than follow her or join the other girls playing in the street. When Sister Jeanne came down the stairs, Sally kissed the little nun but, more and more, begged off their old routines. Sister Illuminata hid her pleasure in this. She turned to her ironing, sighed heavily to disguise a thin smile. Sister Jeanne's sweet goodness was best spent on younger children, she thought. On innocents. An older child, an older child with some spunk like Sally, like her own Mary Pat Shea, might prefer a little devilment in her friends.

A small table was borrowed from an upstairs hallway and carried to the cellar so that Sally could do her homework there, in Sister Illuminata's company (the iron thumping and hissing), rather than, more sensibly, at the well-lit table in the convent kitchen or the dining room in her own home. For if a case of the giggles overcame her here, or if she recalled some incident from the schoolyard this morning that she longed to re-enact, or even if, bored with sums, she drifted to the donation baskets and tried on a few clothes, Sister Illuminata, fondly, would abide.

IT WAS LATE AFTERNOON and her mother had gone to the shops. Sally was nearly thirteen. She was helping Sister Illuminata fold the last of the day's clothes. One of the freshly ironed tunics belonged to Sister Jeanne, and Sally, laughing, held it up against her. The nun looked at the girl over her shoulder. Sally said, "Let's fool my mother."

It was not the first time she had dressed in the habit of the Little Sisters. It was a custom at her school to hold "vocation days," when the students were asked to dress up as priests and nuns and to parade about the schoolyard as miniature ecclesiastics. Because of her status as a convent child, and because she was a good and quiet girl, Sally was chosen every year to represent the various orders of nursing Sisters in the modified habit that Sister Illuminata herself had made for her—and then altered each year as she grew. But on this afternoon, Sally eyed Sister Jeanne's full habit, the clean, consecrated cloth. "Come on, Sister," she said. "Just for fun."

Against her better judgment, Sister Illuminata helped the girl into the tunic. Since she had no cincture handy, she tied a linen bandage around the girl's thin waist and then brushed and smoothed the shoulders and the wide sleeves, shaking her head all the while at their transgression, but loving, too, the nearness of the girl, the coiled energy of her narrow body, the sweet buds of her breasts, the faint pattern of freckles on her nose that, this close, appeared to ride beneath the surface of her skin, as if under a milky veil.

Sitting on her ironing chair, Sister pressed the coif over Sally's bent head, tugging the thing into place over her ears, tucking her hair away with a busy mother's gentle brusqueness. Sally closed her eyes and placed her hands on Sister's swollen knees. Her breath smelled of milk and crackers. She was laughing when they began, her crooked teeth catching at the cloth of the tunic as it went over her head, but now she grew solemn, her eyes closed, as Sister smoothed and tucked, moving her scarred fingertip gently along the girl's forehead and her cheeks. She tugged the cloth into place and leaned back to look at Sally in the basement sunlight.

Sister shook her head, as if she disapproved of the charade and had no part in it, but what she was shaking off, in truth, was the bare beauty of the girl's plain face inside the white linen, a face pure and ageless and as innocent as if it had just been formed. She pushed Sally away a bit, taking the weight of the child off her sore knees, and fitted the bonnet over the coif. Then she lifted Sister Jeanne's black veil, newly ironed, and gently placed it over Sally's head. Took a pin from her own veil to hold it in place.

When Annie came down the stairs just after five o'clock, winded and apologizing that she had taken longer than usual because she had just run home to drop off a few things, Sister Illuminata, in her chair beside the ironing board, said casually, "Oh, Sally's already gone."

"When?" Annie asked. "I didn't see her on the street. When did she leave? I never passed her on the street."

The girl stepped out from the shadow of the furnace, into some streaming light from the high basement window. In perfect imitation of Sister Jeanne, she had her hands tucked into her sleeves, her eyes cast down. Stepping forward, she ducked her head in Sister Jeanne's own way, a way that implied tremendous shyness as well as some futile, last-ditch effort to suppress—like a lid on a boiling pot, Annie sometimes said—the rushing impulse to break into laughter.

The perfume of sunlight arose from Sister Jeanne's clothes. The late-spring afternoon threw a shaft of gold into the high window. It landed at Sally's feet.

With her head bowed, she could not see her mother, but she could hear her pause. "What in the world?" Annie whispered.

Sister Illuminata said, "Allow me to introduce a new member of our community. This is Sister St. Sally. Sister St. Sally of the Smelly Socks."

The nun's laughter was low and deep, and Annie's, after a pause, was full of warm impatience. "You are a pair," she said. She was slipping out of her spring coat. "The two of you. Is that Jeanne's habit? Don't you think it's a sacrilege, Sister?"

Sally moved forward, just a step or two, into the full corridor of spring sunlight.

The golden sunshine through the high basement window was like the light in holy cards—Sally felt it fall on her the way the painted light in holy cards fell over the bowed heads of saints. She held out her arms and marveled at their elegance within the wide sleeves, her wrists so slim and white against the black serge. She was filled with what seemed Sister Jeanne's own confidence and peace. Without a mirror to consult, with only her mother and Sister Illuminata's silly laughter to guide her, she understood, nevertheless, that she had been transformed. That even her voice, muffled as it was by the linen over her ears, the voice the two had so often warned her to soften, was now something else altogether, something solemn and graceful and profound. She knew she was meant to be a nun.

That night, when Sally whispered her intentions to her mother, speaking into the darkness, in the bed they still shared, Annie wondered if she might do well to point out that her daughter's ability to imitate to perfection snooty Mrs. McShane and harried Mrs. Odette, and even nosy Mrs. Gertler downstairs, was no proof at all that she was destined to become a city councilman's wife or a convent cook or a Jewish landlady with a dozen wigs.

But with the girl's bright eyes shining from the pillow beside hers, she resisted the impulse to tease.

She said instead, "Are you thinking already about how you'll leave me?"

And never meant to sound so pained.

WHEN SALLY WAS STILL SMALL and lifted down from the carriage in order to accommodate another of Mrs. Tierney's serial infants, she gripped her mother's skirt as they made their way along the streets. Under the rough cloth, the movements of her mother's hips and legs was always firm, without hesitation, and even as a small child, Sally felt the confidence of those quick steps as if her own feet drove them. When her mother reached for her hand because the crowds on the street were growing dense or the sun was setting and the streetlights coming on, or because there was something, or someone, they had to hurry past, the broad, strong grip of her fingers was not reassuring—it was solid assurance itself.

All her life, Sally had known that assurance.

She had watched her mother's hands dispatch a pile of piece-work in an evening's time. Seen them transform a knot of jumbled linen into a tall straight stack ready for the cupboard, architectural in its beauty. Her mother could set a springing mousetrap in a flash, dispose of the broken varmint—out the back window into the yard—and then light a match with the flick of her thumb to disperse the sweet and sickly dead-mouse smell.

Her mother could deftly wring a chicken's neck, pluck and wash and baste and serve it. She could mix a poultice, a bucket of wallpaper paste, a batter for bread, a batter for cake.

Her mother could soothe a torrent of tears with the brush of her rough thumb. She could send her daughter into an infant's deep sleep with the gentle drumming of her fingertips all along the girl's spine.

In the basement laundry, Sally watched her mother pluck potions from Sister Illuminata's tall shelves, handling with ease even those brown bottles that bore what Sister called the devil's mark: a nightmarish skull and crossbones.

She watched her mother sew—thumb and forefinger moving quickly, lightly, up and down, the other three slim fingers extended elegantly, flashing silver needle and the winking gold of her wedding band—her quick, sure hands, and stitches so fine, so even, you'd think the cloth (Sister Illuminata once said) had healed itself.

Sister Illuminata, glancing up from the ironing board or the scrub brush or the mangle, observed her mother at work. The nun's admiration went mostly unspoken, and yet, in their quiet underworld, Sally saw it.

She saw as well how Sister Jeanne lifted her chin at the sound of her mother's laughter, as if to catch a warm sun. How approvingly Sister Dymphna, Sister Eugenia, any of the nuns, scanned her mother's secondhand suit, beautifully altered and repaired, or Sally's own donation-basket Sunday clothes, whenever they met on the street after mass. From behind their horse-blinder bonnets, the nuns' admiration was palpable and clear.

And even fearless Mrs. Tierney sat back in her chair in pure amazement as her mother related a tale of how she had spoken up: when the butcher had his finger on the scale or the hot water at home was running tepid or the insurance man failed to properly mark his note. "You spoke up," Mrs. Tierney would say, flabbergasted, admiring, proud, and her mother would reply, all strength and assurance, "I certainly did."

Mother and daughter still shared the same bed, as they had done since Sally was born. They woke together, and together went down the apartment stairs just after dawn. The early-morning strolls with Mrs. Tierney ended when all the children were swept into school, but Annie's impulse toward routine was strong and still she stopped most mornings to see her friend—often in yet another, only slightly larger apartment; the six Tierney children growing so quickly that the new place was always immediately tighter still. Chaos and mess, as always, in Liz Tierney's place. And then the walk to school, the Tierney children swarming. And Sally coming down the basement stairs just after three, swinging her books, a story to tell. And then, when the day was done, mother and daughter returning home at dusk, under Mrs. Gertler's watchful eye, to the small dinner they would eat together at the dining room table. Then the cleaning up and the hour on the couch, Annie with piecework and the radio, Sally with her books or the newspaper or, if the paper bore bad news or the day had been dark, a rosary said together in alternating voices.

The repeated prayers, handed off between mother and daughter, always spoken clearly and loudly, as if to reach someone in the next room.

They put out the lights, checked the stove. In winter, Annie stood on a chair to pull tight the transom above the door. In summer, she stood to open it. Mother and daughter undressed together—routine eliminating all self-consciousness, if not the demure turning away—and then climbed into bed, Annie always on Jim's side. They held hands beneath the covers, or spooned, or merely put fingertips to the other's shoulder or arm. A whispered exchange in the dark: Let's remember the rent money, those dresses from the donation box that will surely fit the Tierney twins, a dime for the missions, darning thread for the

Sisters' stockings. Let's remember first Friday tomorrow—no breakfast.

Mrs. Gertler took to saying when she saw them in the hall, "More and more like sisters than mother and child," and both of them blushed, reluctant to decide which was preferable.

They had dinner at the Tierneys' apartment, Christmas and Easter for certain, but any number of Sundays in between, and Mr. Tierney, Sally saw, was a smiling man with a thick mustache, the source of much of Mrs. Tierney's conversation on weekday mornings when he wasn't there, but, in the flesh, hardly presence enough to make a difference. He sat at the head of the long table, he carved the turkey or the ham, he was gracious to her mother and included Sally whenever he addressed his daughters, but once the meal was over, he retreated behind his newspaper or stood out on the fire escape with a cigar or disappeared into the bedroom for so long that Sally was always startled to see him back again, sometimes dressed in his regal doorman's uniform like an actor on a stage, epaulettes and fringe, the cap tucked under his arm. "No rest for the weary," he said. And then he would be gone, the crowded household unchanged by the loss of him.

As a child, Sally believed she would marry a uniformed man and preside over a crowded apartment like the Tierneys', but the appeal of the dream had nothing to do with the lack of a male presence in her life. She felt no such lack. The dream arose merely out of what she recognized as her mother's pleasure in the Tierneys' bustling, comical household—the music and the drama of the talk, the argument, the settling of scores. Her mother took the Tierney children into her arms, the younger ones especially, as if they were her own. She brushed her lips against their hair or rode them on her knee. In Sally's experience, the Tierney household was the only place on earth where her mother agreed to take a drop. Where her cheeks flushed red with laughter. As a girl, Sally took pleasure in imagining herself someday presiding over a household like the Tierneys'—if only because of what a fine gift such a crowded, restful life would make for the mother she loved beyond all reason

"ARE YOU ALREADY THINKING about how you'll leave me?" her mother asked her in the familiar darkness of the room they'd always shared.

There were tears in her mother's voice, and the sound of them brought tears to her own eyes. The truth was, she hadn't thought of her mother at all in that moment when the holy card sunlight fell over her head, or in the hours since.

"There's no room for novices here," her mother said. "They'll send you to the motherhouse in Chicago."

Sally said, "I know."

"It's a dirty town, I think," Annie said.

Sally said, "I'd like to see it."

"You'll have to study nursing. Is that what you want?"

"It is," the girl whispered.

"And then you'll have to go where they send you. No guarantee you'll come back home."

"Yes," Sally said.

"You'll leave the world behind," her mother said.

"I know." Placid.

"You'll leave me behind."

In the pale darkness of the room, Annie turned her head on the pillow. Streetlight shone through the worn shades, so she could just make out the tears that were welling in her daughter's eyes. She saw them spill—a shining, gray, liquid light—and knew in an instant that her words had only honed her daughter's vague resolve.

It was the same mistake her own widowed mother had made when she raised every good objection to Annie's leaving home to follow Jim. He had no job, no prospects, and no promise of marriage had been made. He was—her mother's word—peculiar: laughing and charming in one minute, gone blackly silent the next. His mother, too, was strange.

Sensible, sensible, everything she said against him. But at the core of every reasonable argument the old woman made, Annie heard her fear. Her need. Annie's two sisters were in London. One brother was in Liverpool. Her elder brother lived just down the road, but he had a brace of small children of his own. Her mother wanted to keep her last unmarried daughter for herself—a stay against the loneliness of her final years.

Annie grew bolder with every good warning her mother spoke. Her resolve swelled, feeding not on the perfect sense her mother made but on her own new disdain for the woman's weakness. Her selfishness. Annie had, until then, thought her mother stronger than that. More capable of great sacrifice for the sake of her child's happiness.

In her mind's eye, she saw a crone's hand reaching up as if from a grave, reaching up to catch the skirt of a girl who had already danced away.

"Oh, we'll see each other again," Sally said calmly, into the darkness. "Life is like the blink of an eye."

Of course, it was Sister Jeanne's voice entirely.

SOON ENOUGH, the wider world had the child bound for sanctity. Annie saw how the Tierney kids, always rough and ready and full of mischief, began to change in Sally's presence, to gentle themselves, as Annie thought of it, to hush their voices, smiling at her shyly. Soon the Tierney girls began to encircle Sally as they walked to and from school, as if she were the plaster Madonna in a processional. Now the boys, Tom and Patrick, hung back, newly hesitant, nearly awestruck, although—Annie made note—they bumped and elbowed their sisters still.

Annie heard from Sally's teachers how the girl had begun to spend her recess in the church, not the play yard. How she led the eighth grade in the rosary but refused, all modesty, to crown the statue of Mary in May—gave the floral crown, in fact, to a deaf child in one of the lower grades, a child friendless and shy.

"Overdoing it," Annie told Mrs. Tierney.

That fall, when Sally moved to the high school, the Tierney girls reported to their mother that some nasty boys had called her "Sister"—and Sally had disarmed them all by saying, "That's right. Sister St. Sally of the Smelly Socks."

She eased away with gentle explanations the few boys who pursued her in those years—mostly serious or unpopular boys who hadn't gotten word of her vocation—and rose above the romantic dramas of the other girls—young Matilda Tierney had an operatic heartbreak at sixteen—with benign sympathy, her hands tucked into her sleeves.

"Promised to Christ," Sister Illuminata said over her ironing board, full of admiration. Annie silenced the turning mangle, put her wet hands to her hips. "What man accepts a promise from a girl so young?"

A beautiful newcomer passed briefly through the convent—Sister Augustina, elegant and thin, olive-skinned, sunken-eyed, gone back to her family with a collapsed lung in three weeks' time—and Annie saw how quickly Sally adopted the doomed nun's ethereal glide. She knew a romance was brewing in her daughter's brain, the tale of a girl called by God and a selfish widowed mother who barred the door. It was a tale straight out of the Lives of the Saints—the young female saints, anyway, who were always met with opposition by parents or suitors, or who went to their deaths—eyes raised—in their stubbornness to heed the Lord's call. Jesus Himself playing the part of the lovely-eyed beau, dangerous and strange and so alluring. Jim.

Sister Illuminata understood the case Annie made against her daughter's vocation. She understood the logic of mere mimicry. Who among the Sisters knew better than she how Sally's true nature leaned toward silliness and laughter? But Sister Illuminata had also seen the holy light pass through the basement window. She had seen the girl's face transformed. She told Annie, "My mother used to say, 'A friend's eye is a good mirror.'"

Now, on her afternoons alone with Sally, while Annie was out at the stores, Sister Illuminata whispered her encouragement. She told the girl that it was not sacrifice that had driven her own vocation, not the sacrifice of life and family and the world— "giving up this and that and whatnot" was how she put it, dismissive. It was the notion that Christ Himself had called her to become, in a ghastly world, the pure, clean antidote to filth, to pain.

All things human bend toward it, Sister Illuminata said. They were alone in the basement in the waning afternoons. Because of original sin, she told the girl, all things human bend toward filth, decrepitude, squalor, stink. She pointed to the basement's high windows. "Look out there, if you have eyes to see."

All things mortal bend toward ruin, Sister said, which means toward pain, toward suffering. It had always been the devil's intention, she said, to convince human beings they were no more than animals, never angels. Which is why there's nothing like pain to turn a person into a howling beast. Nothing like disease to wear a soul thin. Stink to discourage us. Dirt to drag us down.

The life of a nursing Sister is the antidote to the devil's ambitions. A life immaculate and pure.

A Sister makes herself pure, Sister Illuminata said, immaculate and pure, not to credit her own soul with her sacrifice—her giving up of the world—but to become the sweet, clean antidote to suffering, to pain.

"You wouldn't put a dirty cloth to an open wound, would you?" Sister Illuminata said.

Sitting on her chair beside the ironing board, her knees beneath the black tunic swollen with arthritis, she cocked her bonnet toward the pile of white handkerchiefs, newly ironed and stacked like cards, as if they illustrated her point. Sally, knowing the routine as she knew every ritual of the convent laundry, took the handkerchiefs from the end of the ironing board and set them carefully in the wicker basket on her mother's sewing table. Her mother would carry them upstairs when she returned, distribute them to each narrow dresser in each of the Sisters' narrow rooms.

She lifted the basket of linen tablecloths and napkins her mother had taken in from the line before she went out. In the hierarchy of her tasks, Sister Illuminata always saved any household ironing for the end of the day, in case her energy flagged. Her best work was done in the morning and was dedicated to the Sisters' habits, or to whatever was going back to the homes of the sick, or to the refreshed donations meant for the poor. Her own habit she washed and ironed on rare occasions. "The last shall be first," she said then.

"It's been a long time since I was out nursing," Sister Illuminata said as Sally helped her to spread the wide tablecloth over the ironing board. It was a plain rough-spun cotton meant for everyday use, redolent now of the line. "But down here the work's the same, isn't it? A kind of healing." And she chuckled at the thought, and then shook her head as if to dispel her own vanity. She directed Sally to fetch the broader, old-fashioned iron that was sitting on the furnace grate. "Down here, we do our best to transform what is ugly, soiled, stained, don't we? We send it back into the world like a resurrected soul. We're like the priest in his confessional, aren't we?" And chuckled again at her own fancy. Sally's vocation had made her expansive.

Sister Illuminata sprinkled the cloth. These days she used an old Coca-Cola bottle with a perforated rubber stopper. She licked her scarred fingertip and tested the iron. Attacked the cloth in broad strokes, her elbow pumping. "We send the Sisters out each morning immaculate, don't we? A clean cloth to apply to the suffering world."

Standing on the other side of the ironing board, Sally said softly, "It's true."

The two worked together in silence, moving the tablecloth across the board, folding it carefully, Sister pressing the hot iron along each of the folded seams. Finally, when the ironing was finished, Sister said, "There's a name for you." She was arranging the still-warm cloth over Sally's forearm, to be carried to the dining room upstairs and laid out in the bottom drawer of the server. "Mary Immaculate," she said, still a little breathless from her work. "There's a lovely name for a woman. A great name for a nun."

Orders

THERE WERE the Little Sisters of the Sick Poor, the Little Sisters of the Assumption, the Nursing Sisters of the Sick Poor of the Congregation of the Infant Jesus, the Sisters of the Poor of St. Francis, the Dominican Sisters of the Sick Poor of the Immaculate Conception, the Poor Clares, the Little Company of Mary. There were the Sisters of Divine Compassion, of Divine Providence, of the Sacred Heart. There were the Little Nursing Sisters of the Sick Poor of the Congregation of Mary Before the Cross, *Stabat Mater*, their own order.

But there were also the Daughters of Wisdom. The Daughters of Charity. The Sisters of Charity. The Benedictine Sisters, the Sisters of St. Joseph, the Sisters of Reparation of the Congregation of Mary. There were the Grey Nuns of the Sacred Heart.

The Visitation Nuns. The Presentation Nuns. The Handmaids of the Holy Child. The Sister Servants of the Holy Spirit.

Sister Eugenia admired the Sisters of Mercy. Their foundress—"like our own," she told Annie, as if courting her native pride—was an Irish woman, a daughter of wealth, called by God to serve the sick poor, first in Dublin, then all over Ireland, England, America. "A wonderful order," Sister Eugenia said. She named the hospitals they ran, the schools, the very sanatorium upstate where Sister Illuminata had been cured.

Sister Joseph Mary, who kept the convent's small library, mentioned St. Rose's Free Home for Incurable Cancer, right across the river and run by the Dominican Sisters of St. Rose of Lima. Their founder was the daughter of Nathaniel Hawthorne, Sister Joseph Mary said proudly. Not a Catholic himself, she explained to Annie, but a great writer nonetheless.

And wasn't there wonderful work being done for the lepers in Hawaii by the Sisters of St. Francis out of Syracuse? Sister Dymphna kept a scrapbook of inspirational things. Annie was shown a folded newspaper clipping that mentioned Mother Marianne Cope. Most of the article was about Father Damien, the priest to the lepers who had first invited the Sisters to Molokai, but Sister Dymphna had underlined in black ink every good word about the nun. There was a photo of a young girl with leprosy—she had a ruined face, a monstrous face, but she wore a cunning skirt and jacket, as good as you'd see on Fifth Avenue. All Mother Marianne's doing, the article said. The nun, the article said, had a flair for fashion.

Wouldn't Annie be proud to see her own child bringing beauty to these suffering souls?

A consensus arose among the Sisters in the convent—perhaps because they had seen the girl helping Sister Illuminata up and down the basement stairs—that Sally would do well with the old folks. The French Little Sisters of the Poor—the order Sister Jeanne herself had once intended to join—did marvelous work in this regard. And the Sisters of Charity had a home for aged domestic workers, immigrants mostly, men and women who had outlived their usefulness and their employers' largesse—faithful servants of the city's faithless titans. Wouldn't Sally be great with them?

Or indigent widows. The Carmelites were mentioned. They had a place on Staten Island.

And then there were the missionary orders to consider: the Foreign Mission Sisters of St. Dominic, the Missionary Sisters of the Immaculate Heart of Mary, of Our Lady of Victory, of the Most Precious Blood. There were the Charity nuns as well, who seemed to be everywhere, doing everything. There were the teaching orders. There were the contemplatives and cloistered, although none of the nuns in the convent believed that such a life would suit Sally—who, they had observed, still fidgeted in the chapel, played with her hair at Sunday mass. Who, even now, despite her call, had to be hushed by her mother when her giddy laughter rose up the basement stairs.

One of the walking orders, then, like their own. An order that would get her out among the poor, out in the air. She might help to care for orphans, childlike as she was. The Sisters of Charity ran the Foundling Home in Manhattan. ("Aren't they a busy bunch?" Annie asked Mrs. Tierney.) Given her youth and her innocence, her spark of mischief, Sally might, as a Sister, inspire and uplift certain fallen women. The Good Shepherd Sisters had a place for them.

"Give her to the prostitutes," Annie told Mrs. Tierney. "Send her to China or Africa. Or to Hawaii with the lepers. That's what they're proposing. Let her work in an orphanage, they're saying, after everything I've done to keep her out of one."

When Sally's high school days were drawing to a close, Sister Lucy ran her yellow eyes over the girl and then told Annie, "Let her follow me for the week. Let her get a glimpse of the work."

On that early morning in June, mother and daughter entered the convent through the front door rather than the back. They waited for a moment, feeling like visitors in the hushed hallway, until Sister Lucy swung toward them, sweeping down the corridor from the kitchen. She wore her cloak and carried her black satchel. She produced a white postulant's veil. "Wear this," Sister Lucy said. "You don't want to look like a tourist." And smiled thinly at her own joke. "Come with me," she said.

Annie helped her daughter fasten the veil and then kissed the smooth top of it as she sent her off. Sally took small, hurried steps, following behind Sister Lucy, as if a long skirt bound her ankles—not her own gait at all. Her mother wondered which of the nuns she was imitating now. She turned. Sister Illuminata was there in the hallway, standing before the basement door, leaning on her cane.

"Baptism by fire," Sister Illuminata said.

Sister Lucy

ALLY TOUCHED THE NEW VEIL, once, twice, three times, as she followed behind Sister Lucy. On the avenue she turned her head briefly, trying to capture her own reflection in the various shop windows—watery, she looked, in the morning light. She could barely glimpse her face through the flash of new sun. She'd worn her simplest dress and sensible oxfords from school, but she wanted to see herself with the veil on her head. Wanted to study the transformation. At a corner, she glanced around, hoping to find someone she knew, someone to witness who she had become. "Stop your gaping," Sister Lucy said as the light changed and she forged on. Sally followed, her head bowed.

At a gray, four-story apartment building, they turned in. The steps were brick, chipped with wear, a pane in the front door was cracked and repaired with brown tape. The door was unlocked. There was a dirty perambulator in the vestibule, its under-carriage full of rust. A knotted plywood board covering its bed. A smell of cats and damp plaster. Sister Lucy climbed the bare stairs, Sally behind her.

The key to the apartment door was on the ring of keys that was tied to the nun's belt and stored deep in the pocket of her tunic. She fumbled not a bit, finding the right one, opening the door to a spare, neat room: two upholstered chairs, a table, a yellow light through the drawn shades. She spun a bit as she reached to remove her cloak, placed the cloak on one of the chairs, and called out at the same time, "Good morning, Mrs. Costello."

A small voice from the next room answered, "Good morning, Sister. I'm awake."

Now the nun was tying the apron she had pulled from her bag around her waist. She rolled up her sleeves as she passed through the living room, Sally following, and into a tiny bedroom—darker still, with drawn shades and drawn drapes—an odor of camphor. The woman was in the bed, stirring. Sally saw in an instant, and with a shudder, the absence under the coverlet, the leg gone below the knee.

"I always know when you're awake, Mrs. Costello," Sister Lucy said, correcting her. "I wouldn't call out if you were still asleep."

The woman was struggling to get up on her elbows. Her long hair was tied into an awkward, uneven braid, and her white, browless face, misshapen from sleep, was small, heart-shaped, finely creased. "I know you always know," she was saying, her voice thin and childish, childishly exasperated. "But I don't know how you always know. Who is this?" Sally smiled with Sister Jeanne's smile, but it didn't warm Mrs. Costello's expression.

97

Despite the woman's pallor, her face conveyed a hot disdain. "Why is it always another one coming into my room?" she asked, and thrust out her lower lip. "One of you in here is enough."

Sister Lucy made no reply, but bustled. With a sweep of her arms, she opened the drapes, then the shades, and then moved a cane-backed wheelchair from a corner of the room to the side of the bed. "Were you well through the night?" she asked.

"No," the woman said, still looking unhappily at Sally. "Not at all. Terrible pains in my stomach and not a bit of sleep the entire night."

Sister Lucy said, "Then you were awake when Mr. Costello went out."

"Heavens, no," Mrs. Costello said, petulant. Plucking at the blankets even as Sister Lucy began to draw them away. There was a brief tug of war. Sister Lucy won. The woman's voice became shrill: "Do you have any idea what time my husband must leave in the morning, Sister? Who would be awake at that hour?"

Neatly, Sister Lucy removed the edge of the counterpane from Mrs. Costello's grasp. Neatly, she folded down the blankets. The woman's nightgown had risen above her knees. Her legs were chalk white, furred with pale hair. Both the full leg and the shortened one looked lifeless. The woman seemed determined not to move. Suddenly, without preliminaries, Sister Lucy bent down and wrapped her arms around Mrs. Costello, lifted her from her pillow, moved the one full leg to the edge of the bed and then the other. Underneath the blue nightgown, the dull stump of her amputated leg, shining with scars, seemed to thrash about on its own. Sally found herself turning away.

"That accounts for your stomach pains," Sister Lucy said. Sally looked again. There were bloodstains on the white sheet, blood on the hem of the nightgown.

"Oh bother," Mrs. Costello said.

Sister Lucy turned to Sally. "Go run a bath," she said. "Heat some water on the stove."

Everything about the small apartment was neat and spare. The bathtub was in the kitchen, draped with a clean white tablecloth that made it look like an altar. A wooden milk box stood beside it, where Sally found the soap and a scrub brush and a box of Epsom salts. She found a cast-iron pot and filled it with water, lit the flame beneath it. She had only begun to run the water for the tub when Sister Lucy wheeled the woman through the doorway.

Mrs. Costello was still in her nightgown, her loose braid over her shoulder. She held a pair of thin towels on her lap. Sister Lucy, with practiced motions, pushed the chair back and forth until she had gotten it over the threshold and, to her satisfaction, beside the claw-footed tub. She added the hot water from the stove, tested it, added a splash more. She took the towels from Mrs. Costello's lap, handed them to Sally, and then, in an instant, lifted the nightgown over the woman's head. Sally turned away, but Sister said, "Get cold water on those stains." Sally dropped the towels onto the floor and brought the nightgown to the kitchen sink. She ran cold water over the streaked blood. At the sound of Mrs. Costello's cry, she looked over her shoulder to see Sister Lucy with the naked woman struggling in her arms. The contrast of the nun's broad black back, solid and shapeless in her veil, and the woman's thin, bare, flailing white extremities was grotesque, startling. They might have been two distinct species: an ostrich in the arms of a great black bear, a grasshopper in the beak of an enormous raven. Over the nun's shoulder, Sally could see Mrs. Costello's mouth opening and closing. She was making a shrill, piping sound, and as she struggled, she caught

Sally's eye with her helpless, panicked own. Her torso was bucking. She seemed determined to knock away Sister's bonnet, to climb over the nun's head. There were long tufts of pale hair, the color of smoke, under her outstretched arms, and again between her thin thighs. "I'm afraid, I'm afraid," she was crying, and she glanced down at the tub as if it were a wall of fire. Sister Lucy said harshly, "Stop it now. Stop your nonsense," but lowered the woman into the water with amazing gentleness, making hardly a splash. Her sleeves caught briefly on the edge of the tub, but her veil was expertly tied back with a black ribbon—when had she done that?

Once she was immersed, Mrs. Costello quieted. There was only a whispered, sucking kind of sobbing. Sister Lucy looked around and then barked, "Take those towels off the dirty floor."

Sally obeyed—although she noticed with some resentment that the worn wooden floor was not at all dirty—and then stood with the two rough towels clutched to her chest. The woman, naked in the water, was awful to see, and yet Sally could not draw her eyes away. She had, on occasion, glimpsed her mother's solid body in the bath, but she had never before seen another human being so exposed. The woman's throat and arms and small puckered breasts were thin, raked, as if the flesh had been scraped away by a dull knife, whittled from Ivory soap. Mrs. Costello's one full leg floated, the other flailed weakly as she moved, now, suddenly, placid, rubbing the soap between her hands, leaning forward to let Sister Lucy wash her back. The tail of her braid was dark with water. A fine pink stain rose into the bath from between her thighs.

"Stand watch," Sister said, straightening up, and then left the room.

Once more Mrs. Costello turned her blue eyes on Sally. Her eyes were sunk into her skull, and the surrounding flesh had a dark hue, but the irises themselves were vivid. Her pale nakedness made them more striking still. Sally smiled at her. She could think of nothing to say. Expressionless, the woman stared for what might have been a full minute, and then turned her attention to the soap. The word *brazen*—her mother's word—came to mind: there was no impulse on the woman's part to cover herself, to apologize, to beg forgiveness for her sorry state.

When Sister Lucy returned, she had Mrs. Costello's clothes in her arms. A simple dress, wool stockings, underwear. She had a white cloth on top of it all, four safety pins in her mouth. Expertly, Sister pinned the napkin to the inside of the underpants, and then took the towels from Sally's arms. She placed one on the seat of the wheelchair, threw the other over her shoulder. She lifted Mrs. Costello smoothly out of the tub—now the woman was as trustful as an infant—placed her in the chair, and dried her flesh with a vigorous rub. She dressed her, lifting and pushing. At one point, Mrs. Costello began to sob again, but Sister hushed her and she remained hushed. Then, with an abrupt tilt of her head, Sister Lucy told Sally to follow her back into the bedroom, where she maneuvered the chair to the window so Mrs. Costello would be facing out. She lifted the hairbrush from the dresser and handed it to Sally. "Do a nice job" was all she said. Then she stripped the linen from the bed and left the room.

The woman's long fair hair was coming out of its tangled braid. Even Sally could tell this was the clumsy work of a man. She pulled the damp braid apart as gently as she could while Mrs. Costello fidgeted in her chair, leaning forward abruptly, turning her head to look up and down the street. "Is it a nice day out there?" she asked, and Sally told her it was. She sat back abruptly. "My husband will carry me down this evening," Mrs. Costello said. "We'll sit in the park for a while."

"Won't that be nice," Sally said.

Suddenly Mrs. Costello reached back, swatting at her hands. "Don't pull."

"I'm trying not to, Mrs. Costello," Sally whispered. She ran her fingers through the last tangles, loosening the braid, releasing the human odor of what her mother called "winter scalp." Carefully, tentatively, she began to brush out the wet ends, her hand held beneath them so she would not pull.

She asked Mrs. Costello, "Would you like a braid or a bun?" glancing up as she did, catching in the window before them the faint image of Mrs. Costello's face and, hovering above it, herself, being so kind.

Mrs. Costello said, thoughtfully, "Oh my." She bowed her head. "What do you like?" This was a new voice entirely, gentle and demure.

"I'll braid it first," Sally suggested. "Then I'll coil it nicely. I do this for my mother sometimes." Which wasn't true. Her mother did her own hair. She couldn't have said why she lied.

With more confidence now, she gently ran the brush over the woman's scalp. Mrs. Costello's head was small and her hair was thin—not like Sally's own, she thought, not without vanity, which had a nice wave, or her mother's, which was Irish thick and dark still, her crowning glory, she sometimes said. The brushing stirred the oil on Mrs. Costello's scalp so that the roots of her hair began to grow as dark as the ends that were still wet from her bath. There were gray strands mingled with the blonde and Sally remembered Mr. Tierney last Christmas singing to his wife, "Darling, you are growing older, silver threads among the gold." Three sheets to the wind, Mrs. Tierney had said, turning away from him as he tried to kiss her—his thick mustache and his wet lips—all of them laughing.

Mrs. Costello bowed her head as the brush ran through it. She seemed to purr a little, a pleasant humming in the back of her throat. There were hairpins in a dish on the dresser. Sally reached for them, glancing at the mirror as she did, at her own face under the short veil. There was a small wedding picture on the doily that covered the dresser top. Mrs. Costello was seated in a chair, two feet beneath her lace skirt. There was a bouquet of silk flowers on her lap. Her husband stood beside her, his bowler hat in the crook of his arm. It was a slimmer, darker version of the milkman she knew. Both of them were somewhat wide-eyed, serious, and maybe afraid. He looked very young. She looked somehow lifeless in her solemn beauty, like one of the china dolls that were slumped together on the dresser. The dolls' faces, too, were finely shattered. One had a glass eye askew.

Sally turned back to the woman. Mrs. Costello was sitting calmly now, her hands in her lap. Sally felt a surge of pride: she was doing very well here. She coiled the thin braid into a golden bun and pinned it carefully. She patted it with her palms and then stepped around the wheelchair to look at the woman straight on. She bent down, smiling at her.

"You look very nice," she said.

Mrs. Costello raised her head slowly, almost coyly. Her blue eyes sought Sally's, and Sally stepped back a bit to smile at the woman, but then Mrs. Costello's gaze slipped away, to the rooftops across the street. Her eyes grew distant and then glistened with tears.

"I have a pain," Mrs. Costello whispered, and she pointed to the place where her foot should have been. "I'm in pain." And then she looked at Sally straight on. Her mouth crumpled the way a child's will when it can no longer resist its tears. Sally felt her own lips turn down in sympathy.

"I am abandoned and alone," Mrs. Costello said.

Sister Lucy shouted "Nonsense" as she came into the room with the breakfast tray. She glanced at what Sally had done with the woman's hair, but said only, "Step aside." She placed the tray on the dresser, opened a small tea table that had been leaning beside the radiator. Sister's bustling seemed to bring the woman back to herself. She narrowed her eyes.

"Have you told this girl what happened to me?" Mrs. Costello asked.

Sister Lucy was placing a tea towel over the woman's chest. "What happened to you?" She seemed only vaguely interested.

Mrs. Costello indicated her missing leg with an abrupt, angry gesture. "My foot," she cried. "My leg." She looked at Sally. "I was bitten by a mad dog, in a yard. I startled him and he came after me. He might have gone for my throat."

Sister Lucy was stirring sugar into Mrs. Costello's tea. "That's ancient history," Sister Lucy said placidly.

But Mrs. Costello was now focused on Sally, appealing to her as she spoke. "I grabbed the pole so the devil wouldn't drag me down. I scraped my cheek." She touched her face. "They heard me cry out, the other women in the street did. They came running. A big man was with them. He beat the dog away and carried me home." Mrs. Costello raised her two hands. "Oh, there was terrible blood."

Sister Lucy said, "Eat your breakfast." She turned to the hope chest at the foot of the bed, opened it, and took out new bed linen. There was the brief scent of cedar as the lid closed again—a green scent in the close room. She said to Sally, "That chamber pot needs emptying," and indicated with her chin the wooden commode beside the bed.

But Mrs. Costello took Sally's wrist to keep her there. "They wrapped the rags too tightly, the women did. Those biddies. My toes turned black. My husband had to carry me to the hospital in the milk cart."

Infected by the woman's indignation, Sally asked, glancing at Sister Lucy, who was paying no heed, "Didn't anyone call the Sisters?"

And Mrs. Costello shook her head. "They did not," she said.

"Someone should have called the Sisters," Sally told her.

Sister Lucy spun on them both. "The chamber pot," she said to Sally. And to Mrs. Costello, "Put your thoughts elsewhere, Mrs. Costello. Eat your breakfast and say your prayers."

The nun returned to making up the bed, and Sally and Mrs. Costello exchanged a look that briefly allied them against her. Then Mrs. Costello let go of Sally's wrist and lifted her tea. "This girl should know what happened to me," she said to Sister Lucy, and blew gently over the cup. "Shame on you, Sister. You should have told her. How that dog came after me in the yard."

Sister Lucy shook out the fresh sheet, let it billow over the thin mattress.

"And whose yard was it?" she asked. "Was it your own yard?"

Mrs. Costello waved her hand. "I don't know whose yard it was," she said.

Sister Lucy was smoothing down the sheet, leaning over the bed and spreading her arms like a swimmer. "Then you should have minded your own business," she said. And then she said to Sally, "The chamber pot. Emptied and cleaned, if you please."

Sally held her breath as she lifted the porcelain bowl from

the seat. She averted her eyes from the yellow liquid and the strings of clotted blood. She emptied the bowl into the toilet and pulled the chain, then washed the thing out in the bathroom sink, uncertain if she should use the clean towel on the bathroom roll or find something else. She carried the wet bowl into the kitchen, thinking to dry it with the towels Mrs. Costello had used in her bath, but they, as well as the bed sheets and the nightgown, were already bundled neatly into a canvas bag, ready to be carried to the convent laundry. The kitchen restored to order. She waved the bowl in the air and carried it back to the bedroom still wet, hoping Sister Lucy wouldn't see.

When Mrs. Costello had finished her breakfast, the tray removed, the dishes washed and dried and put away, Sister Lucy sent Sally through the three rooms with a dust mop and a broom, while she once more brought the woman to the commode and changed her cloth. And then placed a glass of milk and a plate of bread with butter and sugar on the tea tray, within the woman's reach.

From the bare living room, Sally heard Sister Lucy say, "One of the Sisters will be back to give you your lunch today. Mr. Costello has some business in the city. He left a note. He'll be home by dinnertime."

There was a silence, and then, slowly, Sally could hear that the woman was crying again. "I'm frightened when he's gone," she said, weeping. "I'm afraid when I'm alone." She cried gently for a while, childish and heartbroken. And then, suddenly, her voice snapped back into peevishness. "Do you hear me, Sister?" she called out. "I said I'm afraid."

"There's nothing to fear, Mrs. Costello," Sister Lucy said coolly. "Say your prayers to pass the time."

And then there was a thump, as of something dropped or thrown. "I have a pain," Mrs. Costello cried out. "Do you hear me?"

Sister Lucy's voice broke like thunder. "Behave yourself, woman," she said. "We'll have no more of that." And then, hissing it: "Say your prayers. Thank God for the life He's given you. Thank Him for your good husband. You'll get no other."

There was a fraught silence. Into it, Sister Lucy muttered, "You might have broken this lamp."

When Mrs. Costello spoke again, her voice was subdued, conspiratorial. "Look at this bun, Sister," she said. "It's a rat's nest. Take it out, won't you? Before you go."

From the living room where she stood, Sally could hear the hairpins going back into the dish.

She walked into the kitchen to put away the dustpan and the broom. Her own eyes were smarting with what she knew were foolish tears.

When she returned to the living room, she could hear Sister Lucy saying, "I would defer to your husband's good judgment. He'll be back for dinner, as always." And then she was walking out of the bedroom, rolling down her sleeves. There was a brush of brown blood on her apron. When she saw Sally, she paused abruptly, as if she'd forgotten her, and then her expression changed again. For a moment she looked at the girl with narrowed eyes, as if she recognized in her a liar or a thief. And then, slowly, a purple hue rose into the nun's stony face. She ducked her head, slipped off her apron, folded it into her bag, and then reached for her cloak. She told Sally to go fetch the bag of laundry.

As they were about to leave, Mrs. Costello called out again. "I'm afraid," she said. "Please don't leave me."

"Say your prayers," Sister Lucy called back.

"I'm in pain," Mrs. Costello said, but with diminished insistence.

"You're fine," Sister Lucy said, closing the door, locking it with her key.

"I'm afraid," Mrs. Costello called again.

Following Sister Lucy down the stairs, Sally asked, "Will she be all right?"

Sister said, without turning, "Of course."

Faintly, she could hear Mrs. Costello's voice still complaining. "Is it her leg that's hurting her? The short one?"

"That's an imaginary pain," Sister Lucy said. "It isn't real."

Sally said, "But if she feels it."

Sister Lucy said, "She wants company, is all. She doesn't like to be alone."

"Maybe we should stay."

They had reached the vestibule. Sister Lucy was sailing out the door.

Without turning, she said, "There are others with greater need."

Out on the sidewalk, in the bustling light, Sally paused. She was aware of her white nurse's veil, the glances of passersby. Sister Lucy was forging ahead. Sally had to call "Sister" twice to get her to turn. Sister Lucy stood for a moment with her satchel in one hand, a man's watch on a black strap in the other. She thrust out her jaw, a formidable jaw above her white wimple. A question, an impatient one, crossed her masculine face. Slowly, Sally walked to meet her. She would speak up.

Two women passing said, "Good morning, Sisters." A man touched his hat. "Sisters." Sister Lucy nodded to the greetings.

"The poor woman," Sally said. "An imaginary pain is still a pain, isn't it, Sister?"

Sister Lucy said, "Don't be proud," with the swiftness of a slap.

She raised her crooked hand. "Suffering," she said, "does not disguise a true nature. It only lays it bare." Inside her bonnet, her eyes were narrowed. "Any woman who wants an excuse to take to her bed will surely find one." She paused. She seemed to consider whether she should continue, and then, with the slightest shrug, continued, leaning so close to Sally that the starched edge of her bonnet nearly touched the girl's cheek. "There are women who marry with no idea of what marriage entails," she said. "Some of them suffer for it. Babies coming every year. Others impose the suffering on their men." She stepped back as if to see if Sally understood. "If the dog that bit her had been drowned as a pup, still Mrs. Costello would have found an excuse. There's a young woman on Baltic with a withered arm and six children." She raised her eyebrows, which were flecked with gray. "A woman doesn't need two feet to give her husband a child," she said.

Then Sister Lucy turned on her heel, stashing the watch into her pocket. "I'm going in here," she said, indicating another row house, another chipped stoop and battered door. "I'll be with Mrs. Gremelli in the front room. She needs her dressing changed. Catch up with me there."

Sally stood for a moment, all uncertain. Sister Lucy clucked her tongue and turned her gnarled finger to the laundry bag in the girl's hand.

"Take those soiled bedclothes to your mother," she said with exasperated patience. "Then hurry back." Adding, as the girl turned away, "And keep your eyes off yourself if you possibly can."

THIS MUCH BECAME CLEAR TO SALLY over the course of the next week: Sister Lucy lived with a small, tight knot of fury at the center of her chest.

It had formed itself—a fist clenching—when her mother died of peritonitis, caused by a burst appendix.

Sister Illuminata, Sally learned, was not the only one tempted to tell stories of her time in the world.

Sister Lucy's mother had died of peritonitis brought on by a burst appendix when Sister Lucy was seven years old. Appendicitis, Sister Lucy said, is indicated by a terrible pain in the lower right abdomen, fever, vomiting. She told Sally: Waste no time getting the doctor in.

Sister Lucy said the appendix itself is useless. They were waiting for the trolley together. Sister Lucy did not believe in wasted time. "Why God put it there is a mystery," Sister Lucy said.

The peritoneum, Sister Lucy said, is a membrane that covers the organs in the abdomen like a piece of fine silk. "Our Creator is fanciful, perhaps," Sister Lucy said, not amused.

For three days Sister Lucy, seven years old, had run, sleepless and terrified, between the kitchen and the sickroom, bearing the wide bowl, empty and then filled, filled and then empty. Filled with a bitter fluid that grew thinner and darker as the days progressed, that smelled of salty bile, and then of blood. The terrible retching. The blackening of her mother's skin.

It is a loss like no other, Sister Lucy said.

She said, Life itself is a bleak prospect to a motherless child.

She was seven years old.

In these matters, Sister Lucy said again—"Are you listening to me?"—when there's pain in the abdomen, fever, vomiting, never hesitate getting the doctor in. "Sister St. Saviour, God rest her soul—your namesake"—Sister Lucy said—"knew how to put the fear of God into any physician who was dismissive of the poor." They were negotiating the reeking hallways of another tenement house. "I'll give her credit for that much," Sister Lucy said unhappily, a little breathless.

Sister Lucy said her older brothers had already left home when her mother died. Her father was a county tax commissioner who had given them all a comfortable life. A good man, but a serious, withholding man, a man of his times. He brought his mother from Germany to raise his only daughter. Sister Lucy said she was a smart girl in school but mostly silent at home after her mother's death: a clenched fist.

Her German grandmother told young Sister Lucy that it was easier for a camel to pass through the eye of a needle than for a tax collector to avoid the torments of hell. But it could be done, if she prayed for her father's soul.

"So that's what I set out to do," Sister Lucy said. "Save my father's soul. All of seven years old."

A rare smile disrupted that straight tight line that was Sister Lucy's mouth. The two were on a bench in the park, sharing the bread-and-butter sandwiches Sister Lucy had brought from the convent.

She and her grandmother visited nearly every church in Chicago, determined to save her father's soul. She knelt patiently beside the old woman. She prayed patiently at those cold altar rails, hour after hour, until her knees grew numb. In the gloom, the gaslight and candlelight, her eyes drifted to the holy scenes and statues behind the altar or over her head. Her eyes grew keen.

As a child, Sister Lucy said, she came to know the beige hills behind the mount called Golgotha as if she had walked them herself. She knew the tufts of weeds in the far distance, the shape of a small enclave of tombs farther still. She knew the feel of the yellow skull at the base of the cross as if she had run her own fingers over its dome; knew the flavor of the dust that covered the ground beneath the horny feet of the centurion. She saw the pallor that engulfed the world the moment Our Lord took His last breath.

Kneeling beside her pious grandmother, young Sister Lucy studied, too, Mary's assumption into heaven, not merely blue sky and upturned eyes and hands, but the certain fold of cloth at her girded waist, the delicate toe touching a cloud, the brown and gold of a seraphim's curl.

She knew the streets depicted in the Stations of the Cross— uneven paving stones and dark archways—the way the women Jesus greeted touched one another's shoulders as they wept.

Kneeling beside her grandmother in churches all over the city, knees and feet grown numb, hands and face grown cold, young Sister Lucy entered so fully into these holy pictures (she knew the sharpness of the steel that pierced the Virgin's heart, the velvet flesh of the Savior's throat) that afterward, after she and the old woman left the church and went on with what had to be done, she found herself impatient to return. She found herself annoyed by any ordinary hour, angry to be detained by the petty things that concerned the world. She felt whoever stood before her stood in the way of what she most wanted to see: those places where the essential moments were unfolding, where time and eternity were doing battle, where the terrible death gave way—the stone moved from the mouth of the tomb—and breath returned, flesh grew warm again.

"However," Sister Lucy said: those keen eyes that had brought her so vividly into the life of Christ could not be averted at will. When she returned to the streets after her hours of prayer, she saw with the same intensity the raw heel of a shoeless child, the pallor of a consumptive. She saw how the skim of filth, which was despair, which was hopelessness, fell like soot on the lives of the poor.

She saw what needed to be done. Saw that God expected her to do it.

Sister Lucy told Sally that she would have preferred the silence and the beauty of a contemplative's life.

She said her heart clenched at what God asked of her. But she did not refuse.

Sister Lucy held Mrs. Gremelli's swollen, shapeless leg in the palm of her hand. "Edema," she told Sally, "when there is an accumulation of fluid like this," and pressed a gentle thumb into the flesh. "See how the impression holds. Too much water."

The leg was mottled with sores, some of them seeping. Kneeling before the old lady, Sister Lucy peered carefully at each lesion. "From the Latin," Sister Lucy said, "*laesio*, injury." Mrs. Gremelli was a small, heavy woman who smiled toothlessly at Sally and the nun, her hands folded complacently over her mounded belly in its black dress. She had little English, and the small room where she lived was crowded with two beds, a couch, a small table and chair, an avalanche of boxes and newspapers. There was a table shrine with a statue of the Blessed Mother in one corner, squat votive candles crowded around it. There was the odor of garlic and garbage and candle wax. The son who lived with her was at work all day.

Sister Lucy cleaned the woman's awful flesh with exquisite

gentleness and then wrapped it in the fresh bandages that Sister Illuminata and her mother had rolled.

She pulled a clean black stocking up over Mrs. Gremelli's neatly bandaged leg, up over the old, loose flesh of her thigh. She carefully straightened her skirt. Rising from her knees, Sister Lucy placed her hand on the woman's head. Mrs. Gremelli, toothless, eyes clouded with cataracts, looked up at the nun, lifting her spotted arms into the air in gratitude and supplication. Mary at her assumption.

Leaving Mrs. Costello's apartment on another morning, the woman crying softly behind them, Sister Lucy said, A woman's life is a blood sacrifice. This was, she reminded Sally, our inheritance from Eve.

Although, Sister Lucy said, poverty and men made a bad situation—to be born female—worse still.

Sister Lucy paused on the sidewalk, Sally at her heels, to exchange a word with a pretty young woman who had greeted them warmly. Within minutes, the nun discovered that the girl was newly landed and looking for work. Sister wrote down the name and address of one of the women in the Ladies Auxiliary—a wealthy lady looking for domestic help. A good and safe job, Sister Lucy told Sally as they walked on, something to keep the girl from a premature marriage.

Going up the stairs of another tenement, they met a pregnant woman coming down with two small children before her and an infant riding her big belly. Sister Lucy stopped to look at the children. She clucked her tongue and circled her pinky over the bald patches on their scalps, the round red rash on the baby in its mother's arms. "Ringworm," she told Sally. "*Tinea* is the proper term. Latin for a growing worm." Sally felt herself shudder at the phrase. She looked at the inflamed flesh, the

missing hair, and then looked away. "I like to use a paste of vinegar and salt," Sister Lucy was saying. "Sister Jeanne adds a straw
from the Christmas manger. Which is nonsense." And then she
said, reluctantly, "Although she does quite well with it."

Sister Lucy took down the woman's apartment number and
promised that one of the nursing Sisters would be in to see her.
"We'll fix that," she said.

And then she turned her attention to the mother herself,
whose dress was slick with dirt and oil, whose hair was pinned
up haphazardly under a grimy hat. "Is your husband good to
you?" Sister Lucy asked.

Sister Lucy told Sally that a good husband was a blessing—a
good husband who went to work every day and didn't drink away
his salary or lose it at the racetrack, didn't beat his children or
treat his wife like a slave—but a rare blessing at best.

She said, Even a good man will wear his wife thin. She said,
Even a good wife might transform herself into a witch or a lush
or, worse, an infant or an invalid, in order to keep her very good
husband out of her bed.

Sister Lucy waited for Sally's blush to fade—they were
having another lunch, this time in the newly cleaned kitchen
of the old widower Sister Lucy had just fed and bathed—before
she added that some women, wealthy women as well as poor,
chose the pretense of illness or delicacy, even madness, over the
rough and tumble, the blood and strife, the mortal risks, of a
married woman's life.

She said, her keen eyes on the girl, "I will never encourage
the vocation of a young woman who comes to us just after seeing
a sister or mother die in childbirth. No woman should enter the
convent out of fear."

Sister Lucy said that the best of men—Mr. Costello came to

mind—sought the Sisters' help when their wives took ill in this way. They stood in the doorway looking lost and afraid while the nuns sailed in to assess the limp woman on the bed.

"Anemia, you'll often find," Sister Lucy said. "Pallor. Weakness. From the Greek this time, *anaimia*, lack of blood."

You can douse her with castor oil, Sister Lucy said, and then send the husband, or one of the children, off to the butcher for a piece of liver while you do your best with the place. Send the filthy laundry to Sister Illuminata, bathe the children, comb the nits out of their hair, open the windows, beat the rugs. Feed the family a decent meal, after which, perhaps, the mother will stir herself to sit up at the table and chew some small pieces of the liver.

The life might return to her then, iron restored to her bloodstream. Or it might not.

Sister Lucy told Sally that never having had a lazy mother herself, she might not know that there was a distinction between the wife who was sick and then recovered and the wife who was recovered but not yet willing to give up the pleasures of being sick.

"Never waste your sympathy," Sister Lucy said. They were going into Mrs. Costello's once again. "Never think for a minute that you will erase all suffering from the world with your charms."

"The poor we will always have with us," Sister Lucy said more than once in the week that Sally followed her. She said it without kindness or even resignation. She seemed only annoyed. "If we could live without suffering," Sister Lucy said, "we'd find no peace in heaven."

THEY WERE ON THEIR WAY BACK to the convent at the end of a long day, when Sister Lucy, walking ahead of Sally, stopped abruptly. There was a small girl on a stoop, wearing what looked like a bigger sister's nightgown, a pair of rough shoes on her bare legs. As Sally caught up, she heard Sister Lucy asking her severely why she wasn't in school. She called the girl by name, Loretta. Little Loretta said she hadn't gone to school today because her sisters couldn't take her. And when Sister Lucy asked why that was, the girl lowered her chin to her raised knees. Sister had to say, "Speak up, child."

The little girl spoke up reluctantly, all in a rush. "Charlie got mad at us this morning because we were laughing too much," she said. "He locked up Margaret and Tillie and wouldn't let them out."

Sister Lucy looked to the building behind the girl. "They're still inside?"

And the girl, big-eyed and tangle-haired, nodded slowly.

Sister Lucy shook back her sleeve and, without another word, climbed the stairs. Wordlessly, Sally and the little girl followed.

This was a nicer building. There was carpet on the stairs. A radio playing gentle music somewhere. The smell of floor polish. At the door of the little girl's apartment, Sister Lucy raised her fist to rap, and then, with hardly a pause for a reply, reached for the knob and let herself in. There was a long corridor with little light, airless and hot. At the end of the corridor, a pretty room with dark furniture trimmed in knotted tassels, a table draped with a velvet shawl, a large gilded mirror. A small pile of schoolbooks was spilled across the plush seat of a chair.

Sister Lucy stood for a moment to call out, "Girls?" but then turned down another, shorter corridor to a closed door. Again she knocked, and again she reached for the knob without a pause. She opened the door and said, "Glory be to God."

Sally looked over the nun's shoulder into the dim room. She

saw two girls about her own age sitting at either end of a rumpled bed. One, somewhat bigger, was in a skirt and a satin slip; the other, thinner and younger, wore a white nightgown like Loretta's. Both were tied to the iron bedposts by dark leather belts that crossed and recrossed their wrists. The girls struggled to sit up when they saw the nun. As she rushed toward them, they both began to cry piteously, saying together, "Oh, Sister." It was clear from their faces that they had been crying all day. There was a smell of urine in the airless room. The smell of sweat.

Sister Lucy was already untying the belt that held the bigger girl to the head of the bed. Sally fumbled, pulling at the belt that bound the other—two belts, in fact, one a man's long belt with a solid buckle, the other the thin strap that might have held the schoolbooks in the living room. Both were wrapped tightly around the peeling iron rail and the girl's thin wrists. Both belts had raised fiery stripes on her skin, turned her fingertips purple.

Through their tears, the girls told Sister Lucy that they had laughed too much this morning, getting ready for school, and made their brother angry. They rubbed their wrists. The younger girl had wet through her nightgown and blushed in shame. The older, in a gabardine school skirt but no blouse, only her satin slip, cupped her hand to her neck. Sally saw she was trying to hide a bruise there—it looked like a rosebud, a small coin. She saw that Sister Lucy, too, was assessing the mark. Her eyes narrowed. Sally wondered if it wasn't a bit of ringworm on the girl's throat.

As they moved off the bed, still whimpering, Sally followed the nun's sharp eyes to the series of raised red welts on their calves and their thighs. Strap marks.

Sister Lucy said, "Where is your mother?"

"Working," the girls said together. Gone with her family, they said, the family she cooked for, to their summer place for the week. They said Charlie was in charge.

Sally saw the anger pull at Sister Lucy's lips and at the corners of her eyes. She imagined it rising up like something awful, undigested, from her throat, from that knot of fury in her chest.

Sister Lucy told Sally, "Take Loretta to the kitchen. See if there's anything for her to eat. Wash her hands and face while you're at it."

The little girl drew back as Sally reached for her. "Do as I say, child," Sister Lucy said. Cold. Insistent.

Sister Lucy closed the door behind them as they left. Sally heard her say, "Let me see your neck."

The kitchen was large, neat and charming, although the remnants of a breakfast were still on the table: half-eaten eggs in egg cups, dregs of milk, and crusts of cold toast. The laughter that had angered their brother must have begun here.

The table itself was covered with a clean linen cloth decorated with cross-stitched flowers in blue thread. There were crisp blue curtains at the window. A pretty ceramic kettle on the stove. A nicer apartment altogether, Sally noticed, than her own, but, she gathered, a widow's apartment nonetheless. Another mother who went out to work. The icebox was well stocked with milk and cheese and a small ham. While Sally made the girl a sandwich, Loretta explained again that Charlie was her brother and he was in charge whenever their mother went away. Her mother was a cook for a family in New York City. Charlie, Loretta said, spanked her sisters when they were bad, but never her. She was his favorite, she said happily.

Suddenly the little girl paused, kneeling on her chair, her chin in the air. Some uncertainty, or perhaps fear, crossed her small face. Sally heard footsteps in the long hall, and then the boy himself appeared in the kitchen doorway. He was a tall, dark-haired boy no older then she, in a white school shirt rolled at the sleeves, a loosened school tie. He said to her, only a little surprised, "Hello, Sister," even as Loretta flew into his arms, her bare legs going around him. "Hiya, pipsqueak," he said. His arms beneath the rolled-up sleeves were brown and muscular. He was as big and broad as a grown man.

And then, over the child's head, he asked, "What's up?"

Loretta whispered, "Sister Lucy is here again. She's talking to the girls."

Charlie said, "Oh yeah?" He lowered the little girl to her feet and then looked at Sally. He was close enough that she could smell the perspiration from him. A scent she associated with the subway or the trolley, with the workingmen who boarded late in the day, carrying lunch pails. His eyes were dark blue, and one strand of his thick black hair fell across his forehead. Casually, he reached up to smooth it back. There was a deep dimple in his chin, the trace of a five o'clock shadow, handsome on a boy so young. He was handsome. "You a novice?" he asked her. She said she was just following Sister Lucy today. Learning things.

He nodded. Put his hands in his pockets and then leaned in the doorway, one foot kicked up on its toe, still watching her. His shoulders were broad beneath the white shirt. He was tall, over six feet, she guessed. He cast his eyes around the room, smiling with straight white teeth. His eyes were the color of deep water. He was as handsome as a movie star. "Sister Lucy's a pistol, ain't she?" he said. "Six-shooter Lucy, I call her."

Sally saw Sister Lucy herself come through the room behind him. She was carrying her black bag. The two girls followed at some distance, cowering, it seemed, at the entrance to the short hall. They were both dressed now, their hair combed.

Sally had not realized that Sister Lucy was such a short woman, dumpy, even, in her dark habit, until she stood before Charlie and raised her crooked finger toward his face. He looked down at her.

"You lay a hand on these girls again and I'll have the police here," Sister Lucy said.

The boy only smiled. He seemed both kind and tolerant. "They were acting up," he said patiently. "My mother told me to spank them when they act up. I'm in charge," he added. "They have to learn to behave."

"Your mother told you," Sister Lucy repeated sarcastically, hissing it. "I know your mother. She told you no such thing." Her finger was trembling. Even her bonnet and her veil seemed to be trembling. She pumped her elbows in her dark sleeves: bellows to the fire of her indignation. "Locking them up all day," she said, growing shrill. "Keeping them from school." Her voice broke: "You've left welts on their flesh." Even her jowls were trembling against the tight linen of her cowl. She closed her hand into a fist, shook it in his face. "I know what else you've done to these girls," she said, nearly shrieking it. "Sinful."

Handsome Charlie shrugged, uncrossed his legs, folded his arms across his chest, stood even taller. "When my mother is away at work," he said again, "I'm in charge here."

His smile was a kind of sneer, but it was lopsided, too, which made it boyish, even charming. His bare forearms were covered in dark hair. Above the casually rolled sleeves, there were muscles beneath the white cloth. His legs were long. His hips narrow. He said, "Lookit, Sister," and then paused. He glanced at Sally, waved a hand in her direction. His eyes were deep blue. "These girls ain't obedient, like this holy one. They need to be disciplined." He shook his head sadly, amicably. Then he shrugged again and added, "I'm sorry to have to tell you what you don't know."

Sally felt her cheeks burn.

"You brazen boy," Sister Lucy said evenly. She had gotten control of her voice. Little Loretta was at her brother's side, looking up at the nun with big eyes.

Glancing at the child, Sister Lucy said, "I'll have the police here if you so much as touch these girls again." She said, "I'll go straight to the Monsignor."

Now there was no avoiding how helpless, how foolish, Sister Lucy seemed, shaking a fist at him, trembling with rage in her long black skirt and her silly bonnet.

Charlie reached down to take little Loretta's hand. "Okay, Sister," he said easily. "Calm down now. I had to teach them a lesson and I did." He narrowed his glistening eyes, still smiling. "You can go mind your own business now."

"Beast," Sister Lucy whispered, turning away. She said, "Come," to Sally, and Sally brushed past him to get through the door. He might have been laughing under his breath. Loretta said, "Bye-bye."

In the living room, the two girls were leaning together like victims from a storm. Sister Lucy told them, "If he puts another hand to you, you go over to the convent at St. Ann's. Immediately."

The girls said they would, but Sally wondered how they would go over to the convent at St. Ann's if they were tied with leather belts to their bedstead. "Don't hesitate," Sister added weakly, as if she understood this, too. Her eyes went to the elder of the two, whose hand was once again cupping the mark on her neck. "Don't let him touch you," Sister said.

Going down the apartment house stairs, which were well

tended, not a trace of cobweb or dust, Sister Lucy said, "If I were a man, I'd take a strap to him myself."

When they reached the street, Sister Lucy said, "Come," once more, and then turned away from the trolley stop that would have taken them back to the convent. Sally followed her, walking rapidly—"Good evening, Sisters," people whispered— four blocks, six blocks, until they came to a squat red church with a sprawling school. They passed them both, passed the empty playground, and then climbed the steps of a brown rectory. Sister Lucy rapped at the door and waited on the doorstep with her head down, her foot tapping impatiently. The woman who answered was plain and gentle-looking, her salt-and-pepper hair curled tightly to her head. She wore a calico apron over her dress.

Sister said, "Hello, Trudy, is he in?" and the woman nodded, "Just upstairs," and then added, as a warning, "He's just about to sit down to his dinner. He's got a Holy Name meeting at seven."

"Only a minute," Sister Lucy said, and the woman, reluctantly, invited the two of them in.

The vestibule was chilly, despite the June weather, and as dim as winter. There were two leather chairs, thin-backed and slim, flanking an icon of a glowering, dark-eyed male saint. There was a rich Persian rug over the tiled floor. The vestibule held the stone smell of a church, although there was a whiff as well of seared meat from the kitchen. Sister Lucy told Sally to sit, but she continued to stand. She paced, moving her free hand, flicking it back and forth as if she were dealing cards or quickly saying her beads, although the hand was empty.

Sally had never before seen Sister Lucy expend so much energy on what seemed a pantomime.

Beyond her, the doorway through which the housekeeper had

disappeared offered promise of a warmer part of the house. There was a table with a Tiffany lamp in a narrow passage, and then a high-backed couch and a mullioned window. Sally glimpsed the turning of a staircase, and after what seemed more than a few minutes, she saw the black shoes and the cassock hem of a priest descending.

The priest was another large man, perhaps even taller than Charlie. He filled the doorway when he appeared—large chest and big head and thick dark hair; a belly, covered by his black soutane, that seemed to precede him into the room. He looked as if he'd just finished shaving. His fair face was flushed around the jaw, a pinprick or two of fresh blood. He greeted Sister Lucy by name and gave a thin smile to Sally. There were black hairs on the backs of his big hands. His eyes were very small in his large face. Sister Lucy said, "A word," and indicated the passageway behind them.

The priest held out his arm, and Sister Lucy walked ahead only a few steps before she turned to look up into his face. Sally saw the priest bend to put his ear toward Sister's bonnet. She saw him glance her way as Sister spoke. He may have winked. Sally looked away. This secrecy on Sister Lucy's part seemed foolish since Sally had been there herself to see the girls with their wrists tied and the strap marks on their skin.

She heard Sister Lucy say his name, Charlie. She said, "Tied by their wrists."

Sally realized that she could not bring herself to imagine it, that handsome boy—how sweetly he had called his sister "pipsqueak"—wielding his belt like Simon Legree. She wondered if it could be possible, if there hadn't been some misunderstanding. Perhaps the girls had been very bad.

The nun's sibilant whispering into the priest's big ear gave way to something more solid. "Tonight, Father," she said, insisting. "I'd hate to have another morning go by. Their mother won't be back until Sunday."

The priest said, "All right, Sister." Now he had his hand on her elbow, he was guiding her to the door. "I'll go over there tonight," he said. "Put the fear of God into him. As soon as I've had my dinner."

Sister Lucy said, "Thank you, Father." But Sally knew she was not appeased.

It was growing late as they walked back to the trolley stop. Although the sky was light blue, a sense of the coming night was already pooling at the feet of the people going by—"Good evening, Sisters"—pooling along the cobbled streets, along the silver trolley tracks, at curbs and in the alleyways. "A cruel and evil boy," Sister Lucy said, shaking back her sleeve as they waited for the trolley. "Cool as a cucumber. Brazen." She seemed to be trembling still, and Sally realized, standing beside her, that they were now shoulder to shoulder. That Sister Lucy, ramrod straight as she always was, as Sally had always known her, might even be shrinking.

Telling it later, our mother said, "Sister Lucy didn't scare me so much after that."

"If I were a man," Sister Lucy muttered once more, "I'd wipe that smile off his face." She added, over her shoulder, as they climbed the steps into the car, "And you standing there making eyes at him was no help to me at all."

AT THE END OF SALLY'S WEEK with Sister Lucy—on a morning her mother let her stay in bed—the nun came halfway down the basement stairs, pausing when Sister Illuminata and Annie both looked up at her. "If there's a vocation there," Sister Lucy said, "I'll eat my hat." She shook her black sleeve and touched her back. Under her arm, the basket woven of unblessed palms. Sister Lucy would be taking her turn to beg today. A duty she despised, silently. "I love her like a daughter," Sister Lucy said with no change in the harshness of her tone, as if love, too, was an unpleasant duty. "Marriage might settle her. Not the convent."

Annie smiled, but when she turned to Sister Iluminata, the old nun was hunched over her ironing.

"And what do you say, Sister?" Annie asked her when Sister Lucy was safely upstairs.

Sister Illuminata shook her head, shook the iron against the board. "I say give God what He asks for."

Reparation

SISTER JEANNE FOUND ANNIE in the convent's drying yard. She gestured that the two should sit, and Annie pinned the last cloth to the line and then joined her on the wrought-iron bench that had been tucked into this corner of the yard ever since the convent was a rich man's house, elegant and new. The story in the neighborhood was that the house had been bequeathed to the Little Nursing Sisters in Chicago fifty years ago, when its owner washed up there, having lost his family's fortune to drink and depravity. The story was that the man died in the Little Nursing Sisters' care, and had asked on his deathbed that they take his house in Brooklyn in reparation for his sins.

Sister Illuminata dismissed this tale when Annie asked about it. Said the house was a gift from a good man who wanted only to help the poor.

The bench was under a narrow arbor, now overgrown with honeysuckle vine and curling ivy, fitted with a statue of St. Francis. The folds of the saint's robes were tinted green with oxidation; ivy had grown up around the creatures at his feet. The black leaves were repeated in the carvings on the bench, which were also touched with a blue-green dust. Annie made note to brush down Jeanne's veil for her before they went inside.

The shade gave little relief from the day's heat. Annie watched as the nun found her handkerchief and wiped the perspiration from her temples, from the pale down above her lip. That any of the nuns could bear their habits on these hot city days, could bear especially the starched linen at their throats and their chins, filled Annie with admiration—and some pride that she and Illuminata were able to keep most of them smelling sweet, at least through the first hours of these stifling mornings.

Annie had opened her own blouse three buttons more than was modest as she came out into the yard with the wet wash. With the clothespins in her mouth, she had glanced down at her breasts as she pinned the nuns' summer shifts to the line. She recalled without irony or shame the pleasure of his cheek against her skin.

Poor Sister Jeanne had a sunken look about her. Broad creases were pressed into her face, just under her eyes. She had been out of the convent for a string of days, and she recounted her casework: a widow grown blind had been resettled in the French Little Sisters' home for the aged, a young mother with milk fever was restored, her baby thriving once more. Those First Communion dresses Annie had bleached and mended were much appreciated by an Italian family of seven girls—four of their own and three orphaned cousins. Although one of the girls was determined to wear red shoes. Mr. Bannister, the old veteran, the old bachelor, had both Sister Jeanne and Sister Agatha with him as he went through his last agony, which had taken four long days. But he had not died alone.

Annie, for her part, said she'd met the new president of the Ladies Auxiliary, nicer and younger than Mrs. McShane. She wanted to raise money through a dinner dance at a fine hotel in the city, not the usual bridge party here at the convent. Both women pulled down the corners of their mouths and raised their eyebrows, their familiar, unspoken conspiracy against the society ladies who did so much good. *Fancy-dancy*, their expressions said.

Annie knew these women called her "that poor widow" when her back was turned. To her face they said "Annie, dear."

"Have you had an afternoon to yourself all this while?" Sister Jeanne asked her.

And Annie nodded. "You know me," she said. "I catch my breath when I can," evoking Sister Lucy.

Sister Jeanne nodded. The unspoken forbearance the two afforded Sister Lucy was a joke they'd shared since the first days of their friendship.

They were in the shade of the narrow arbor, although bright sunlight was moving leisurely against the white shifts on the line. The back of the convent rose over the yard, the sky reflected in each of the convent's windows. Sister Jeanne's white hands were resting in her lap. Annie saw her own work on the edge of the nun's worn sleeve, the black stitches small and neat. Both women wore gold wedding bands. Annie reached for Sister's hand, patted it affectionately. Something miraculous about how familiar and smooth it was, despite the years of hard work.

They had been friends for a long time.

Annie nodded toward the building. "Which was St. Saviour's room?" she asked, and Sister Jeanne looked up, smiling.

"First floor," she said. "On the corner there."

Annie knew she'd been told this before.

"When she died," Sister Jeanne said softly, and with her childish amazement, "there was the most beautiful scent. Like roses it was. I know I've told you."

Annie nodded again. She'd been heavily pregnant with Sally on the day St. Saviour died. Another hot day like this. Sister Jeanne had come to the apartment that morning as she always did, with fresh milk and clean linens and an alcohol rub to keep her cool. There were no tears between them, only laughter, as the little nun bathed her swollen ankles with cool water and the two considered St. Saviour in heaven, imperious and proud, all her pain ended.

It was Sister Jeanne who suggested Annie give her baby the nun's name in baptism. A formidable patroness for the child.

Wide-eyed, Sister Jeanne had described for Annie that morning the nun's last breath, the peace of it, and then the odor of sanctity filling the hushed room. The beauty of heaven in the scent, Sister Jeanne had said. Just the smallest notion of it—of what is promised. As much of heaven's beauty, Sister Jeanne had said, full of wonder, as we on earth can bear.

Annie didn't doubt the report. Sister Jeanne couldn't tell a lie. But Annie was inclined to reconcile such miracles with the sensible world. Sister St. Saviour died in July. The windows were surely open—or, if they weren't, Sister Jeanne, who held on to the old superstitions, would have opened one the moment the old nun passed. Surely roses bloomed somewhere in the neighborhood.

Annie imagined that St. Saviour, who disdained all superstition, would have said the same.

Looking up at the room—whose was it now?—Annie said, "You're here to tell me I should let Sally go."

Sister Jeanne said, "Let her try."

"Did I ever believe I could stop her?"

Sister Jeanne laughed and lifted both their hands. She brought their entwined fingers to her lips, kissed Annie's knuckles, her lips warm and dry, and then dropped their hands together into her lap. She looked up, tilting her chin so the sun that filtered through the ivy could reach her face.

"I was going to enter a teaching order," she said, "but when I finished my novitiate, God asked that I go out among the poor, to nurse. My confessor suggested the French Little Sisters. But that's not the address he wrote down." She laughed. "He was busy with many things, Father was, I don't blame him. And so I presented myself here. When I realized the mistake I'd made, Sister St. Saviour said, 'God's will.' So I stayed where He'd brought me."

"It wasn't Chicago," Annie said.

Sister Jeanne said, "It could have been the moon. I'd never been to this part of Brooklyn before. I grew up in the Bronx."

Annie glanced at the nun. It was as much as Jeanne had ever said about her life in the world. She was no Illuminata, with her tedious childhood tales. Annie wondered where they were now—her people in the Bronx, a mother or a father surely, siblings perhaps—were they all dead or merely forever unspoken of? Was there a difference?

Annie cast her eye over Sister Jeanne's small frame, the short lap, the childish black shoes, neatly tied, just touching the sparse grass at their feet. She wondered what had convinced her as a girl to be confined to this lonely life of hard labor. What had made her believe she was capable of such long sacrifice—tiny as she was, gentle as she was, no training, no idea what she would find in this part of the world, much less in the hidden rooms of the city's most desolate? What drove her to think she could endure this life?

"How did your mother feel about your vocation?" Annie asked her.

Sister Jeanne paused. And then said, tentative, "She was happy in heaven, I'm sure." She raised her handkerchief again, delicately blotting her lips and her chin.

"If Sally goes to Chicago," Annie said simply, "it will break my heart."

Sister Jeanne turned her white bonnet toward the convent. The rattle and shout of the street reached them faintly. A garbage can falling. The grinding of gears. In an interval of quiet, Sister said, "I saw him. When Sally was young. Here," and she bowed her head toward the convent's windows, lit blue and white by the sky and the summer clouds. "Jim, I mean. In his brown suit. Looking like himself. Solid as stone."

Annie nodded. Sister Jeanne could not tell a lie. "It was Jim?"

"It was," Sister Jeanne said, full of regret.

"You never saw him alive," Annie said.

And Jeanne shook her head. "No, I didn't."

"But you recognized him."

She whispered, "I did. Poor man." And she followed this with a sudden breath, taken through her teeth, as if in response to a sharp and sudden pain in her side. "What worse suffering can there be for a soul?" she said. "To be trapped forever in these bodies of ours. No relief."

There was another spasm of street noise, and then Sister

Jeanne turned Annie's hand over in her own. She bowed her head and placed a finger into Annie's palm, gently tracing a line as she spoke, like a child enumerating a fragile logic, giving it careful voice.

"What I wanted to tell you is this," Sister Jeanne said softly, cautiously. "Here's redemption, see? Here's forgiveness. Through his child. Through her vocation. Here's the forgiveness of sin."

Annie raised her eyes to look over her friend's bowed head, looked to the winding vines above her. For a moment, an image of him trapped, his body trapped in the tangled shade, flitted across her eyes. A glimpse of his pale forehead, his dark brows, the black corner of his grin.

He'd lost a tooth in the days before he died—how long since she remembered this? His teeth were always trouble to him.

What greater torment for a man whose sin was suicide than to be trapped forever in the body he'd sought to shed?

The sun moved through the leaves. She felt it touch the top of her head, her throat. The pale skin beneath the opened buttons of her blouse. Jim, too, had put his warm cheek to her breast, even on the last night of his life. Sally inside her then, no bigger than a heart.

She took her hand from Sister Jeanne's. Sat up straighter, looking out across the yard.

"What you're telling me," she said. And paused. Sister Jeanne's face was attentive but weary. It was full of affection. They had been friends for a long time. "What you're saying is that I haven't suffered enough." She paused again. The perspiration was once more beaded on Sister Jeanne's pale lip. A drop of it, the size and shape of a tear, gathered at her temple, rolled down her cheek. "These eighteen years," Annie said. "You're saying they haven't brought me suffering enough. Loneliness enough. You're saying

I should lose my daughter, too. My own. So that God can for-give him."

Only a narrow ray of sun, filtered through the black leaves of ivy, caught Sister Jeanne's white bonnet. Inside its depths, shadow and light, she was smiling, her eyes sunken and drawn and the perspiration sparkling on the fine hairs above her lip. It was the way she might smile at a misbehaving child—the repri-mand hardly outlasting the fond absolution. She reached again for Annie's hand, took it in both of hers. "Oh no," she said. "Not Jim. I'm not talking about Jim. He's a lost soul, poor man." She paused. "I'd never have seen him here if there was any hope of heaven for him." And she shook her head—resigned to the fact, but still not without pity. "What I'm saying is, it's so you can be forgiven, see?" And she bit her lip, as if to suppress a laugh, to suppress her own wonder and delight at this turn of good for-tune. "It's your sin I mean. Your soul."

It was the first Annie ever knew that Sister Jeanne had made note of how she spent her afternoons.

Overnight

I N LATE SEPTEMBER, Sally went with her mother and Sister Jeanne to Pennsylvania Station. An overnight train. There was no money for a Pullman, so she would have to sit up in the open coach, but she was young, as the Sisters were always reminding her. She would be fine.

Her nearly new valise was on the rack above her head. It was secondhand but quite lovely: lacquered beige rattan with caramel leather trim, a gold clasp repaired, free of charge, by the shoemaker who served the convent. It contained only what the Sisters at the motherhouse had required her to bring: six pairs of stockings, six pairs of knickers, three muslin nightgowns without ornamentation, four chemises, woolen gloves, black shoes.

Sally had five dollars in her wallet and fifty pinned to the lining of her purse, to be turned over to the Sisters in Chicago when she arrived.

She sat on a bench seat beside the window. Looked out to see her mother on the platform, her arm through Sister Jeanne's. They were leaning together, the two of them, Sister Jeanne coming only to her mother's shoulder. Her mother looked nice in her hat and her gray Sunday suit. The unaccustomed scent of the face powder and lipstick she donned only for a trip to Manhattan lingered on Sally's cheek. They could have been something from a movie, her mother and Sister Jeanne, they both looked so polished and clean. Sally waved and blew a kiss, and her mother touched her gloved hand to her heart, then lifted it, the way you might release a bird into the air.

Sally looked around the train, felt the energy of its silent engines, poised to move. People were settling themselves. She did the same.

The windowsill was not grimy in the way of subway cars. The upholstery was plush. It was all very lovely. Her mother had packed her a sandwich for dinner and a roll for breakfast. A pear and a chocolate bar. The Sisters had told her that if she waited until the tail end of the dinner hour, she could go to the dining car for a nice cup of tea. She had three books with her: her missal, *The Story of a Soul* by Saint Thérèse, and the novel the Tierney twins had given her as a going-away gift. She looked out again. Her mother and Sister Jeanne were still on the platform. The engine gave up a tremendous sigh and then the trainman cried out. The train began to move and the movement thrilled her. Goodbye, goodbye, she cried silently, as if it were a prayer. Touching her gloved hand to the window until the two women had passed out of its frame.

A plump lady with two bulky shopping bags made her way

down the aisle, bound, Sally could tell, for the seat beside her. She watched the woman back into it, big rump and dark coat and short struggling arms. Sally smiled up at her, weighing her disappointment at not having the seat to herself for the long ride against the promise of companionship. She was thinking of the Thunderbolt in Coney Island, when the man in charge sometimes lifted a stray kid into your car. The Tierney twins always resented this, but Sally preferred to feel even a stranger's shoulder against her own as the roller coaster began its climb.

The woman took some time getting herself arranged. She wedged the shopping bags between her knees and the seat in front of them, sat back to observe the arrangement, and then leaned forward to fuss with them again. Each time she moved, her clothes gave off the smell of artificial violets and, just behind it, cooking oil. Then she sat back again. She was breathing heavily, but with an odd rhythm—not the rhythm of a woman catching her breath after running for the train, but the quick, deep, agitated panting of an animal in distress.

Sally glanced at the brown bags, their handles tied together with dirty string, glimpsed the unconscious motion of the panting woman's bosom, and felt the most peculiar brush of panic— like the wing-stroke of a bat against her hair. It was not, merely, a failure of courage at the start of her great adventure. It was a throat-catching, spine-seizing fear, as startling as a dream's sudden misstep, that reflexive start, that abrupt intake of breath.

She turned to the window. The train was making its way through the tunnel that would lead them out of the city, passing through flashing columns of darkness and light. Of course, she had been riding subways all her life. She was as accustomed to being underground as any New Yorker. But that wing-stroke of terror—she actually reached up to touch her hat as if it had been somehow altered—reverberated. It seemed to rattle through her bones. Never before, gone underground, had she thought to wonder about the capacity of the steel beams and the concrete, or the genius of the sandhogs and the engineers, to keep earth and rock and water from coming down on their heads.

She had never before considered the fearful, foolish miracle of moving through this hollowed-out place.

Never before equated its rushing darkness, its odor of soot and soil and steel, with the realm of the dead, the underside of bright cemeteries—the cemetery, for instance, where her father was, had always been, in sunshine and in rain, through all her bustling days as she went blithely down the subway steps or down into the convent basement . . .

She looked through the train window to the hollowed-out darkness.

She told herself the soul rose, of course, but until the last day, didn't the body pass its time here, in this dark underside of the bright world? Why had she never thought of this before? Her father's body waited down here, in stillness, looking much as it had when it last saw the sunlight: same clothing, same hair, the same patient, folded hands. No shoes—someone at school had told her this—and, slowly, of course, flesh fallen away from bone.

And then full daylight broke suddenly upon the train— explosive, thunderous. She may have jumped.

The woman beside her, leaning into her shoulder, breathing on her neck, said, "You headed for Chicago?"

Sally turned to her. "Yes," she said, grateful for the daylight now at the windows, the orange hue of the late afternoon. "I am."

"Me, too," the woman said. Her wide face was rough-skinned, well-powdered, scattered with coarse hairs. She was younger than she had first appeared. Something supple in her cheeks and chin, which gleamed softly with sweat, indicated this. She wore bright lipstick. There was lipstick on her small gray teeth as she smiled.

"Are you running away?" the woman asked.

"Oh no," Sally said. It took an effort of will to meet the woman's small eyes, not only because her face was so close, but because Sally so wanted to turn once again to the window, to the lovely light of dusk. They were no longer underground. But she had been raised to be polite. She had been trained by nuns to offer kindness to every stranger. "I'm going to a convent," she said. "My novitiate. I'm going to be a nursing Sister."

The woman sat back a little, moving her short arms, kicking the bags at her feet. Her hands, Sally noticed, were very small and plump, the short fingers all coming to little pale points. The woman smiled broadly, with real delight. "Mercy!" she said to the air above their heads, and laughed, a kind of rumbling, staccato laughter. "Mercy me. A nun." Then she reached down again to adjust her shopping bags. "Well," she said, "I'm sure that's very nice for you, but I, for one, am running away."

She straightened up again. "From my husband," she added. There was something avian—was it pigeon or owl?—in the way she turned her head on her thick throat, moved chin and eyes in Sally's direction. "He thinks I'm going to see my sister in Chicago, where I'm from, but I am going on through, all the way to California." She nodded, smiling still. "He'll never find me. He'll never see my face again as long as he lives." She raised her eyebrows, which were thick and wiry, all askew. "What does a little nun have to say about that?"

Sally hesitated. "I'm very sorry to hear it," she said, imitating Sister Jeanne's sunny sympathy. "I'll pray for you."

The woman smiled again. She was growing younger and younger in Sally's estimation, growing closer to her own age, which seemed odd given how old she had first seemed. "We were married for six years," the woman said. "I can hardly believe it. Six," she said again. "Six years. I was just a girl." She laughed again, moving from side to side in her seat. There was something sweetly unpleasant on her breath. A decayed tooth, perhaps. "And while I'm sure," the woman was saying, "that a little baby nun would know nothing about these things, I can tell you with assurance that he had the tiniest penis known to man." She held up her pale pinky. The nail, the flesh itself, came to a point and was rimmed with grime. And then the woman slipped the pinky into her mouth, pursed her lips around it. She widened her eyes as if in surprise. When she withdrew the finger, it was wet and stained at the base by her lipstick. Then she put her hand, with the fingers curled into her palm, over her wide lap. She wiggled the wet finger against the dark fabric of her skirt. "Can you imagine," she said casually, "a girl the size of me spending her life riding a thing the size of that?"

Sally pulled her eyes away, her face burning. The woman touched her with her elbow and nodded down, drawing her eyes again to the dark lap, the wet pinky moving spastically like some pale blind thing.

"Of course," the woman went on, closing her hand into a fist, "a little nun would know nothing about any of this, but when you get to your convent, ask around. Or ask your own mother when next you see her. Is your mother still living?"

Sally was shocked and embarrassed and confused enough to give a courteous reply. "Yes, she is," she whispered.

"And your father?" The woman asked. "Is he still with us?"

Sally shook her head, once more averting her eyes. There was a man reading a newspaper just across the aisle. She thought he might have, briefly, glanced around it to see them. "My father died before I was born," she said, even though, as untraveled as she was, her instinct told her to stop this conversation, to move to another seat, another train. To call to the man across the aisle for rescue.

The woman laughed again, a deep slow chuckle, even though, Sally saw as she glanced at her once more, her chest was rising rapidly, up and down, with the odd pace of her breathing. "I suppose a case could be made that a teeny weenie is better than none at all, as would seem is your poor mother's case."

Just then, the conductor reached them, "Good evening, ladies," and took their tickets. Her companion said, "Good evening, kind sir," leaning forward a bit as she reached for her ticket, which was wedged into a corner of one of her bags, and then bringing her head up too close to his belt buckle. She looked at Sally as she handed her own ticket to the man and then shifted her gaze back to the trainman's blue pants, nodding, as if Sally should consider what was hidden under the gabardine.

She had an image of the woman's wriggling wet pinky, writhing in the darkness, and felt herself blush again. She turned her face to the window.

"Did you ever read *The Teenie Weenies*?" the woman asked her in what suddenly seemed a pleasant, conversational voice. "They were in the Sunday funnies? Adorable little pixies, they were. Little spools of thread for chairs and chestnut leaves or some such for clothes. Did you ever see it?"

Sally shook her head. "No," she said.

"It's really quite charming," she went on. "I'm a great reader of the Sunday funnies. I love Orphan Annie, being orphaned myself. Almost like you. And that big Daddy Warbucks with his beautiful bald head. I also love Li'l Abner. Do you go to the pictures much?"

"Sometimes," Sally said.

The woman turned her head, doubling her chins, and cast her eyes over the girl once more. "You really want to go through life all alone, without a man to protect you?"

Sally shrugged, smiled. Instinct told her not to squander her belief on this dirty woman, but still she struggled with the impulse to say, Betrothed to Our Lord.

The woman was studying her. "But you're just a baby," she said without waiting for a reply. "You'll see what I mean soon enough."

Then the woman reached up to unpin her hat, getting further settled. She fluffed her hair. "I'm going to go bleach-blonde when I get to California," she went on. "I think it will suit me. Do you think it will suit me?"

Sally smiled politely—it was the response she'd been trained for—and said, "I think so," wanting once more to turn away from the woman, toward the window, both to see where they were going and to put this conversation to an end. But she was uncertain about how this was done.

"Of course, the muff gives it away," the woman said. And again she touched her elbow to Sally's side. Sally, still smiling, shook her head. Her mother had once found a white muff made of rabbit fur in the donation basket, but Sally had refused it—she was old enough by then, maybe ten or eleven. She had, by then, become aware of the haughty eyes of other girls, on the street, even in church, when they saw her wearing their own outgrown clothes.

But the woman was nodding toward her lap, speaking to her as if she had suddenly lost her hearing. "A muff," she said. "Don't you get it? Down below. I'm not about to bleach that." And she laughed into the air, once more moving her bottom from side to side to get more comfortable in her seat. Her arms were too short for her body. She crossed and then uncrossed them over her broad chest. "The way I figure it," she went on, "by the time you've got a man eye-to-eye with your muff, he's not worried if you're a natural blonde or not."

Sally shook her head, uncomprehending, and the woman laughed again, panting still. "Oh, you baby," she said, all-knowing. "You'll find out one of these days."

Sally turned her burning face to the widow. The train was moving through the flat outskirts of the city. There were still tenements and long avenues in the distance, lights coming on here and there, although the sun had yet to set. She was vaguely aware of the woman leaning forward again to arrange her bags, pushing them out into the aisle, drawing them back in again, over the high insteps of her small feet.

And then her voice was at Sally's shoulder again. Hot puffs of words on her neck. "One time," the woman said, "I was riding the train from Chicago and a man came down the aisle selling nuts. Have you heard this one?"

Sally shook her head—misunderstanding once again.

"He was selling nuts, yelling out, Peanuts, roasted almonds, cashews. So I said to him, 'Do you have any pecans, kind sir?' And he said, 'Pee cans? Back of the train, lady.'"

She laughed. Her exhalations gave a taste to the air between them. "Do you get it? Pee cans. Toilets." She waved her little hand. "What I'm saying is, I'm going to go find the pee can," and Sally, the habit of politeness so well engrained, smiled and nodded, as if their conversation thus far had been refined. Suddenly the woman gave her a long, penetrating look, not kind. "Keep your hands to yourself while I'm gone," the woman said. "Lay off my stuff."

She had some trouble maneuvering out of the seat. Once again, the way she moved—shuffling, heavy-bottomed—gave the impression of great age. As she moved away, the man across the aisle lowered his newspaper and looked at Sally with a kind of amused sympathy. He was an older man. Or maybe a young man made old by the vague shadow of his hat brim over his eyes. Her face flushed again to think he had overheard.

A small child appeared in the aisle beside her. Or small-bodied, thin-limbed, but with a large and dirty face. His head was unevenly shaven, down to white scalp in some places, prickly with dark hairs in others, which made his skull seem battered and misshapen. There were scabs on his scalp and on his chin and nose. He stood beside her for a moment, a bit wobbly because of the movement of the train. And then he put his hand on the armrest of the empty seat and smiled, his crooked teeth nearly green. She smiled at him and said hello. He said hello. "Are you going to Chicago?" she asked. He shrugged. There was a fine white crust around his nose. "Would you like a piece of chocolate?" she asked him.

He raised his pale eyebrows. She noticed another maroon scab along one of them. It seemed to crack dryly as the skin moved. She reached into her bag for the dinner her mother had made, and just as she put her hand on the chocolate bar, another hand, reaching upside down and backward from the seat in front of her, clawed the air until it touched the boy's arm, then his collar, and then pulled him out of sight, nearly off his feet. She heard a woman's voice say "Sit," and the crack of a hand against flesh. No sound from the child, but the man across the aisle again looked up from his paper, observed what she couldn't see, and then again looked at her and shook his head sorrowfully.

The dirty woman was some time in coming back, and when

she did return, and once more maneuvered herself rear-first into her seat, the unwashed odor beneath her violets and cooking oil was vivid.

Sally had taken out her missal by then—much as she would have preferred opening the novel, she feared what conversation it might lead to—and the woman leaned over elaborately to see what she was reading. Then she sat back again.

"Ever had a boyfriend?" she asked.

Sally turned a page and nodded with a small, apologetic shrug, as if she were too absorbed in her prayers to speak aloud. But already she was rehearsing how, if the woman pressed her, she would use the name and the personality of Patrick Tierney, whom she had known all her life, to create an image of an adoring boyfriend, finally refused. In the story she would have told the woman, had she pressed her, her imaginary Patrick Tierney was better looking than the real one, something like tall Charlie with his blue eyes, and with a flourish to his background (his father a soldier, not a doorman) and his profession (a medical student, not a laborer). She would tell the crude woman that this Patrick Tierney held back his tears—stoically—when he saw her off at the train station today, rather than, as was the actual case, merely saying last night when he came over with his two sisters to tell her goodbye, "You'll be back, I guarantee it. That's not the life for you."

But the dirty woman didn't press her. She waved her hand in the air as if she knew the girl's nod was a lie and then leaned forward to rummage through her bags. She took a sandwich from one of them—now there was the smell of liverwurst and onion—and ate hungrily, but silently, panting as she did.

All over the car, as the world outside lost light, people were bringing out food, odors of canned meat and cheese and old apples. Cigarette smoke gathered like mist over the hats and the heads of the passengers. A shouting argument erupted at one end of the car. She saw the conductor stop in the aisle to wave a finger at the culprits. The bald-headed child walked by again as if in a trance, balancing himself between the seats. Some minutes later, when the train lurched, he let out a wail that could be heard even over the noise of the tracks and the engine. His mother, whom Sally could only see from behind, a crushed cloth hat over a tangle of thin and graying hair, was slumped against the window. She sprang from her seat and raced down the aisle in a stooped, hunchbacked way. A second later, she was dragging the boy through the aisle. He was wailing. He had his hands over his eyes, his little mouth a moldy circle. The mother threw him into his seat and dove after him. Again there was the crack of her hand against his flesh, but to clear effect this time: the boy's outraged cries reached another register.

Someone on the train said, "Shut up."

The woman beside her said, "Serves them right."

The man on the aisle folded up his paper, neatly, and tucked it under his arm. Then he pulled his hat down over his eyes.

When Sally finally got the courage to get out of her seat and use the toilets, the floor there was wet. The soles of her shoes were tacky when she returned to her seat. When she went to the dining car—at the tail end of the dinner service, as the Sisters had advised—she was made to wait in the swaying corridor, and while she did so, a man, smelling of alcohol, passed by her too closely and rubbed his chest against hers, breathing into her face. A girl her own age—she was certain this one was her own age—was already at the table where they sat her, finishing her dinner. She wore a smart dark suit and a hat with a veil, and at first Sally feared she might be a rich girl, the daughter of a prosperous father, the kind who would snort through her nose, even in church, when she looked Sally's outfit up and down. But it took no more than a minute for Sally to see the shine on the fabric of the girl's jacket, the pale threads at the edge of her cuffs. Sally knew secondhand when she saw it. There was a tear in the veil as well. The girl had tried to hide it with a hat pin, but the material had come undone and now stood up stiffly, showing the hole to anyone who looked—as if the hat itself disdained this unworthy owner. The girl's outfit, Sally recognized, was all effort.

When Sally ordered her tea, the girl asked for the same, and a bowl of vanilla ice cream.

Then she smiled warmly across the small table. "Going to Chicago?" she asked, and Sally only nodded warily. She had learned the first lesson of her first journey from home. But the girl barely registered the reply. She began talking, leaning into the table as she did, as if without it between them she would crawl, talking, into Sally's lap. There was something endearing about the tumble of her words. She was from the Bronx, she said, going to Chicago to meet her husband, who had, at last, found work there. He hadn't had work, she said, for two years. As long as they'd been married.

Here she straightened up to allow the waiter to set down their tea and her silver dish of ice cream. She opened the purse on her lap and began to rummage through it, talking all the while.

She missed him so much, she said. Missed him like crazy. "It's like an itch," she said.

Mrs. Tierney sometimes said, "An itch where I've never had a bite," which always got her mother laughing.

"I'm just going crazy with it," the girl said. "I'm so lonesome for him."

Talking, she extracted a small perfume bottle from her purse and tipped a little of the clear perfume into her hot tea. Without pause, she reached across the table and poured some into Sally's cup as well.

Astonished, Sally put out her hand.

"It's good for you," the girl said, merely as an aside to her tale.

When they were first married, she said, they lived with her mother in the Bronx, but they were always fighting because he couldn't find a job. So he left for Chicago. (The girl licked the ice cream from the back of her spoon.) She didn't even know where he'd been living. Her mother said he must live on the street. She wrote to ask him if he lived on the street, but he never answered. For six months, all she had was two letters that said, No luck, still looking. She said again, "I was going crazy, missing him so much."

She sipped her tea and pursed her lips. "It's good," she said, and nodded that Sally should try hers. "Better than cream and sugar."

Reluctantly, Sally lifted the warm cup. She was expecting the taste of lavender or rose water—the taste of perfume—but what hit her tongue was hot and clenching; it seemed to sear, simultaneously, her nose and her throat. Her eyes watered. She coughed.

The girl laughed.

"This is whiskey," Sally said. She knew something of the taste of it—given to her by her mother, on a spoon, when she had a cold. Or rubbed on her gums for a toothache.

The girl agreed. "Sure it is," she said. "It's good for you," and then she reached for the sugar cubes on the table between them. She tossed two of them into Sally's tea. "Now try it," she said, and Sally did. Again the watering of her eyes and the impulse to cough, although the sweetness helped.

The girl said, "So, as I was saying." Finally, her husband wrote to tell her he had work—he didn't even say where—and a room. The stationery he used was from a Chicago hotel, it had the name and address printed right on it. That was good enough for her. She got the letter only yesterday—but, she said, she was never one to let grass grow under her feet. She was going crazy, missing him so much.

Through her tea-induced tears, Sally saw the girl smiling at her. She had a pleasant, square face. Sally thought of the stationery Mrs. Tierney used for the notes she sent to school when one of the Tierney children was sick—lovely white stationery marked with the address of the St. Francis Hotel. "Purloined paper," Patrick Tierney called it, teaching Sally and his sisters the meaning of the word.

Sally took a third sip. The taste was the taste of her mother's warm finger, dipped into a capful of whiskey and rubbed against her gums.

The girl said she just walked out of her mother's apartment this morning, tried to pawn her wedding ring (she held up her ringless hand), which turned out to be gold-plated, not gold. She shrugged. She went back to her mother's place and looked around. Her mother had a silver tea service they never used. Never. Not once. Just sitting there. She took the tea service back to the pawnshop and got enough to buy her ticket. And here she was.

"I bet you think I'm something awful to steal from my own mother," she said from behind her teacup. "But I know I'm going to send the money back as soon as I can. And I swear to you on a stack of Bibles, my mother never once used that teapot."

"I don't think you're awful," Sally said softly.

The girl was saying she had a very nice sleeping berth, and asked if Sally had a sleeping berth, clucking her tongue sympathetically when she said no. She was a pretty girl with a small face, pale brown hair, a tiny mouth that hung open when she wasn't talking. She seemed puzzled when Sally told her she was on her way to the novitiate, and then shrugged when Sally explained this meant she was going to be a nun.

"I'm not Catholic," the girl said, suddenly dull-eyed, without interest.

When the white-jacketed waiter brought the checks, the girl reached across the table and took Sally's wrist. She began to speak urgently across the small space. Once more, Sally wondered if she had misjudged a stranger's age. "Help me out," the girl said. "I haven't got any more money. Now they'll throw me off the train."

Sally had the five dollars in her wallet, the fifty more pinned to the lining of her purse, meant to be given to the Sisters on her arrival. She smiled as Sister Jeanne would have smiled and put two bills on the little silver tray to cover the girl's dinner.

But then the girl took her wrist once again.

"If you've got a little more," she said, and paused, and then said in a rush, "What I mean is, if you could lend me a little more. If you've got it." Her grip tightened. "See, I don't know how I'll get to the hotel. Maybe there's a subway or something. I don't know. And if my husband isn't there, I don't know what I'll do. Where I'll stay. What if I can't find him? What will happen to me? I'll be out on the street."

The girl pressed her fingertips into Sally's flesh. Her nails were bitten.

"I'm sure your husband will be there," Sally said, trying to soothe her. It was the voice she had used with Mrs. Costello. "He sent you the letter." But she was thinking of Mrs. Tierney's purloined stationery.

The girl leaned even farther over the small table, pressing her breasts against the narrow wood. The ripped veil of her hat seemed to rise up, to reach out imploringly, a beggar's thin hand. "But what will I do if he's not?" she said. "Can't you just lend me something? A little more?" She eyed Sally's purse. "I swear I'll pay you right back," cooing it. And now her voice grew to a whine. "What will I do out on the street?"

Sally recognized, reluctantly, what was happening here: her vocation was being tested. First the dirty woman with her vulgar talk, and now this girl. It hardly seemed fair that God would measure her worth so soon. She thought of Sister Lucy, who had wanted a contemplative's life. Who did not refuse.

Unhappily, Sally said, "All right." She extricated her hand from the girl's clammy grip. She opened her pocketbook and reached into the slim tear behind the satin lining, felt for the safety pin, aware of the girl studying her all the while. She knew she should have the grace to give the girl all she had, as Christ would have done. Certainly as Sister Jeanne would have done. She knew the Sisters in Chicago would applaud her generosity. But she knew, too, that she didn't want to. Didn't want to give up what her mother had so carefully saved. Didn't want—even more fiercely—to be mocked by another dirty stranger. She slid out two ten dollar bills and passed them across the table, fighting her own regret even as she gave them up. "That's everything I have," she said piously. Stubbornly. "That's all I own."

The girl reached for the money. "Write down your address," she said, and took the receipt from the silver plate, pushing it toward her. "I'll be there tomorrow to pay you back."

She was tucking the bills into her own purse when she suddenly looked across the table. "I didn't know nuns were allowed to have money," she said. It seemed a reprimand.

As Sally was leaving the car, headed in the opposite direction from the Bronx girl, the white-jacketed waiter took her arm. "Pardon me, miss," he said. "That lady a friend of yours?"

And Sally, somewhat breathlessly, as if he had caught her in a lie, said, "Yes."

The man shook his head. He was a bald black man with large and sympathetic eyes. "I just hope she was no trouble to you," he said kindly. "That's all."

Sally said, "Thank you." She was about to walk on when she added, abruptly, as if to return his kindness, "My father worked on a train, too. The Brooklyn Rapid Transit." She was surprised to find her tongue had grown thick.

The man smiled and nodded. This might have been something he already knew. "Is your father with you tonight?" he asked.

And she said, "Oh yes," the two words running together sloppily. She indicated the open corridor. "He's just back there," she said. And imagined him briefly, a man with a fedora pulled over his eyes.

The porter said, "You both have a nice evening, then."

When she returned to her seat, her companion was once again chuckling inside her panting breath—no telling at what.

Outside, there were only small bits of light, moth holes, as she thought of them, in the heavy darkness. The taste of the sweet tea, the aftermath of the alcohol, lingered at the back of her throat, made her eyes ache. She leaned her head against the window.

The stations they pulled into were a relief at first, golden and bustling, but as the hour grew late and she woke from a shallow sleep to see them, they offered only a yellowed, nightmare tableau of weary shadows: a lonely stationmaster lifting a heavy arm, a single passenger with a suitcase and an abandoned air, a newspaper blown against a wall. Weary shadows that were quickly lost again as the train moved on, into the cavernous night.

Her father was a trainman on the BRT.

All her life, as she moved over bright sidewalks and green grass, he had been in his coffin, the narrowest of corridors—of lightless tunnels meant to keep out rock and stone and damp earth. Why had she never thought of this before? Why had she never pictured him there as she blithely went up and down the subway stairs, rode nonchalantly through the darkness. A trainman on the BRT, now long returned to the place where he had plied his trade: the damp underground, the dirt and carved stone, the brittle dark.

At one point, she woke to see the little boy standing in the aisle again. Her companion slept lifelessly beside her. He swayed with the movement of the train. Even in the dimmed light, now thick with smoke, she could see the goose egg on his bald skull. As he shifted with the train's shuddering, she could see a line of dried blood on his cheek just below it. She had only half her chocolate bar left, but she found it in her purse and handed it across the bulk of her seatmate to the child. He took it from her and then, wraithlike, walked on. His mother's head was slumped into the window.

She was going to give her life to others, in the name of the crucified Christ and His loving mother. She was going to join the Little Nursing Sisters of the Sick Poor, Congregation of Mary Before the Cross, *Stabat Mater*, which Sister Jeanne thought the most beautiful name of all the orders. Because it reminded us all, Sister Jeanne said, that love stood before brutality in that moment on Golgotha and love was triumphant. Love applied to suffering, as Sister Illuminata put it: like a clean cloth to a seeping wound.

Sally had understood the image in the basement laundry of

the convent, when she watched Sister Illuminata put a hot iron to the nuns' clean clothes—perfume of starch and of soap, of the heavy linen itself, dried in the courtyard's sun. A clean cloth—immaculate and pure—to place against mankind's wounds. She had felt, the fragrant steam rising, the joy of it, the rightness of it. No help in putting a soiled, sullied thing to what was itself debased and infected. One kept oneself, one made oneself, pure—dressed in these immaculate clothes, moved about these simple rooms, prayed the Hours, spoke softly, kept still one's idle hands and kept gentle one's thoughts, to offer relief to the wretched world, to assuage the seething wound, the lesion, *laesio,* of human suffering. The suffering that all things mortal were heir to, Sister Illuminata had said.

In her lovely habit, she wanted to be that pure antidote to human pain.

But she wanted, too, in some equal, more furious way, not to be mocked for it; not to be fooled. Sister Lucy had told her, Don't think you can end all suffering with your charms.

The next time she got up to use the toilet she had to climb over the solid bulk of her sleeping companion. As Sally awkwardly crossed her lap, trying to step over the brown bags at her feet, she felt the woman grab at her hip and then poke a dirty finger at the seat of her skirt. Sally cried out, nearly tumbled, but swiftly caught her breath as she gathered herself in the aisle. She looked back at the woman, who had once more closed her eyes. The man on the aisle reached out to steady her, and briefly, although she didn't need to, she gripped his hand. Warm and broad and very strong. She said, "Thank you."

In the toilet, the odor of someone's bowel movement was overwhelming. She stumbled out, walked to the thin corridor between the cars to get some air. Out here, the rattling echo of the

steel over the tracks seemed to bounce off the darkness that surrounded them, as if the darkness itself were made of black stone.
As if they had once more gone underground.

She saw a man approaching from the yellow light of the next
car, a sleeping car—she could see a porter moving behind him.
The porter was buttoning down the curtains on each berth,
securing whoever was inside for the night. The girl from the
Bronx, asleep on the money Sally's mother had labored to earn.
The man approaching seemed to smile at her, and, afraid, she
stepped back inside just ahead of him. He followed her, even
reached over her head to hold the door, pressing—was he
pressing?—himself into her back. He went into the toilet and she
made her way down the aisle. A card game was going on among
four smoking men. They looked up indifferently as she passed.
One of the men held the black stump of a cigar between his fingers; the end of it, blacker still, was wet. Everything reeked. Of
smoke and sweat and the human gas seeping from these mounds
of flesh. She put the back of her hand to her nose and her own
flesh reeked.

Unsteadily, she walked past her seat, to the end of the car—
"pee cans," the dirty woman had said, vulgar—and then she
turned around and walked back again. Here in the dim and
smoky light were, for her consideration, a sampling of "the others"
she was giving her life to: vulgar, unkempt, ungrateful. Pale,
sleeping faces with gaping, distorted mouths, sprawled limbs, a
hollow-eyed soldier looking out into the night, a khaki rucksack
clutched to his chest, a yellow-skinned old man folded into himself, gazing forward with a murderous look. A young woman in
a jaunty hat, chewing gum ferociously, reading a magazine,
picking her nose and then flicking her fingertips into the aisle.

She passed the seat in front of hers, where the little bald boy now slept pressed up against his mother's back, which was turned to him. His hands were between his knees, as if for warmth. He looked like the bums who slept beneath the elevated, like a little hobo curled against the concrete wall of a warehouse. There was a dirty, bloodstained handkerchief on the floor at his feet.

"Excuse me," she said to her companion when she returned to her seat. The woman was sprawled and did not move. The man on the aisle was watching, smiling still. "Excuse me," she said again, and now the woman merely turned her face away with a small snort and bubble. The man across the way said, helpfully, "You might have to poke her." She looked at him straight on for the first time. An older man with a five o'clock shadow, balding, almost handsome, some missing teeth in the side of his smile. A look of weariness about him, too, of course, at this hour, but a kind eye. Did she really want to go through life without a man to protect her? He reached across the aisle to touch the woman's thick elbow. "Madam," he said. And louder, "Madam." Again someone in the car called, "Pipe down."

Sally, weary herself, screwed up her courage and shouted, "Excuse me!" She reached out—even to her own eye her movements had grown weird, as if weirdly weighted—and pressed a finger into the woman's shoulder. The flesh beneath her coat seemed barely to give. Her wide thighs, straining against her dark skirt, twitched a bit, but continued to block the way. The man on the aisle said, "Madam," once more.

Struggling to keep her balance in the aisle, Sally looked at her empty seat on the other side of this fleshy obstacle. She had never in her life so desired a single destination. She wanted only to curl into it, turn her face to the cool window. She wanted only to be left alone. Suddenly, in a kind of desperation, she reached down and slid the shopping bags off the woman's feet and into the aisle. One of them toppled, an orange and a gold compact and a bit of bright silk, a scarf or a slip or a nightgown, spilling from the top, causing, at last, the woman to stir. She reached out her spiked hands in the startled way of sleepers, and in an instant of fear and rage, Sally swung her fist into the woman's palm, made contact with it, and then swung again, striking this time the inside of her fat wrist, touching the bone beneath the ringed flesh. And then, it seemed all the same, continuous motion, although in truth it was choppy and abrupt, like pounding laundry, she swung again—the woman tried but failed to raise her elbow in defense. Sally felt the hard surface of the woman's dry teeth against her knuckles, felt, too, the tacky lipstick and the humid breath.

"Keep your damn hands to yourself," Sally said, stepping over the woman's feet, kicking the greasy bags with her heel. "Stay away from me."

She cleared the woman's lap and drove herself into the seat, her heart pounding. Turned her face to the window.

There was an astonished pause, and then the woman shouted, "Mercy!" Panting more forcefully. Or not panting now, but sobbing. Sally glanced briefly over her shoulder. The woman, her awful fingers pressed delicately against her mouth, was now leaning out into the aisle to retrieve the bag. The man across the way had bent down to help her, and the little bald boy appeared, handing her the escaped orange and the thick gold compact. An act of betrayal on both their parts, Sally thought. "Thank you, sweetheart," she heard the woman say as she wept. "Thank you, kind sir." She told them, "You'd think butter wouldn't melt in her mouth."

Sally turned her face to the window. Once again, she felt the woman's breath on her neck. "A fine Sister you'll make," she hissed.

Sally raised her shoulder against the sound, against the woman's breath. She was now the one who was panting. Her anger a clenched fist in her chest. And yet there was pride, too. She had, after all, spoken up.

"You're a devil," the woman said into her ear. Without turning to face her, Sally bared her teeth at her own reflection and whispered, "You are."

The windowsill of the train was now as sooty as any subway's.

The smell of soot, in fact, was lofting through the car. She put her forehead to the glass to see if there was a refinery outside, a house fire, a blazing garbage dump. Fire and brimstone. It seemed the right smell for this hellish train, this terrible journey that could not have taken her farther from the convent's clean laundry and the pretty joy she had felt just this afternoon about the consecrated life she was called to.

There was only darkness beyond the train window, her own vague reflection passing over it. She wondered how many miles they had gone and, with the thought, felt the flood of tears she had not realized she'd been keeping at bay, had been keeping at bay since she last glimpsed Sister Jeanne and her mother through this very glass. She put her fingertips to the window. Her mother and Sister Jeanne had once stood framed within it. The tears came, bitter and unrelenting. Life a bleak prospect to a motherless child.

At her back, she heard the dirty woman say, "Serves you right."

It was three in the morning.

By the time the train came into the station in Chicago, she had done her calculations: she had the money in her wallet, and the remaining bills pinned to the lining of her handbag. She also had a dollar in each shoe—following the Tierney twins' advice. She would get herself a sleeping car for the journey home.

There was the scent of morning air inside the beautiful station—the familiar scent of early-morning city air that made her feel for just a moment that she had not arrived but returned. There was something lovely in the bright beams that poured in from the skylights, touching down here and there on the wide floor.

There was the bustle of many busy people, the trailing presence of the dirty woman, whose breath she could still taste. She saw the two nuns who were there to meet her, their clean and simple forms, arms folded, idle hands tucked into their sleeves. One was young, one older. They both smiled as she approached. Their skin, after the heavy powder of the woman on the train, looked pure, newly formed, despite the peach fuzz and wrinkles on one and the scattering of blemishes on the other. She recognized the smell of sunlight and starch on their habits. She recognized the offer of friendship in the younger one's shy brown eyes.

She would love the companionship of nuns for the rest of her life.

"Here you are," the old one said, holding out her immaculate hands, welcoming her. "We're so happy you've thought to join us."

Sally put her suitcase down. She might have seen the Bronx girl walking quickly past from the corner of her eye. "The truth is," she said, "I've thought better of it."

Stabat Mater

THERE WERE NO NURSING SISTERS on the street when
she walked up from the subway. No Patrick Tierney,
either, to call out, "What did I tell you?" when he saw
her lugging herself home. That was lucky. She had
slept only briefly on the train coming back—buttoned into a
lower bunk, but no less terrified going east than she had been
going west. The torment on the trip out had been those awful
people. The torment of the trip home was the utter loneliness of
that dark, narrow berth.

The movement of the train was with her still, in her back and
under her feet, as she walked down her own block with her suitcase and then up the familiar steps. There was no one in the
entry. No Mrs. Gertler perched in her window on the parlor
floor. That was lucky, too. She climbed the stairs. It was early

afternoon, but her lack of sleep, her unplanned return, made the hour of the day seem uncertain and strange. Just forty-eight hours ago, she had said her goodbyes to this place, folded into her view of herself the romantic notion that many years would pass before she saw it again. It would not take much imagination, tired as she was, to believe that time had, indeed, intervened and she was returning like some Odysseus, much older and much changed.

Life goes by in the blink of an eye. It would not take any imagination to convince herself that it already had.

Her mother's voice reached her through the open transom above the apartment door. Her mother's laughter. Distinct and familiar and yet, as well, indistinguishable from the man's voice that ran just beneath it. A man's voice low but rising, rising and falling in a kind of enumerating rhythm, the rhythm of a tale being told, a joke or a story. Inside the apartment, a man was telling her mother a story and her mother was laughing, laughing here and there. There was always something enviable about her mother's laugh. Ever since she was a child, Sally flew to it. Put up her arms, put her hands to her mother's broad cheeks to say, What? What?

She thought of Sister Jeanne, raising her face to the sound of it, as if to a warm sun.

Sally eased open the door. Placed her suitcase beside the couch. From the living room she could see that the man had drawn a dining chair into the kitchen doorway. He was sitting in it crookedly, his back to her. He was in shirtsleeves and had his hands in his pant pockets. Her mother was in the kitchen just beyond him, at the stove, but in easy reach. She was frying something in a pan—the spit and sizzle of ham. She was laughing. He was talking. Never in Sally's experience had a man in shirtsleeves sat in the kitchen doorway in this way, talking to her mother in this way. Not as a visitor would, but as one who was utterly at home in, utterly familiar with, these few rooms. She moved closer, through the living room, to the long sideboard.

From where she paused she could see him better. His hair was black and touched with gray, thick over his neck but thin at the top. His shoulders in his striped shirt were wide. He was collarless. In the glass of the kitchen's single window she could see a vague reflection of his face: broad forehead, pale, and dark eyes made shadowy by the reflection. "'Are you telling me?'" he was saying, and Sally recognized the brogue. "'Are you telling me,' I asked him, 'that after all this time . . .'"

"After all that time," her mother said without turning, laughing with him, her hips moving, the hem of her long skirt moving, moving with her laughter, and her voice—what was it about her voice that was so new?—bright, easy, warm. Both of their voices so familiar in the exchange. When had she ever heard such a thing in these rooms? When had she ever seen such a thing?

Telling us later, she said, "I had to rub my eyes."

And then she saw, with an intake of breath, a cry of surprise, that the man's thin white feet were bare on the linoleum floor.

"Glory be to God," her mother said, and the man, turning, sat up in his chair. Not Jim at all, not her father returned to them, to her, returned to life in the interval of her departure, but Mr. Costello, the milkman, struggling to stand now, politely, long bare feet and all.

In the bedroom, the sheets and the coverlet were folded down. There was the smell of cigarette smoke in the air, the smell of flesh, some paler, warmer version of the human air of the train.

The man's worn jacket was draped over a chair. His empty shoes placed side by side at the foot of the bed. Her mother followed her there and closed the door behind her.

"You're back," she said. Her hair was loose. Her cheeks flushed red. She had grown younger in Sally's short time away. "What's happened? You frightened the life out of me." She paused, and together, mother and daughter took in the tumbled room, the counterpane, the white coat, the man's two empty shoes at the foot of the bed.

"You're back," her mother said again, but this time as if she understood it plainly.

Sally took in the room, what had been her room, her own bed.

She turned to her mother. She felt the sensation of a plunge, with not even a stranger's shoulder beside her.

"And where will you go?" her mother asked her.

WHEN THE TWO WOMEN RETURNED to the living room, Mr. Costello—in his bare feet—was standing undecided by the front door with his head bowed, like a man waiting for an elevator. Shyly, he looked up at her mother, and then, as they passed him, he slipped into the bedroom.

Her mother told her to sit at the table. Sally noticed that the dining room chair had been neatly returned to its place. Moments later, her mother brought two plates with the ham and the eggs. She sat down with her daughter. Mr. Costello appeared in his shoes and his white coat and his hair combed down and his cap in his hands. He said, "I'll be going, then," politely, and her mother only looked up briefly—and the affection in her eyes was both brand-new and immediately familiar, a reminder of something Sally had always known: the strength of her mother's capacity to love, the assurance of it.

"Goodbye, dear," her mother said.

They ate in silence. All was tasteless in her mouth. She felt again the movement of the train beneath her. If she closed her eyes, she knew, she could make herself believe she was still on board, in the suffocating darkness, looking out to this dancing light—this room, this day, her mother's sure hands, her living presence, her happiness—looking out at it all with what might have been her father's own eyes: envious, lonesome, buried, bereft.

The Substitute

MRS. TIERNEY SAID, "Take Patrick, then. He's got his name."

Mr. Tierney said, "I will."

It was the end of the argument. They were both red-faced. Both licked the spittle of shouted words from their lips, satisfied. His parents' arguments, our father said, erupted suddenly, like a street fight, and then, just as rapidly, concluded. Peace descended. Something like happiness.

Their six children came to understand that a certain satisfaction might be found in setting a beloved's blood boiling.

A telegram had arrived from Poughkeepsie: Mr. Tierney's father was dead. Mr. Tierney said he must go to the funeral, and Mrs. Tierney asked if he was going to do her the indignity of expecting her to accompany him. He said no, but he would take the children. She said she would not have them missing school for a man they'd never met. He said he would take only the boys, then. She said Michael's job was already hanging by a thread.

"I won't stay long," Mr. Tierney said.

Mrs. Tierney said, "You're a fool to go at all."

"I'm his only child," Mr. Tierney said.

"Didn't he know that himself?" Mrs. Tierney replied.

"I won't be plagued by his ghost," Mr. Tierney shouted.

"He had no use for you when he was alive," Mrs. Tierney said coolly. "Why would he be coming to you dead?"

"There's ice water in your veins," he said.

"There's sawdust in your head."

"He's dead."

"He let your mother die without you."

"I didn't know."

"The bastard didn't tell you."

"He was bitter."

"He was hateful. He hated me."

"Us."

"Us, then."

"Have a heart. There was a monkey on his back. That cripple in the room upstairs."

"Where's my violin?"

"Have some pity."

"Have some sense."

"I'll go alone, then."

There was a pause. He had spoken the one word she could not abide: alone. All through his growing up, our father said, he couldn't walk to the corner for a newspaper without his mother urging him to take someone along.

"Take Patrick, then," she said. "He's got his name."

"I will," he said.

It was the laughter in her voice when next she spoke that signaled to their children that the fight was over. That it had brewed some pleasure for them both. "If the bastard's going to haunt anyone," she said, "it will be Patrick."

Mr. Tierney said, "A ghost could do worse."

And so our father found himself on the train to Poughkeepsie for the funeral of his grandfather, and namesake, a man he'd never met.

Although Michael Tierney was wearing what he called his "civilian clothes"—starched collar, vest, fine dark wool suit with a thin, pale violet stripe, gleaming shoes, brushed bowler—he retained nevertheless his erect and elegant doorman's bearing throughout the ride. There was a gold watch and a fob, subtly displayed across his trim middle. A smooth cheek newly shaven and redolent of bay rum. A fine chestnut mustache, gleaming like polished wood, trimmed and combed.

The suit Patrick wore was also fine. It had been purchased from a Jewish tailor on the Lower East Side—one of his father's "cronies"—for his older brother's high school graduation just the year before, but because Tom had found work at the Navy Yard, and not in an office, it had been stored ever since in a linen suit bag, weighted with mothballs and cedar blocks.

Given the short notice—the telegram had come from his grandfather's maiden sister, Rose, just two days ago—his mother had only a single sunny afternoon to air it at the window, and so it retained a whiff of what his father called "its hibernation." Comically, Mr. Tierney sprinkled his son with cologne before they left the apartment, making the sign of the cross and murmuring in Latin. And so they had gone off to the train in good humor.

His mother had refused to come. Perfectly understandable, Mr. Tierney said, given how the man had stood against their marriage. Because she was an immigrant. Because she was a servant girl in the home of an Upper West Side family who summered in Poughkeepsie—a wealthy family that his own father had admired and envied and aspired to imitate. It had been an elevation for his father, a schoolteacher, the child of immigrants himself, to be invited to the summer home of such people. A confirmation of the schoolteacher's growing status as town sage, as cosmopolitan man-of-the-world, to be invited to converse with a city man of such wealth, in his own summer place, about business and politics, philosophy and learning.

And an irreconcilable insult that the schoolteacher, so honored, should bring along a son—"Yours truly," Mr. Tierney told Patrick on the train to Poughkeepsie, "and not much older than you are now"—who, rather than attending to the after-dinner conversation, rather than seizing the opportunity to make himself remarkable to this businessman from Manhattan, a man who might do him some good, put his eyes on a buck-toothed servant girl and refused to draw them away.

"Of course your mother's not buck-toothed," his father said on the train, "she's a beauty beyond compare—but that was my father's anger speaking, his disappointment and his rage. He didn't want me coming down in the world, he wanted me going up, up, and up." On the train, Michael Tierney thrust his right hand into the air as if he were elevating a great weight. Then he dropped it, casually. Shrugged.

It was a fine spring day, and as soon as the train left the city, the smell of new grass and rich earth, sweet country air, began to fill the cars. At each station stop, the sun was morning-bright and full of lovely, floating things, white seed pods and green insects, butterflies and bumblebees. There were urns of vivid flowers at each train station, and the men and women who disembarked seemed all to be greeted by handsome children and happy dogs. His father had given him the window seat when they boarded and then sat with regal bearing on the aisle, tipping his hat to every new passenger. "Lovely day," he said. "Madam." "Sir." "Good morning." "Fine weather." The doorman's trade.

A woman who had already been greeted rose into the aisle to wait for the station ahead. Michael Tierney touched his hat to her again, and she beamed at the two of them. She was not a young woman, but she wore a pale spring suit and a summer fur and there was a gold bracelet over the wrist of the gloved hand that gripped the back of the seat in front of them. "Is this your son?" she asked, and his father said, laughing, "I stand accused."

"He's very handsome," she said, and his father looked at him and feigned a start. "Is he?"

The train was coming into the station. "You are a very handsome pair," the woman said, her eyes all on his father. Once more his father raised his hat as she left them, smiling, for the door. Father and son exchanged a look of chagrin, and then his father, dear man, put out his hand and patted the boy's knee. There wasn't a chance, they both knew, that an estrangement of any sort would ever drive them apart.

The station at Poughkeepsie bustled somewhat more than the others, but it was a country station nonetheless. His father knew the way. It was a small brick church, already filling up with what appeared to be the town's oldest citizens. Gray-haired men and stooped women in floor-sweeping skirts. The mothball scent of hibernation all about their clothes. The pallbearers—the coffin was a gleaming mahogany—seemed the youngest of the attendees, but even they were thick about the middle. Patrick heard their straining breaths as they carried the coffin down the aisle. They were followed by only two mourners. One was a tiny woman smiling like a bride behind her black veil, and beside her, walking slowly, with practiced patience, a one-legged man who leaned on a crutch, the sleeve of his missing arm pinned neatly against his shoulder. His hair was the pale orange of an ancient redhead, with a streak of pure white on the right side, above a gnarled patch of silver scar tissue, the twisted remains of an ear.

"Aunt Rose," his father whispered from behind him. "My father's sister. And Red Whelan. My father's substitute in the war."

After the funeral mass, a flushed and heavy man, a friend of his father's youth, recognized him in the milling crowd. He offered them a ride to the cemetery in an open car that was an adventure for Patrick since there was no need to own a car in Brooklyn. Patrick, in the back seat, stretched himself along the leather upholstery. The day was brighter still, growing warm, the green landscape, lawns and fields and budding trees, was luxuriant, wide open, a painted stage set to his city eyes: there was a simple red barn, comical black-and-white cows, a cartoon silo. Over the whir of the engine and the jostle of the springs, he heard his father say, "And I see old Red is still with us." The friend wore a straw boater, much like Patrick's own. "A tough bird," the man cried. "But no tougher than Rose. Still his caretaker."

His father turned to shout into the backseat. "Red Whelan," he began, but the car swerved a bit, avoiding a hole in the road, and an impatience passed over his father's face, as brief as passing sunlight. He began again, "Red Whelan is the man who served in the Union Army so my father didn't have to. Saved my old man's skin. Made it possible for me to be born."

The friend behind the wheel shouted a laugh at this, and then nodded, as if the connection had taken him by surprise. "Isn't that the truth?" he said. And added, more solemnly, "No truer words," as if to amend his surprise.

Michael Tierney threw an arm over the backrest, so he could get a better look at his son, lounging as he was in the wide backseat of the jaunty car. He aimed a finger at the boy's chest, added, "Which means Red Whelan made it possible for you to be born, too."

Patrick sat up straight, as if in response to a reprimand. But the landscape was not a serious landscape, it was full of broad greens and bright blues and clichéd farmsteads. The car puttered and squeaked like something in a circus. The scenery, this talk of the past, the day itself, was straight from the funny papers. He took none of it seriously.

The stout friend was shouting back to him, eyes on the rearview mirror. "Think of that, my boy. You might never have been. You!" he called out. "The first-born son." Patrick resisted the impulse to correct him: Tom was the first-born. "The finest fruit of Red's sacrifice," he went on, enjoying himself. "You. A barefoot boy with cheeks of tan. Here only by the grace of old Red Whelan."

That shadow of impatience passed over his father's features once again. He was, perhaps, remembering how little he liked this old friend. "Nothing is certain," he said, sober and annoyed. "My father might well have survived the war unscathed if he'd gone. If Red Whelan hadn't replaced him, he might have survived nonetheless. No one knows." He turned to face the windshield again, and then, after a few moments of consideration, turned to his son once more. "Although I suppose you should thank the man," his father said. "If you get the chance."

At the gravesite, Red Whelan was already seated, so old and thin he looked sunk into his clothes. His uniform. In the sunlight,

Patrick now noticed the faded stripe on his one outstretched leg. Sunlight caught as well the golden buttons on his jacket and a medal on his chest. With his broad face and his thick hair, his skull at the top of his narrow shoulders seemed as big and as buoyant as an outsized balloon. Seemed, in fact, to lift him out of the chair when the service was ended and the casket—no flag because it was Red Whelan who had served—was lowered into the freshly dug earth. But in fact it was the little woman, his father's Aunt Rose, who got him standing, got him steady on his crutch, even in the soft uneven grass. Even though, despite how stooped he was, she came only to his shoulder. His caretaker.

Driving back to town, the friend of his father's youth was full of regret—he clucked his tongue at every other sentence—for the lost years of their acquaintance, for the lost time of their boyhoods together. Without inquiring about their plans, he drove Patrick and his father to the house in Poughkeepsie for the luncheon. It was a pretty house, narrow and tall, brick-red shingles and white trim. A small front porch, a spreading oak, fading daffodils with their heads bent in the front yard, and a not-yet-blossomed row of lilacs along the side, under a bowed picture window hung with lace.

The funeral guests were parking their cars all up and down the shaded street or walking along the sidewalk, as father and son and the clucking friend made their way up the flagstone path. As they reached the painted steps, the black funeral car pulled into the rutted drive and stopped. The driver stepped out to open the door for Aunt Rose, and then she, in turn, put out a hand for Red Whelan. Together the two slowly crossed the lawn. His father's friend, greeting them, said, "Miss Tierney, Red," and then stepped back to show them Patrick.

The boy swept off the straw boater and placed it over his

heart, waiting to be introduced to this frail man who had once been a soldier. But no one said a word. His father had moved away, was already up the steps, standing at the front door, with his own hat against his chest. He had opened the door for them and was standing, waiting, holding back the screen. The corpulent friend of his youth was chuckling, but so quietly, so deeply in his throat, that the sound seemed to come from something nattering in the trees.

Aunt Rose smiled, her hand on Red Whelan's arm. Only her teeth and her eyes shone behind the black netting of her veil. With no introductions made, Patrick said, "How do you do?"

Red Whelan was concentrating on the slow movement of his crutch as he lifted it from the grass of the lawn to the blue slate of the walkway. This close to the man, Patrick saw that the injury that had plowed his flesh, taken his ear, turned his hair all white on one side, seemed only a part of the general redness nature had given his skin, the general havoc that time had played with his ravaged old face and neck and single, skeletal hand.

"I'm Patrick Tierney," our father said, addressing the man. He threw his head back. "You went to the war for my grandfather. You went instead of him." And did not know why, since he'd never met his grandfather, his namesake, he was suddenly overwhelmed. He felt his face grow warm, felt in his throat the hard knot of rising tears. Felt, too, in a flash of imagination that set his teeth on edge, the pain—churned flesh and mud and howling blood—this man must have endured. The suffering.

"I'm Patrick Tierney," he said again, more boldly. "I'm the grandson."

Aunt Rose patted the shoulder of his fine suit. "You are," she said, a kind of encouragement.

But Red Whelan said nothing. The small eyes in his broad

face looked up briefly, passed over him, and then fell again to the tip of his crutch. He moved the crutch to another part of the slate, hopped a bit to follow it, his one shoe broad and worn, his breath laboring. Aunt Rose gripped his arm. Something of the mothball odor of his own clothes as Red Whelan brushed past him.

The two climbed the steps, Aunt Rose beside the old man, her arm across his back. Red Whelan paid no attention to the doorman either, but, head down, back bent, made his way into the black interior of the house, his medal—for it was indeed a medal on a grimy ribbon, although there was no telling (our father told us) if it was his—swaying against the worn fabric of his soldier's coat.

Neither of them, father or son—the handsome fruit of Red Whelan's sacrifice—of any interest at all to the old man, no worthy impediment at all to his determination to go inside and have his lunch.

At the door, Aunt Rose nodded to his father as he held back the screen and then went in with her charge. The corpulent friend went in as well. Patrick, too, climbed the stairs, thinking to follow them, but his father took a pinch of his sleeve and told him to wait. Together, father and son stood at the opened door until all the funeral guests had gone in, Michael greeting each, "Good day," "Fine weather." Some recognized him and offered condolences. Others leaned into their companions even as they crossed the threshold to ask who he was. When the last had gone in, and no more cars moved slowly down the street, Michael Tierney closed the screen door gently and returned his fine bowler to his head, giving its rim, as he liked to do, that extra, two-fingered skim.

"Let's go," he said.

They had only made it to the bottom of the steps when a female voice, thickly Irish, called after them. "You're not coming in?"

Father and son turned to see a dark-haired maid behind the screen, a bundle of women's coats in her arms. She wore a white cap with a black ribbon, and although the screen was a kind of veil, she was clearly a beauty, big-eyed, sweet-faced.

"We're not," Michael Tierney said.

Halfway down the slate path, father and son turned again to see her. She was still behind the screen. The father tucked his hand up beneath his son's arm, pulling him away. "Let's not have you marrying any Irish housemaids," he said wryly. "Let's not have history repeating itself."

The two had lunch together, looking so sharp, in the elegant restaurant of a local hotel. His father carried a flask from which he poured himself two whiskies before their steaks arrived, and then two more to have with his coffee.

On the train ride home his father said—under the influence, no doubt—"I wonder if it irked my father to see Red Whelan outlive him. I wonder if he thought, as he lay dying, that perhaps for three hundred dollars more Red Whelan would take his place again."

He told his son how Red Whelan had come back from the war, a knock at the door one evening while the family was at dinner. His own father but a young man then. How Red Whelan, a young man, too, was brought upstairs to the attic room he would have for the rest of his life. Aunt Rose, just a child, wordlessly taking on the responsibility that she bore even now, and would bear into the future, or at least until that day—not far away, it would seem—when Red Whelan's life finally came to a close. "Lord knows what she'll do with herself then," he said. "She'll be both an old maid and a kind of widow. No family but myself." And then added, "And you children."

As the train came into the city, Mr. Tierney said the last time he saw his father, the man had grabbed him up under the arm as they stood on the very same threshold he had not crossed this afternoon. Michael Tierney was leaving home for the last time. Elizabeth Breen, his Lizzie, was meeting him at the train. They would be married the next morning in Brooklyn, where her family lived. "Is this what Red Whelan threw away an arm and a leg for?" his father asked him. (Our father, telling us the story, added, "Thus coining a phrase.") "So the fruit of his sacrifice can drag us back to the slums?"

The man whispering his furious question, as if Red Whelan, two floors above and without half his hearing, might catch the words.

"You can be sure I didn't whisper my reply," Michael Tierney said as the train returned to the city. "I spoke it clearly, right into his face. I said, 'One life's already been given to save your skin. I won't give you mine as well.' Those were the last words we ever exchanged."

He turned to his son, his teeth bared beneath the polished mustache and his eyes briefly pained. But the pain quickly slipped away. He smiled. "It's all the past," he said, and reached out again to touch the boy's knee. He looked him over fondly, brushed the lapel of the new suit. "Still," he added—the whiskey had made him flushed—"I might have forgiven him. The old bastard."

Patrick said, "He might have forgiven you."

ONE MORE RECOLLECTION of that day:

Late that night, after he'd been some hours asleep, Patrick woke in the darkness. His brother Tom slept soundly in the next bed. No stirring in the room beside them where his four sisters sometimes laughed or fought or tapped the wall in the middle of the night. Street noise, sure, but faint at this hour, and nothing to tell him why he woke so fully and so abruptly, wide-eyed in the darkness. In the darkness, he recalled the wooden coffin, gleaming with sunlight, as it went down into the fresh-cut earth. He thought of Red Whelan's cold failure to acknowledge him, the shining, spiffy, living fruit of the old man's sacrifice. He recalled his mother laughing as she said, If he's going to haunt anyone, it will be Patrick.

He looked to the vague, pale blue—ghostly, yes—light at the one window. Was there a face in the glass? Was that a cat yowling in the back of the house, or a banshee? A lost soul? He imagined his own soul—a pale, startled version of himself—clutched in his bitter grandfather's bony hands like a thin blue rag. He imagined being dragged through the empty streets outside, lamplight and darkness, black wet pavement, fences and fire escapes and tumbled yards—slums, his grandfather had called them—up, up, up, into utter darkness.

Tom waking tomorrow to find only his brother's body in the bed, a hollow shell, empty-eyed, thin-skinned. Only dust. Is this what Red Whelan lost an arm and a leg for?

He felt the prickly heat of fear on his neck, in his spine, at the soles of his feet. He wished with everything in him that his father had never said whatever it was he'd said at their final parting, about one life for another. One life to save your skin.

He had worked himself, under his blankets, into a froth of dread when he heard his father's voice and his mother's in the dining room, and knew he was hearing again what had woken him so abruptly. His father was saying, "Too late, too late," and his mother replying, soothingly, "Nothing to be done, Michael. Nothing to be done." Patrick knew without seeing that his father had his hand around a glass. He heard—impossible, of course—the glass go to his father's lips, the soft swallow. And then his father's voice rose abruptly and Patrick recognized the phrase that, just moments ago, had pulled him out of a deep sleep. "I loved the man," his father said, moaning it. "I loved him."

There was another silence. His father was crying.

It all would have been too terrible, his own fear, his father's sorrow, the cats yowling in some distant yard, the face of the old man at his window, if his mother's voice hadn't, at last, broken the spell.

"You did," she said. He recognized her tone: the smooth voice richly amused: the end of the argument. "But love's a tonic, Michael, not a cure. He was a bastard still."

TWO WEEKS LATER a letter came from Aunt Rose. Beautifully composed—the lines written straight in black India ink and the handwriting, Spencerian script, so beautiful, their father called the girls to admire it before he read out what the letter had to say. Aunt Rose was very sorry that he had not come into the house after his father's funeral. She had not anticipated the depth of his anger. Righteous anger, she said, to be sure. My brother was an unhappy man, she said. Weighed down all his life by the burden of gratitude.

Gratitude, their father pointed out, glancing at their mother. "A monkey on his back."

Now, the letter said, Red Whelan was gone. She was composing this in his attic room, which was full of his absence. She had lived out her life at his side, she said, and she had done her duty gladly. She had no complaints to make. She had been his companion through the years and he hers. Now she was alone. One generation passes away, she wrote. And then she gave their

father instructions to contact a lawyer on Water Street. In reparation for their estrangement, she was giving him everything his
father had left her. She would move out of the house, take an
apartment in town. She would make do on what she and Red
Whelan had saved together over these many years. She asked
only that he write to her now and then. She said she would do
the same. She said she would pray for him and his family every
morning and every night for the rest of her days.

Liz Tierney said, "She's looking for someone to take care of
her when she grows feeble."

Wasn't she the soothsayer? our father said.

Four months later, the family moved again. This time to a
three-story house on Second Street. Their own home, purchased
with the inheritance. It was a row house, nothing pretty, but five
bedrooms—five. One for the two boys, one for the twins, one
for the two younger girls. A wide bedroom for the parents, and,
after all that spreading out, an empty bedroom left over, suitable
for a boarder or a guest.

Suitable for Sally when she came to the door, late in the afternoon of the day she returned from Chicago. Beside her was the
same rattan suitcase she had carried on the train, containing still
the four chemises, six pairs of stockings, three muslin nightgowns without embroidery or decoration—the immaculate clothes
that were to bring her to her new life.

Behind her stood Sister Lucy, who could insist.

True

WITH OLD AUNT ROSE ensconced in our attic, Sister Jeanne raised her eyes to the ceiling. Here's a story, she told us.

This happened in France, in the last century. Jeanne Jugan was a kind woman who worked in the homes of the wealthy. One day, she came across a blind widow who had been put out on the street by her family. Put out on the street to die. Jeanne Jugan took the old woman to her own home, bathed her and fed her. She tucked the old lady into her bed and moved a pallet to the attic just above her head, where Jeanne Jugan slept within earshot of the poor soul.

Not long after that, Jeanne Jugan came upon another old woman who had been abandoned on the street and she took that woman in, too. And then another. And another.

Life was very hard for the old in those days. For poor widows especially. Who needed them? The small and the weak and the old. They got in the way of rushing, robust life, see? They were a pain in the neck. Always frail and sick. So people asked themselves, Who needs them?

Word got out, and people around the town began to bring their old folks to Jeanne Jugan. But there are always as many good people as there are bad. Better believe it. Soon other women who were as kind as Jeanne heard about the work she was doing and asked if they could help her. Some of these good women moved into Jeanne's attic, too, so they would be available any time of the day or night. The community expanded. The number of old folks who were cared for grew and grew.

Jeanne Jugan went to the priest. She asked if the women could form a religious community of their own, to help guide their lives as they did this good and difficult work. They held a meeting in Jeanne's attic and there they drew up their plan to become the Little Sisters of the Poor.

Every day, Jeanne put her basket over her arm and went out to collect food and money for her people. She would never take no for an answer, see? One rich man got so angry at her persistence—Sister Jeanne waved a fist in the air, imitating him—he punched her right in the face. Knocked her down.

When she got up again, she said, "Yes, but my ladies are still hungry." Then he gave her all the money he had.

Whenever people said to Jeanne Jugan, "Oh good Lord, Sister, I gave you money yesterday," she said, "But my ladies are hungry again today."

Jeanne Jugan became famous. The President of France gave her a gold medal for her good work, and what do you think she did? She melted it down and used it to buy a bigger house for her ladies.

Sister Jeanne said, I heard this story from my spiritual advisor when I was a young nun: One day, Charles Dickens came to see Jeanne Jugan. Maybe he had read about her in the papers, I don't know. But what do you think she said to the guy?

We couldn't answer.

She said he should put his money where his mouth is. So he gave her a big donation.

And then he wrote somewhere or other that she was the holiest person he had ever met. Isn't that something?

We said it was something.

But all the while good Jeanne Jugan was busy doing her work, the priest who had advised her was off scheming. He went to Rome and told them *he* was the one who started the order. He said he was the one who found the first blind widow on the street and he was the one who told Jeanne Jugan to take care of her. He was the one who invited the other women to help out. And the priests in Rome fell for it. They made him the head of the order. And they put up a plaque on Jeanne Jugan's house that said HERE FATHER SO-AND-SO FOUNDED THE LITTLE SISTERS OF THE POOR.

And that wasn't the worst of it, Sister Jeanne said.

There was a very young nun in the order, and this priest liked her better than Jeanne Jugan. He put her in charge and told Jeanne she could no longer go around with her basket. She could just stay inside, do some housekeeping, train some novices. Jeanne said to the priest, "You have taken my work from me." And then she said, "But I gladly give it to you." And that's how she lived the rest of her life. Staying inside.

As the years went by, people forgot that Jeanne was the founder of the order.

But, listen, Sister Jeanne said, life is like the blink of an eye.

The young nun the lying priest had put in charge became an old woman herself, and as death approached, she knew she had to set the record straight. An investigation was made, and sure enough, the plaque on Jeanne's house was changed to say HERE JEANNE JUGAN FOUNDED THE LITTLE SISTERS OF THE POOR.

Sister Jeanne sat back in her chair, the light of the fading afternoon just behind her. We sat back, too, satisfied, as children will be, at any tale that is resolved with the restoration of order. Children who know, without instruction or study, what is fair.

But then we saw that old Sister Jeanne was laughing inside her bonnet. It's all silliness, she said. Don't you see?

Jeanne Jugan was already in heaven with Our Lord.

What in the world would she care about a plaque on an old building in the country of France? Whatever glory was taken from her here on earth had already been restored a hundred times, a million times, and more.

More happiness than any of us can imagine, Sister Jeanne said. More beauty than any of us on earth can bear.

I'll never see it, she said. But all of youse will.

The point to remember, Sister Jeanne said—*pernt*, she said—is that truth finds the light. Lies, big or small, never stay hidden. She pushed the air with the palm of her hand—a comic gesture that said *Go on with you*— So don't even bother telling lies, she said.

Truth reveals itself. It's really quite amazing.

God wants us to know the truth in all things, she said, big or small, because that's how we'll know Him.

In all her simplicity, old Sister Jeanne told us, "It's really that simple."

A Tonic

ON HER FIRST AFTERNOON at the sanatorium upstate, Sister Illuminata left the porch where the pa-
tients were lined up like bolts of linen and wandered
through the wings of the cottage. She wanted only
solitude. She had already endured the crowded crossing in steer-
age, the filth and the sickness. She had endured the constant
entreaties from every poor Catholic on board, and had brushed
from her veil and from the hem of her skirt the traces of spit that
had been directed at her from those who were not. She stood in
the knocking crowds on Ellis Island, elbow to elbow. And although her habit earned her only a cursory stethoscope to her
lungs—through her bib, no less—from a harried and blushing
doctor, she'd had barely a night alone in her convent room when

Dr. Hannigan, less afraid and more thorough than the government doctor had been, sent her to the sanatorium.

When a nurse there—a Sister of Mercy herself—tried to stop her from going off alone, Sister Illuminata said, lying, that it was a stipulation of her own order that she say her afternoon Office on her feet. She wouldn't be long.

So it was that she found herself drawn by the luxury of silence to a section of the cottage that was not currently in use— the back of the house, where a winter sunroom she had seen from the drive had now, in midsummer, been given over to storage. Her beads in her hand, she turned from the darkened hallway into the bright space. The air here was hazy, full of dust motes and vague sunbeams, stiflingly hot. There were bed frames and wicker chaises piled haphazardly. A green-and-white linoleum floor that was glazed with sunlight. The dull silence was exactly what she had sought. But then a human sound disturbed it: a long sigh that rippled across the stifling air like breath on water.

In an instant, her eyes found them: a man and a woman, half kneeling, half crouching. They were pressed together in a corner of the hot room, pressed up against each other, behind an iron bedstead that seemed to enclose them. Both had slipped their white robes from their shoulders. Both moved with the same slow, stuttering rhythm. Sister could see the woman's bare throat, corded and straining, the white flesh of her breasts and the brown of her nipples. She could see the man's shoulder blades, the short bones of his spine as they pressed themselves against the paper-thin skin. He rose up over her, she arched herself toward him. He was an old man, white hair on the back of his head, across his shoulders, and all along his skeletal arms.

Briefly, Sister thought there was something angelic about their pale struggle, the winged shoulder blades, the tangled bodies, the soft folds of their white robes, and the dusty, streaming sunlight. But then she saw how their mouths were wide open, black and straining. Opened helplessly as if in sudden reflex—as if to expel the short, ragged breaths they were taking. Precious breaths in this place.

Sister Illuminata saw them for only a moment before she turned away. There is a hunger, she thought.

The woman was a young mother from a wealthy family—Sister Illuminata's own age. She died within the month. The old man was a doctor from Syracuse, New York, who went home with his family the same week Sister Illuminata returned to the convent—both of them, he said, with lungs forever scarred by their ordeal.

There is a hunger. It was a lesson she had learned and then forgotten across the years she had labored in the convent laundry. But she remembered it again when Sally returned from Chicago and Sister Lucy explained to a small coterie of the nuns: Illuminata and Jeanne, Sister Eugenia and old Sister Miriam, what the girl had discovered.

They were in what the Sisters humbly called the refectory; it was, in fact, the rich man's former drawing room. It was elegant still, high-ceilinged, paneled, with the same thick silk draperies he had paid for. It was where the Sisters took their simple meals, but it was also the site for card parties and ladies' teas, Christmas gatherings for the neighborhood poor, visits from the Bishop. A room the nuns used to impress both the indigent and the hoi polloi.

The small bulbs in the chandelier above the polished table where the nuns now sat reflected prettily in the dark wood, like starlight on a pond. As Sister Lucy spoke about the arrangements she had made to remove Sally from the scene of her mother's "indiscretion," Sister Illuminata recalled that she had seen such a pond, such dancing starlight, at the sanatorium upstate. She recalled the pond, the bracing cold night, the tall black pines in the distant darkness, and the flavor of pine on the air. She became aware once more of the ache in her scarred lungs. She recalled the old doctor.

She remembered the lesson she had learned on her first afternoon at the sanatorium, had learned but forgotten: There is a hunger.

Now Lucy was speaking of the property that was to be left to the Sisters, an estate out on Long Island. A rambling house the order would convert to an old folks' home, the acreage that might accommodate a hospital someday. This was a realm of convent business Sister Illuminata had little to do with—upstairs business was how she referred to it—the stuff, as she saw it, of ambition and vanity as much as it was a part of the Sisters' mission to serve the sick poor. There was goodness in it, of course, and the generosity of the Catholic family who had left the Sisters the land. Sister Lucy said the property would not come to them free and clear. But the motherhouse in Chicago would work with the diocese here. The Bishop approved. Some of the good ladies of the Auxiliary had volunteered their husbands, Wall Street men, bankers, men of the world.

There was goodness in it all, of course, but there was greed, too. Sister Illuminata heard it in Lucy's eager voice: acreage and a house and banks and mortgages, the Bishop, the Cardinal.

More good, Sister Lucy said, than any one Sister could do on her own, going door to door.

It was the kind of worldly ambition, Sister Illuminata thought, that well suited Sister Lucy's mannish face. And then prayed to be forgiven for the unkindness.

This was no time, Sister Lucy was saying, to disturb the ladies in the Auxiliary, or to stir gossip in the neighborhood, by throwing out onto the street a widow known these nearly twenty years as the laundress in the convent.

Sister Illuminata raised her eyes from the electric starlight reflected in the dining table's shine. She felt that old ache in her lungs. And in her swollen knees. She knew the time would come, soon perhaps, when the trip down to the laundry, the trip back up again, would be impossible for her. She was well aware that even now, without Annie's help, she could not manage half the tasks, most of the tasks, the convent needed her to do. If Annie was to be dismissed, no doubt another, younger nun would be assigned to take her place, or perhaps another needy widow from the neighborhood. The long hours Sister Illuminata spent in her chair beside the ironing board, sometimes—with Annie's good indulgence—just dozing, would be exposed. Sister Illuminata, all other usefulness gone, would be brought every morning to an office lobby or a drafty subway entrance or to the vestibule of some busy store, a woven alms basket to hold on her lap. The cane she now used an extra added attraction.

Sister Lucy was saying, "If Sister Illuminata will have her."

They all directed their eyes toward Sister Illuminata.

Caught by surprise, she only nodded gravely.

"I suggest we keep her here, then," Sister Lucy said. "Whether she amends her life or no."

And then they called Annie into the room. She stood with

her hands folded before her, her back straight. "No" was the answer.

ONCE MORE, the cathedral light, the light of painted holy cards, streamed from the high windows to touch the girl's shoulders and her bowed head. Sally was crouched on the floor beside the nun, leaned into her lap. The Ninth Hour prayers had just ended. Sally visited now only when her mother was out—at the shops, they continued to say, as if the truth of what her mother was up to on these afternoons could not assail the custom of their belief, their determined innocence.

There is a hunger, Sister Illuminata told the girl.

"A hunger to be comforted" was how our mother recalled it.

But the nun's language in these matters—matters of the body, of the flesh, what went on between women and men—was limited. Her experience limited as well.

She put her hand on the girl's head. Leaned as close to her familiar, sweet-scented hair as the starched bonnet would allow. "We can pray for your mother's soul," she said. "We can offer up our work, the way we do for the souls in purgatory." She paused. Felt the old assurance of words she understood. "Maybe there are some extra works of mercy you could do. Something you can offer up to God in the name of your mother."

"I don't like nursing, Sister," Sally said. Stubborn. "I'm no good at it."

"It doesn't have to be nursing," Sister Illuminata said. "It doesn't have to be religious life." Sally was leaning against her lap, looking up at her warily. Sister could feel the quick impatience in the girl's young bones. A coiled energy that had been there since her childhood, that Sister only now was willing to acknowledge was proof of Lucy's assessment that marriage might settle her.

"You could simply do some good in your mother's name," she said. "Until your mother's ready to do something for herself."

Sally narrowed her eyes, as if to see Sister's point. Her plain lovely face was not as childish as it once had been. Today she wore some face powder that obscured her fading freckles. Some rosy color on her chapped lips as well. Mr. Tierney had found her a small job in the tearoom at the hotel, three afternoons a week. Sister Illuminata took the makeup to mean the end of the girl's vocation.

"A kind of penance," Sister said. "A way to gain some indulgence for her. For her soul."

Above them, the sound of the Sisters' footsteps as they were leaving the chapel. Only a few of the nuns had returned to the convent today, most had stayed out on casework, need being what it was in the neighborhood.

"Maybe we can find some poor creature you can help. Maybe an old woman who would love your companionship. Maybe a young mother nearby who needs help with her children. We can ask the Sisters. We can find you some good you could do. For your mother's sake. You can offer it up. For the salvation of her soul."

Sister Illuminata heard Sister Jeanne's light step on the basement stairs. Sally placed her cheek on the nun's wide lap. "She won't," she said. And Sister heard Annie's own determination in the girl's voice. "She won't change. She calls him 'dear.'"

"We'll find some good work for you to do," Sister Illuminata said once more, raising her voice, hoping that Sister Jeanne would hear her, even as she understood the vanity of this, this long, silly competition for the girl's affection. "Prayer and good work together will surely move Our Lord to grant you what you ask for."

Sally raised her head again. Sister Illuminata was surprised to see there were no tears—only, in her searching brown eyes, what would have been, when she was young, the prelude to mischief. "Mrs. Costello," Sally whispered. She said, "Sister Lucy thinks she's a faker, but I don't. I could go sit with her when she's all alone. She hates being alone." She raised her pale brows, her eyes full of childish mischief. "I could sit with Mrs. Costello while her husband's away," Sally said. "What would my mother think of that?"

Sister Illuminata was about to object—the notion both confused and dismayed her—when she looked up and saw Sister Jeanne leaning over the banister. In the bright afternoon sunlight Sister Jeanne was mostly silhouette, her hand to her heart.

Sister Illuminata placed her arm around Sally's shoulders. She touched the girl's soft hair. It was sinful, the way she competed with Jeanne—a sin she could never confess or define. Her need to be the girl's favorite, to be loved beyond all the other nuns in the convent by this confused and mortal child, was inexplicable, even to herself. A hunger.

"That's a fine idea," Sister Illuminata said.

Mercy

THE LAUNDRY at the St. Francis Hotel was a far cry from the dark and efficient realm of the convent basement, but Sally felt herself drawn to it nevertheless. She passed it by in the afternoon when she arrived at the hotel and made her way toward it at the end of the day, just to smell the steam and to observe the noisy industry of the workers—mostly Chinese men who only glanced up at her when she wandered past, glanced up quickly and then looked away.

She had a mean and accurate version of the way they argued, which she had already performed for Sister Illuminata. The nun had not been amused. "Stay away from those men," Sister had told her. "They'd as soon put a knife in you."

The job Mr. Tierney had found for her was in the tearoom, helping to serve three days a week, from two in the afternoon to six in the evening. It was the best he could get for her for now. She wore a smart gray dress and a white apron, a cap and a hair-net and solid black shoes, and the outfit, given to her in the basement locker room where the workers gathered and dressed, immediately told her everything she needed to know about how to behave upstairs. She was a quick study, the supervisor said. A lovely girl.

Mornings, she waited on the steps of Mrs. Costello's apartment house.

When the Sister arrived, Sally followed her up the stairs, then made herself useful in the neat and barren household, and then lingered after the Sister's work was done, keeping Mrs. Costello company through those lonely hours of the late morning and early afternoon, the hours that filled her with such fear.

Hours during which Mrs. Costello chatted aimlessly, sometimes scolded her, sometimes drifted to sleep in her chair by the window.

On those days, while Mrs. Costello dozed in the silence that followed the Sister's busy presence, the small apartment filled with an awful light—the color of bile. Wherever Sally's eyes fell, there was something to make her shudder. Mr. Costello's hairbrush on his dresser, threaded with his dull black hair. A poorly tatted bureau scarf Mrs. Costello had made at the Sisters' urging: work for idle hands. The wedding picture. A dark sock turned in on itself, forgotten beneath the nightstand—was its partner beneath her mother's bed? The man's underpants and long johns—she opened drawers while Mrs. Costello slept—and handkerchiefs tucked into neat rows, a worn missal placed among them. The dresser itself was stained a dark, nearly black, mahogany, but the interior of each drawer was pale, startlingly pale—like something you should turn your eyes from—and redolent of fresh-cut wood. Her nightgowns and stockings and underclothes carefully folded. A marriage license in a brown envelope. Twenty years they had been married. Mrs. Costello's baptismal certificate from St. Charles. She was forty-two years old. A cemetery deed for Holy Cross Cemetery in Brooklyn. A paper, many times folded, and with a gold seal like something from a classroom, that said Mr. Costello was a citizen of the United States.

The man's trousers and shirts were in the small closet. Mrs. Costello's few dresses hung beside them. Her two felt hats on the shelf above, side by side with his straw boater and a fedora—further proof, if any was needed, that these two were husband and wife.

Mr. Costello's white milkman's jacket, once, on a hook behind the bedroom door—it was slumped at the shoulders, collar raised, as if the man himself had turned from her, his head hung in shame.

What Sally knew of the physical relations between men and women in those days was vague enough, only words—hastily spoken—when her mother told her "what she needed to know." Only the words some girls at school, and the rough boys who shouted in the street, had added to that mix. Penis. Backside. Tush. Bowels. Down below. The writhing pinky of the woman on the train.

When she was young, she had caught, now and then, and only for the short time it took her mother to hurry her past, a man—drunk, her mother always said—holding himself and splashing his water in the street. She had glimpsed last summer as she followed Sister Lucy more bare flesh than she had ever seen before—backsides and limbs and breasts and chests, baby boys with pink tulip bulbs between their legs, old ladies plucked hairless, their privates as puckered as their toothless mouths.

She gathered that an odd magnetism drew human eyes to even the palest, the foulest, the saddest of uncovered skin. Sister Lucy, giving a sponge bath to an old man, running a soapy cloth over a wretched turkey neck pillowed on two bloated sacks the color of a bruise, shouted, "Turn away," when she saw Sally gaping. "This is not a sight for you."

But what she could not understand was how that strange magnetism accounted for what went on between her mother and Mr. Costello in the bedroom that used to be her own. How it—"a hunger," Sister Illuminata said—was enough to allow her mother to choose this milkman, to call him "dear," to live in what the Sisters, who even now were mostly tight-lipped about the situation, knew was mortal sin.

Her mother lived in mortal sin, skimmed the precipice of perdition with every step she took, every breath. Down the stairs she went in the morning, alone now, out into the teeming street, trolleys and trucks, cars veering, mad strangers jostling her at every corner, and no daughter beside her to serve as extra eyes. This was how her dangerous days now ran. Over to the convent, down another set of stairs. Furnace moaning. Mangle rattling. And what if fire or flood should trap her there? Boiled water scald her? What if the poison on Sister Illuminata's shelves should find its way into her tea? Or pneumonia, tuberculosis, flu, transfer itself to her lungs from the putrid wash water of a dying woman's linen? And the days growing darker now. And the way home sometimes slick with rain. The stolen afternoon with Mr. Costello, ham and eggs and the tumbled bed in the cold and waning light, black sin upon black sin. And then the long night with no one else in the apartment—did her mother check that the oven was turned off, as they always used to do when Sally was young, because of Jim? Was she careful stepping down from the chair when she reached up to the transom above the door? Would anyone hear her if she cried out in the night, clutching her heart?

The devil waited at her mother's heels, his pointed fingertips rimmed with grime, waited to catch her as she moved through her dangerous days, a fruit ripe for the plucking (she had heard the expression in a sermon once). Her mother was in a state of mortal sin, and if she were to die now, nothing would keep her from falling forever into the devil's arms.

And what then of Jim, Sally thought—as if devising an argument no one had asked her to deliver—Jim, who waited for her in heaven?

Nothing to keep her mother from perdition except, perhaps—perhaps—the indulgence earned for her by her good daughter, swallowing her panic and her pride, her desire to be anywhere else (an urge that made her nerves coil and twitch), in order to remain with Mrs. Costello in her lonely late-morning hours, listening to her nonsense, absorbing her scorn, watching these spare and empty rooms—the heart of her own troubles—fill up with mid-morning light that was the color of urine, the color of bile.

The situation was clear: her mother would not change her ways. Mr. Costello was her "dear," and even the Sisters seemed helpless before her blithe determination to keep him. Someone had to do penance for her, for the sin she would not give up. Who else but the daughter who loved her above everything?

THE NUN WHO WAS HERE THIS MORNING, Sister Aquina, had left Mrs. Costello in her chair, wrapped tightly in Mr. Costello's woolen dressing gown. She'd told Sally to be sure she didn't throw it off. Mrs. Costello was chilled and running a fever, Sister Aquina had said. Sally watched the nun stir cream of tartar into Mrs. Costello's morning tea—to help with the constipation, Sister Aquina explained. And then the nun placed a flannel soaked in linseed oil on the woman's chest. Before she left the apartment, Sister ground two aspirins with a mortar and pestle and instructed Sally to mix them into some of the applesauce she'd brought from the convent so that Mrs. Costello in her weakened state would not have to struggle to swallow them whole. "Just the smooth part of the applesauce, please," Sister Aquina said. "Not the chunks and peels."

Sister Aquina was a short, fat tomboy of a nun, with the broad face and the matter-of-fact authority of a cop on the street. Her small black eyes were slightly crossed. She was new to the convent, and so she assumed that Sally came to Mrs. Costello's apartment every morning to learn something about nursing.

"What we want to avoid in these cases is aspiration," she said. She was spooning applesauce into a teacup, and then fishing out myopic Mrs. Odette's famous bits of peel. "And I don't mean aspiring to find yourself a good-looking husband," she added. She laughed at her joke, knowing nothing of Sally's situation. Seeing only her willingness to serve. "We want to be careful that our patient doesn't get food in her windpipe, doesn't choke and breathe it in. Aspirate." Sister Aquina traced a line down her bib, to her dark tunic, indicating her own lungs by drawing a circle under her shapeless breast. "That's how infection can set in. Lung infection. Pneumonia. We don't want that."

Sister Aquina did not stay long. It was late January. All the Sisters were busy in this frozen season. With her cloak on, she put a hand to Sally's arm, moved her head as if to catch the girl fully with her disparate eyes. "Aren't you good?" she said, standing at the apartment door. "To be here like this."

And Sally bowed her head in the old way—the way she might have accepted the praise last year, before her trip to Chicago—as if Sister Aquina's ignorance of the situation, of the penance Sally was doing and the circumstance that required it, had restored her innocence. As if Sister Aquina's ignorance made Sally's goodness, her work of mercy, uncomplicated once more.

While Mrs. Costello napped in her chair, her breaths uneven, tangled with phlegm, Sally made another circuit of the cramped bedroom. The air in the room was a dirty yellow, the ceiling marred by mustard-colored water stains, the seams of the faded wallpaper grown pale brown. Behind the drawn lace curtains, the shades were the brittle color of old paper. The constant hiss and rattle of the radiator was like the gurgle of muddy street water going down a rusted drain.

Sally walked quietly around the bed, which Sister Aquina had left neatly made, around the narrow hope chest at its foot. Casually, she paused to open the chest a few inches—a breath of cedar, the glimpse of folded linen—and then closed it again when she heard Mrs. Costello stir.

She walked to the dresser. The two china-faced dolls were slumped together. They wore similar dresses, long-sleeved and full-skirted, yellowed lace at the neck and sleeve and a vague stripe woven into the faded fabric, one blue, one purple. The doll in the purple dress had an eye pushed back into its skull. The faces of both were shattered with small cracks. Sally picked up the purple one and was surprised to find that its limbs were heavy with sawdust or sand.

Something of Mrs. Costello herself in the doll's limp weight.

It occurred to Sally, just out of her own girlhood, that with only the slightest act of imagination she could bring the doll to life—poor thing, sweetly smiling, lonely here with her sister on the shelf. But some distaste, for the age of the doll, for the rolled-back eye, made her resist her own girlish impulse to animate the thing, to offer it her sympathy.

"Put that down," Mrs. Costello said. Her voice, weakly petulant, was full of congestion. "That's not yours."

Sally returned the doll to the dresser. "It must have been yours," she said, approaching Mrs. Costello in her chair, "when you were a little girl."

Mrs. Costello began to struggle out of her dressing gown, pulling at the lapels, reaching for the flannel on her chest. "I'm hot," she said. "Take this off me."

Sally moved to stay her hand. Over these many weeks of sitting with Mrs. Costello, the nuns had taught her that the woman was as easily distracted as a child. "They're such pretty dolls," Sally said, moving Mrs. Costello's hand away from the dressing gown. She was aware of the thin wedding band, the bird bones of her pale fingers and arms, her flat, narrow chest under the thick gown and the heavily oiled cloth.

Mrs. Costello looked up at Sally. The tiny veins that fed her pale eyelids were vivid. "Those were my mother's dolls," she said softly. "She gave them to me."

"Is your mother alive?" Sally asked, and heard herself imitating the voice of the dirty woman on the train. Imitating her pretend refinement. Butter wouldn't melt in her mouth. She blushed at her own phony pleasantries.

Mrs. Costello shook her head. "Rheumatic fever," she said. "I had it, too, but my mother died of it. I was only thirteen."

"I'm sorry," Sally said.

"After," Mrs. Costello went on, whining, complaining, "I couldn't go to school again. Couldn't sit still. Always walking. Saint Vitus Dance. My father grew so weary of it all, he tied me to a chair." She whimpered a little. "What else was the poor man to do?"

"And you never went back to school?" Sally asked.

"I couldn't sit still," Mrs. Costello said impatiently, aware that she was repeating herself, that Sally had been inattentive. "Even the nuns couldn't get me to sit still. I'd walk and walk until the neighbors banged on the ceiling." And then she pulled at the lapels of her dressing gown once again, and Sally once again stayed her hand.

"What's the use?" Mrs. Costello said, her attention fading from the struggle. Her eyes went vacantly to the window. She shifted in her seat.

"I have a pain," she said softly, her eyes without focus. "I'm in pain."

Sally said, as any one of the Sisters would have said, "I know." It was a familiar call and response. Nothing else to be done, the Sisters had told her. Nothing to be done for an imaginary pain, for a woman touched in the brain; a woman determined to take to her bed. "But you got better," Sally said, aiming to distract her. "You got over the Saint Vitus Dance. You got married."

Mrs. Costello seemed to consider this. Then she nodded, as if it took some effort to recall. "I did. I got better. I married the milkman. He came to the door and my father said, 'You're welcome to her.'"

Mrs. Costello nearly smiled. Sister Aquina had parted the woman's hair neatly this morning, had fixed two tight braids that fell over the shoulders of the brown robe. The braids made her look like a young girl—there was some trace of a delicate beauty. "We were married on December 8," she said, and coughed. "In the Church of St. Peter and St. Paul," and then coughed with more vigor, making her chair shake. Sally put her hand on one of the wheels to keep the chair from rolling. "It was a very cold day," Mrs. Costello said, coughing through the words. "I was very happy."

When the fit had passed, Mrs. Costello went limp, as if her arms and legs were weighted with sand. She dropped her chin, let her hands fall to her sides, and cast her eyes out over her thin lap in a wide and empty stare.

Sally had seen some of the more impatient nuns slap Mrs. Costello's hand when this happened. Some would shake her shoulder and call out her name.

"None of your nonsense, now," Sister Lucy would cry.

And always Mrs. Costello would quickly revive. Proof, perhaps, that the fit was a sham.

But today Sally waited in silence, a little afraid, but also curious about how long this vacancy would last. A few minutes, it turned out, although they were long, silent minutes, filled only with the sound of the hissing radiator and the traffic in the street, the faint trill of pigeons at the window. Mrs. Costello slowly raised her head again and her eyes regained their focus.

"I am abandoned and alone," she said.

There was mucus bubbling in her nose.

"Let me get you a handkerchief," Sally said softly.

She went to the dresser and took out one of Mr. Costello's fresh handkerchiefs, ironed by Sister Illuminata. She held it to the woman's nose, held the back of Mrs. Costello's head as her own mother used to do when she said, "Blow." Mrs. Costello sputtered into the cloth, childish herself in the way she took Sally's wrist in both hands as she did so. The handkerchief filled with a wet warmth. Sally wiped the woman's nose and folded the cloth over. Mr. Costello's initials were embroidered in one corner. Her mother's neat stitches.

It occurred to Sally that she and Mrs. Costello both were left out—left alone and abandoned—by the alliance Mr. Costello and her mother had made.

Impulsively, she bent and put her lips to Mrs. Costello's neat part. The woman's unwashed scalp was hot, the unnatural heat of a fever. The smell of linseed rose from under her clothes.

For a moment, Mrs. Costello sat still and uncomplaining under the caress.

As Sally straightened up again, she saw a pigeon's shadow pass across the shade, behind the lace. She thought of her own sacrifice, her work of mercy flying to heaven to repair her mother's sin.

And then Mrs. Costello's belly rumbled and she gave up some gas.

"Take me to the toilet," she cried. "Hurry up."

Moving quickly, Sally backed the wheelchair away from the window and maneuvered it to the wooden commode, even as Mrs. Costello told her again to hurry, struggling to stand on her one good foot, disrupting the journey rather than aiding it. Once they were beside the bowl, Sally took the woman's elbow, helped her up, then stooped to grab the hem of the dressing gown. As she leaned down, her ear at the woman's waist, Mrs. Costello struck her back, saying, "Hurry, you, hurry." Sally gathered up the heavy dressing gown and the flannel nightdress, raising both above the woman's knees. The crossed scars at the base of Mrs. Costello's amputated leg, the gross marks of the stitches, shone like silver. The flesh was puckered at the center, turned in like a balled sock. The bulk of the dressing gown was difficult to handle. It slipped once or twice as Sally tried to gather it up, and then the nightdress slipped down as well. Leaning into Mrs. Costello's reeking chest, wrapping her arms around her thin frame, Sally managed to gather the skirts of both the dressing gown and the nightgown at the woman's back, above her pale backside. She maneuvered the woman on her one, hopping leg. Mrs. Costello sat with a small crash and voided—Sally turned her face away from the smell and the sputter of it, still holding Mrs. Costello's gathered nightclothes just behind her.

Mrs. Costello sat, slump-shouldered. "Sorry," she said. And then grunted softly, pushing out another splash of urine and foul air.

Sally wiped Mrs. Costello's pale bottom quickly, holding her breath, nearly bursting into tears herself when the rough paper broke and the wet feces streaked her fingers. She swatted at the mess on her hand with more paper, and then, not gently, stood the woman up, brushed down her skirts, and again guided her back into the chair, holding her breath all the while. She returned the chair to its place before the window.

She wanted only to flee. To plunge her fingers into a bowl of bleach.

"I'll just go clean myself up," Sally said. "Then I'll bring you some broth."

Mrs. Costello was reaching into her nightgown, pulling at the cloth Sister Aquina had made.

"Empty the commode first," she said. Her chin was raised—it made her seem haughty. She was pulling up the sodden cloth, hand over hand. When she had freed it from her dressing gown, she put the limp flannel to her nose and then disdainfully dropped it on the floor beside her chair. Sister Aquina's kind attention.

Then Mrs. Costello pulled the lapels of the dressing gown

back up around her neck and said regally, "Don't leave that mess in here."

THE DOG—in this telling there was only one of them—got hold of her skirt, and when she tried to pull it from his jaw, he nipped her hand. She gave him a good kick and was turning to get away when he caught her foot. She cried out and struck him on the head and—snap snap, she said—he had hold of her ankle, her calf. She cried out again, falling into a pole, scraping her face, her poor cheek, she said, against the rough wood, but holding on to it for dear life as the dog tried to pull her down. She heard the women in the street come running. Shouting from the apartments above. A man in shirtsleeves and suspenders picked up a plank—the yard was a mess of junk—and threw it at the dog. Lifted her. All these years later she remembered his strong arms.

In her wheelchair by the window, Mrs. Costello began to cry again.

He carried her home, this man, jostling her raw cheek against his suspenders. Her stockings were soaked with blood. Her shoe was gone. A rush of women with towels and aprons followed them, they surrounded her in her own place. Linen tea towels and aprons of cambric and rough calico, a box of sterile cotton from somewhere. They tore off her stocking. The flesh was swollen and oozing, blood everywhere. The cotton sticking to her wounds. Someone fetched a basin. Someone poured peroxide from a bottle, and she howled. The marks foamed and flamed.

"That's old news," Sally said softly. "Let's talk of something pleasant for a change." The bowl of broth, grown cold, was on her lap.

Mrs. Costello shook her head. The leg throbbed, she said.

Throbbed and throbbed. When her husband came home, he fell on his knees beside the couch where she lay. There were still a number of women in the room. They told him to leave it be, the bandaged leg. They swatted him away with their towels and aprons. The leg throbbed and throbbed and swelled up against the bandages made of torn rags. Swelled up like baking bread. Green pus oozed. The bandages darkened. Her toes grew black. The women flew about the room.

Early one morning, her husband lifted her, carried her downstairs. The milk cart was in front of the door. He put her on the seat. A stream of neighbors following, drawn by her cries of pain and humiliation.

When her husband brought her home again, he wheeled her through the streets in this very chair.

Sally knew Mrs. Costello's moods. Sometimes the tale of her catastrophe caused her to flatten her lips against her teeth in bitter anger. Sometimes, as now, retelling the tale merely made her weep. Sometimes it was the neighborhood women she condemned. Sometimes it was her husband's fault for standing back when they admonished him. Sometimes she shook her head in sympathy and called him a good, unfortunate man—it was the doctors who cut off her leg without so much as a by-your-leave who were to blame. Sometimes there was only her seething humiliation that he had taken her to the hospital in a milk cart.

On this afternoon, Sally recalled Sister Lucy saying that if that dog had been drowned as a pup, still Mrs. Costello would have found an excuse. She had married without knowing the duties of married life. Duties, Sally knew, her own mother understood. Perhaps relished.

And there was some confused pride in this for the girl—another indication of her mother's power, her endless expertise.

205

"Whose yard was it, where you found the dog?" she asked. The boredom and lethargy of these long hours was in her voice. She planned to repeat Sister Lucy's taut reply: You should have minded your own business.

Mrs. Costello waved her hands. Sally saw that she had not resettled the woman's clothes as neatly as the nuns would have done. Her dressing gown was twisted about her thighs. "I don't know whose yard it was," she said impatiently. "Some woman was looking for a man—a man who had beaten a child, tied a child to a pole and whipped him good. She and some others were on the street when I came along. We all went looking into the yards. But only I got bit."

"Too bad," Sally said. "But you're better now."

Mrs. Costello looked at her. That small, finely shattered face. "Better?" Mrs. Costello asked. "How?"

Her nose was running. Sally put the bowl of broth on the dresser and stood to collect another handkerchief from Mr. Costello's drawer. "How am I better?" Mrs. Costello called after her. "Sitting here all alone day after day."

"I'm here," Sally said, returning. "You're not alone." She put the handkerchief to the woman's nose.

"Abandoned and alone," Mrs. Costello said beneath it. And then, whining, "I have a pain."

Sally folded the handkerchief, wiped at her face again. She had a sudden impulse to stuff it into the woman's mouth.

"I know you do," she said dully. "I know."

Mrs. Costello's troubles were endless. The care of her was endless.

Sally took the bowl of broth from the dresser. The two balled handkerchiefs, full of snot, the yellow towel soaked in linseed, were still on the floor around her. There was straightening up to do. There were still hours to go before she could leave for her shift in the tearoom.

Mrs. Costello squirmed in her chair, broke wind, coughed delicately.

She seemed on the verge of tears again, but then her gaze turned to the window, to the bright cold light of the late morning, and she sank once more into that wide and vacant stare. Sally listened to the traffic in the street. Heard a brush of wind against the building. Her legs and arms ached with the impulse, electric, insistent, to flee. Her own Saint Vitus Dance. "I'm going to leave now," she said.

She went quickly to the kitchen. In the sink, a cockroach darted into the drain, and she poured what remained of the broth after it. In her own household, her mother's household, lost to her now, no food was ever left out in the open, uncovered, but still Sally left the pot with the nuns' soup on the stove. Why shouldn't Mr. Costello clean it up when he came home, his stomach filled with her mother's ham and eggs and toast and tea? Why shouldn't he care for his own wife?

She left the unwashed bowl in the sink. Took her coat from the chair in the living room and slipped it on. Put on her hat and her gloves, and saw as she did how her hands were shaking.

Mrs. Costello called from the bedroom, "Are you there?" Sally could hear the mucus in her voice. The woman coughed and then asked again, beginning to cry, "Is anyone there?" She let out a single moan—childish, despairing, startling in its sudden volume—and then said, angrily, all to herself, "Damn them to hell."

Sally slipped out the door. "I'll be back tomorrow, Mrs. Costello," she called weakly, understanding the woman couldn't hear her at all.

Gaining the cold street, Sally felt the weight of her desertion. She had failed in her fine intentions once again. It was like a thumb pressed into her chest, a smudged shadow on her soul. She breathed deeply, as if to dislodge the discomfort. The winter sun, bouncing off windshields and tenement windows and pale brick, made her squint. But it was delightful, nonetheless, to walk unencumbered in the cold air. To be out of that stifling room.

And then she remembered the aspirin Sister Aquina had left, for the woman's fever. To be stirred into Mrs. Odette's applesauce, the smooth part of it, anyway. She thought of the heat that had risen from Mrs. Costello's scalp. It was an unnatural heat, the sickroom heat of a fever. She imagined how it might continue to burn as Mrs. Costello sat in her chair, crying out uselessly, her temperature rising and rising, sweat running down her small face, mixing with the mucus that covered her lips. She imagined the sound of her voice tangled with phlegm.

And Sister Aquina returning to the apartment, or perhaps Mr. Costello himself, to find cockroaches in a black line across white enamel of the stovetop. Mrs. Costello lifeless in her chair, her face scorched.

Sally reached the hotel two hours early for her shift. She used the service entrance and took the stairs down to the locker room, but then went the long way around, through the basement labyrinth. She could feel the change in the air—scent of bleach, a touch of steam—as she approached the wide doors of the laundry. The humid air throbbed with the banging of the machines. After the cold outside, the sudden heat made her fingers burn inside her gloves. She pulled them off. The big steel doors of the laundry were open, thrown back against the tile walls. She walked past. Inside, the men in their white clothes were busy with their work, pushing baskets, loading sheets into the big machines. They all seemed the same size and shape. Some wore white brimless caps. Two or three had long black braids down their backs. There were four large steam presses on the far side of the room, the size of gray coffins. They belched steam in a way that made the workers surrounding them seem, briefly, to disappear. There were two ironing tables, with men—she still thought this a comical sight—wielding large electric irons whose cords ran upward, to the ceiling.

She stepped inside. Ordinarily, she would just walk past, glance in, breathe the familiar air, gather the details to bring back to the convent—how many sheets did they wash in a day, how many towels and tablecloths, Sister Illuminata loved to speculate—but today she stepped over the threshold. One of the Chinese men looked up immediately, shouted something over the din, and waved her away. She grinned back at him, but stayed where she was. He shrugged and returned to his work. She wondered if Sister was right. Would they put a knife in her if they could? What would her mother say then?

To her left there was a shelf, taller and longer than Sister Illuminata's but as well stocked as hers was with boxes of detergent and bottles of bleach, tubs of Borax and bluing and salt and lime. A tiny skull and crossbones on a bottle of ammonia. Sister Illuminata had called it the devil's mark when Sally was a child. A way to scare her into keeping her hands off.

Sister's Illuminata's sainted mother, Sally knew, had once saved the life of a little boy, the child of another laundress. The boy had swallowed a fistful of alum, and his silly mother, in her panic, had poured water down his throat. The boy would have choked to death or drowned right there on dry land, Sister Illuminata said, if her own dear mother hadn't pushed the woman away and then reached her pinky into the boy's mouth, unstopping him.

That boy grew up to be a priest, Sister Illuminata always said at the end of this tale, well satisfied.

Impulsively, Sally reached up and touched the devil's mark. Again, one of the Chinese men shouted at her, waved her away with a towel as if she were a duck to be chased. She pulled back her hand and noticed as she did a bit of brown grime beneath her fingernails. She could smell Mrs. Costello's stink, even here, where the air was filled with soap and bleach.

She lifted the bottle of ammonia from the shelf and turned quickly, out the door, down the narrow hallway. She went around a corner, through the door of the ladies' room the employees shared. She put the stopper into one of the sinks and filled it with water as hot as it would run. She poured the ammonia into it—the scent rising, stinging her sinuses. Another tearoom girl, a broad, motherly sort, was at the other end of the washroom. She wrinkled her nose as she approached the sink where Sally stood. She asked, "What's going on?" with a slow, bovine curiosity, and then watched open-mouthed as Sally plunged her hands into the water.

It wasn't hot enough to scald, but the ammonia burned her bitten cuticles and she gasped a little. The smell of the ammonia was pricking her nose, crawling up into her eyes. She turned her head, holding her breath, but kept her hands where they were.

"Is this a rule now?" the girl asked with a little more urgency. She pinched her nose. She wore her dark hair cut straight across her high forehead, which made her look stupid. "Are they making us do this now?"

Sally nodded and then, forced to exhale, laughed. She said, yes, all the tearoom girls were now required to wash their hands in ammonia. She said something about the health inspector. She listened to herself tell this lie, amused, but not surprised, to find that she was capable of such a small cruelty. She stirred her hands in the quickly cooling water. Ran one nail under the other and stirred her hands again. "There's a lot of sickness going around. They want us to be careful."

The girl considered this. She was a big girl with wide, droopy breasts beneath her street clothes, a woolen dress, an ill-fitting coat. It occurred to Sally that she looked far better in her tea-room uniform, cleaner, even smarter, in her apron and her cap. A face and body made for service.

Sally saw the girl eye what was left in the bottle of ammonia. "Help yourself," Sally said.

Side by side, the two of them bathed their hands, scooping up the sharply scented water and pouring it out again.

Telling it later, our mother said, "Like a pair of Pontius Pilates."

IN THE TEAROOM that afternoon, there was a lovely couple—a mother and a daughter. They were conferring like businessmen about the daughter's wedding reception here at the hotel, come June. The mother was an elegant lady with her veil drawn down over her eyes. The daughter wore a lovely suit with wide white lapels and a cinched waist. They both gave off a soft perfume. They spoke together, heads bent: orange blossom, she heard them say, stephanotis, lilac, lily of the valley. She heard them say June weather, vanilla cake, iced lemonade.

When they were gone, Sally found a linen handkerchief beneath their table, neatly folded, of a pretty, pale violet shade. It carried the women's perfume. She put it in her purse.

As she changed out of her uniform at the end of her shift, she was still repeating the words in her head, like the refrain of a song, like the words of a prayer: stephanotis, lilac, iced lemonade.

It was dark and bitter cold when she returned to the street. She had thrown her gloves away, and now she kept her raw hands plunged into her pockets, aware of the scent of ammonia that lingered on her skin.

Orange blossom and lily of the valley. Stephanotis. Iced lemonade. It occurred to her as she walked that if Mrs. Costello had died in her chair this afternoon, abandoned and alone, her mother and Mr. Costello would be free to marry. Come June, perhaps.

Holy

MRS. TIERNEY SAID, "Good for you," when Sally told her the next morning, through her bedroom door, that she was sleeping in. "Sure the Sisters can get along fine without you. Get your rest."

Liz Tierney was happy to think that the girl was growing somewhat weary of all her good works: all the holiness and the loneliness and the sacrifice.

Mrs. Tierney understood only that Sally, having had a false start on her vocation, was once again spending her mornings following the nuns. Getting her courage up to try again. The estrangement between her and her mother, Liz Tierney believed, was another matter altogether.

On the following morning, when Sally announced at breakfast that she would not be helping the nuns at all anymore,

Mrs. Tierney smiled. She told her own daughters, who were sitting right there with the girl at the kitchen table, that it was now their duty to make sure Sally had "a little fun at last." She said, sympathetic and forgiving, "It's an awful lot they ask of you, the Sisters. It's a difficult life." She said, "God's not going to hold it against you if you're something less than a blessed saint. Aren't we all human? Aren't we all doing the best we can?"

Elizabeth Tierney was full of admiration for the Sisters, who moved through the streets of the city in their black and white, doing good where it was needed, imposing good where they found it lacking.

She never failed to greet them as they passed—"Good morning, Sisters," "How are you, Sister?"—or to put a penny or two in their baskets whenever she saw them begging. And although she sympathized with Annie's disdain for the society ladies who raised money for the nuns, still Mrs. Tierney went to the bazaars and the card parties at the various convents and spent her husband's money lavishly on aprons and raffle tickets and crocheted blankets, for the sake of the Sisters.

The nuns did more good in the world than any lazy parish priest, she liked to say, especially in arguments with her husband, especially after he learned that she had squandered the week's household funds on euchre and bridge at some convent, or had given what he called "more than their fair share" to some plucky little Sister bound for pagan lands.

The priests were pampered momma's boys compared to these holy women, Liz Tierney would argue. "Princes of the Church, my eye," she would say—if only to get his goat—"Spoiled children they are. It's the nuns who keep things running."

Liz Tierney loved the nuns—adored them, she said—but she also harbored in her heart the belief that any woman who chose to spend a celibate life toiling for strangers was, by necessity, "a little peculiar."

Mrs. Tierney was a devout Catholic, but the kind of Catholic, she knew, who preferred the noise and humidity of the street after mass to the cool dampness of the sacristy, preferred conversation to prayer, sunlight to flickering shadow.

She was a Catholic woman who was more moved by the miraculous blood that colored the cheeks of her six children as they fidgeted in the pew than she was by any injunction from the pulpit regarding the watery stuff that flowed from His pierced side for the salvation of all men.

Liz Tierney had nothing against the salvation of all men. She was as grateful for the fact of heaven as she was sure of her path toward it. She counted the Blessed Mother as first among her confidantes. She loved the order and the certainty the Church gave her life, arranging the seasons for her, the weeks and the days, guiding her philosophies and her sorrows. She loved the hymns. She loved the prayers. She loved the way the Church—the priests and the Brothers and the nuns, as well as the handy threat of eternal damnation—ordered her disorderly children.

But holiness bored her.

She liked chaos, busyness, bustling. She liked a household strewn with clothes and dust and magazines and books, jump ropes, baseball bats, milk bottles. She liked the sight and the smell of overflowing ashtrays, of a man who's had a few drinks, of tabletops crowded with cloudy glasses. She loved falling into an unmade bed at the end of the long day, falling in beside her snoring husband—with maybe a child or two snagged in the covers—and never reaching, because sleep overtook her, the part of the Hail Mary that said: *Now and at the hour of our death.*

It was at the end of everything the Church had to say, in her opinion: Death was. And while she understood the need and logic of this, she had never found the subject of much interest.

Quoting her, our father sometimes said, "Isn't it funny how we all die at the same time? Always at the end of our lives. Why worry?"

Liz Tierney preferred the bright distractions of living. She liked a good fight. She liked a long talk with plenty of gossip in it. She liked her husband when his passions were at high tide, and her children when they were rocking the boat: running, or laughing, full of outrage, full of schemes. She liked the sound of many voices in her house—liked it better still when they rose in a chorus of song. She liked stories of sin far better than tales of virtue. She liked the salty taste of contradiction on her tongue. She hated idleness. And long silences. She hated to see anyone doing anything alone.

When Sister Lucy appeared at her door for the second time in nearly twenty years, Sally all bedraggled beside her, not gone to the convent after all, Mrs. Tierney was quietly delighted by the news of Annie's stolen afternoons—with the milkman, no less.

"You spoke up," she wanted to tell her friend, spoke up against the lousy certainties life had given her: a husband dead, a daughter to raise alone, daily labor, daily loneliness, dull duty. She said, in fact, when next she and Annie met, "An hour or two of an afternoon isn't much of a sin."

And so on the morning that Sally told her, still in her dressing gown and with the breakfast plates and cups and crusts still on the kitchen table, "I'm not following the Sisters anymore," Mrs. Tierney could only smile. It was a cold, dark morning and an icy rain was hitting the courtyard outside the window. Liz

Tierney was delighted to know that the girl wouldn't be going out into such weather, even to comfort the sick. "Oh, it's nice to get up in the morning," Mrs. Tierney said, singing it, as she brewed another pot of tea. "But it's nicer to stay in bed."

And then, not two weeks later, Mrs. Costello came down with pneumonia and Mr. Costello decided to amend his life. Annie told Liz Tierney this news without shedding a tear. She seemed to love the man all the more for it. He'd broken it off with her and then made a good confession, and, Annie said, "That's that."

"And you?" Liz Tierney said. "Have you made a good confession, too?"

Annie hushed her—they were walking arm-in-arm through the cold and leafless park. She said it was hardly a subject she would bring up in church, with a holy priest, no less. Wouldn't the poor man die of embarrassment?

They leaned together, laughing. But knowing, too, faithful as they were, that an immortal soul was at stake. "You could make a quick confession," Liz told her. "You wouldn't have to go into detail."

But Annie, stubborn, shook her head. "There's not a thing I'm sorry for," she said.

THAT NIGHT, a wet night in early February, Sally came back to the Tierneys' after her shift at the hotel and went up to her room. She and the twins were going to the movies in an hour. She had barely taken off her shoes and stockings and was drying her hair with a towel when there was a light tap at the door. Mrs. Tierney entered, and then closed the door behind her, leaning back against it, her hands on the doorknob behind her substantial hips. Her cheeks were bright red, as if she had just come in from the cold herself.

"You should know," Mrs. Tierney said, without preliminaries, "the situation has changed. For your mother." She studied Sally, as if to see if there was more she needed to say. She seemed briefly disappointed to find there was. "She no longer has her visitor. His wife is ill. He believes that's where his duty lies." And then she raised her eyebrows to say, Do you understand me now? And then smiled in relief as if Sally had actually said, I understand.

In fact, Sally said nothing at all.

Mrs. Tierney straightened up, brought her hands forward, drying them, although they were not wet, on her apron. "You are always welcome here, of course," she said. "You can stay as long as you like. But no one would wonder if you want to leave us now to go back to your own place."

She smoothed her apron over her skirt, her voice taut with the emotion she could not conceal. "Your mother is there by herself now," she said. "Entirely alone."

Still

THE LAMPS WERE ALL ON in Mrs. Costello's apartment, although daylight was at the bedroom window. A funereal hush about the place as the two nuns—Sister Jeanne and Sister Lucy today—bustled silently about. Sister Jeanne was putting the clean laundry in drawers and cupboards when Sally arrived. Sister Lucy was just turning from Mrs. Costello in the bed, her stethoscope around her neck, black against her silver cross and her white bib. Mrs. Costello's small face was wan. She was, Sister Lucy told Sister Jeanne, "weak as a kitten." In the corner by the window, there was a bullet-shaped oxygen tank beside a folded oxygen tent that was ghostly pale.

Sister Lucy glanced up at Sally as she stood in the door of

Mrs. Costello's bedroom, and then she said, indifferently, "Good. You're here."

She brushed down her sleeve with her crooked hand. Then reached into her pocket for her wristwatch on its worn leather strap. "All right, I'm off," she said. She took Sally by the arm and steered her out of the room. "Are you here for the duration or just stopping in?" she asked. Her eyes were moving and her mouth indicated that she was already certain no answer would satisfy. "Because I've been told you've abandoned this particular work of mercy," she went on, "which is fine, you're not obliged. You were never obliged to be here. But Jeanne's exhausted. She could use some help until Mr. Costello gets home. The missus is recovering, but slowly." She squinted a bit from the distance of her bonnet. "Mr. Costello will be home as soon as he can get here. Every morning now. Do you hear what I'm saying?"

Sally said, "I know."

Sister reached for her cloak, which was still damp and sparkling with the morning's rain. She swept the cloak over her shoulder, the stethoscope around her neck, tangled now with the chain of her cross. "Mrs. Costello will live," she said, as if she were merely ticking off the day's obligations. "Her husband will mend his ways." She smiled her thin-lipped smile, reaching back to adjust her veil. "I've never believed our God is a bargaining God, but men do. It's nonsense. While he was praying for her to live, she was praying to die. Which one of them struck the bargain?"

Sister Lucy sniffed disdainfully. "We kept her alive," she said. "God knows it."

Now she pulled off the stethoscope and stashed it angrily, as was her ordinary way, into her little black bag. "Mr. Costello returns around ten. Eleven at the latest. No one will blame you if you don't want to run into him. But stay a while and let Sister Jeanne catch her breath."

She lifted her bag, looked around the room. "Take a dust rag to those lampshades," she went on, "and to the baseboards. There's bread and butter in the kitchen. Some boiled eggs, applesauce. Get Jeanne to eat something, too. And put the kettle on. Bring them both a nice cup of tea. Fortify it with plenty of milk and sugar." And then Sister Lucy was out the door.

Sally still wore her coat and hat, and her pocketbook was still on her arm. She stood in the room, briefly uncertain. The nuns had the two lamps turned on and the light in the kitchen as well. New, if gray and muted, sunlight was streaming into the bedroom from the one window. It was nearly 7 a.m. The radiator against the far wall was hissing and ticking, but the draft left by Sister Lucy's exit swept the room, hollowing out the warmth. Sally shivered. In her purse was the violet handkerchief she had picked up from the floor of the tearoom. Tied into it, like a hobo's pack, was a good handful of alum.

Sally put her purse on the slipcovered chair. She took off her coat and her hat and placed them over it. Then she went into the kitchen to put the kettle on for tea. While it boiled, she went back to the living room and picked up her purse. Now she put it on the small kitchen table. She set out on the counter two of Mrs. Costello's teacups, spooned tea into the silver tea ball, and placed it inside the tin pot. When the water boiled, she poured it in. She went to her purse, easily found the violet handkerchief.

She untied the knot and shook the alum into the empty cup. She poured the tea over it and immediately the water grew cloudy. The faint odor that arose was redolent of Sister's Immaculate's laundry. She added sugar and milk and then tasted the

221

mixture from the spoon. There was the bitter sharpness of what was not tea. In the cupboard over the sink, Mr. Costello kept a bottle of whiskey. Sally had seen it before. Quickly she reached up for the bottle and poured a splash into the tea, briefly recalling the Bronx girl on the train. She tied up the handkerchief again and returned it to her purse. She snapped the purse closed, and the sound of the lock reverberated. It echoed, she was certain.

She carried the teacup on its saucer, the spoon rattling, into the bedroom. Mrs. Costello was propped in the bed as she had been. Sister Jeanne was taking her pulse.

"Sister Lucy said to bring her some tea," Sally whispered. "There's some waiting for you in the kitchen, too." She kept her hand over the cup, as if to contain the scent of what she had done. She felt her palm grow damp with steam. There was something painful rising to her throat. She knew she could always drop the cup. Mrs. Costello's eyes fluttered open, that meaningless blue of them. "I don't want it," she whispered. "Go away." She coughed weakly and tried to move down into the bed.

Sister Jeanne was adjusting the pillows behind her head. "It's better for your lungs if you can sit up a bit, dear," she said gently. Sally could tell Sister Jeanne had said this many times before. "I know you are tired, Mrs. Costello, but it's better if you can give your lungs some room."

Mrs. Costello coughed again and then narrowed her eyes like an angry child. "I'm tired of you," she said.

Sister Jeanne said, "You're tired in general, Mrs. Costello. A little tea. Something to eat, and you'll start feeling stronger."

She signaled to Sally to come around the bed. "Just a spoonful," she whispered. "A spoonful at a time. I'll bring some food."

Sally's hand was trembling as she held the cup, and the cup

was rattling against the saucer. The alum was at the bottom. Her plan was to give Mrs. Costello some sips of liquid, and then to spoon up the wet alum from the bottom of the cup and fill her mouth with it. Stop her throat with it. Stop her breath.

Her plan was to exchange her own immortal soul for her mother's mortal happiness.

It was a ridiculous plan. Even this far along, she knew it was ridiculous. She knew it was ridiculous when she first conceived of it—walking home from the hotel on that bitter night, thinking lilac and stephanotis, a wedding in June, and considering how only a miserable woman, blood and stink and complaint, bird bones and pale skin, stood in the way of her mother's happiness, her mother's place in heaven.

She knew it was ridiculous just yesterday when she coaxed Sister Illuminata up the stairs for the three o'clock prayers. ("Wouldn't you rather pray in the chapel, Sister?" she had asked. Butter wouldn't melt in her mouth. "How long has it been since you've spent the afternoon hour away from your ironing board?") And then filled the violet handkerchief with Sister's alum— meant, Sally knew, for making flameproof the nuns' veils, the donated infant clothes, the kitchen curtains. Telling herself all the while her plan was ridiculous. She would never do it. Never find the nerve.

And then waking so early this morning in her bed in the Tierney house. The mad sounds of the morning routine echoing through the walls. Feet pounding on the stairs and Mr. Tierney pounding on the bathroom door. The girls complaining they needed to get in there, too. A refrain of "Can I wear your . . . Can I borrow . . ." passed among the four of them. And Patrick calling to Michael, and Mrs. Tierney calling to the twins. Mr. Tierney singing wordlessly in his lovely baritone as he passed her doorway, going down the hall. The whistle of the kettle and the snap crack of bacon frying in the pan. Toast burning. And smelling again that moment when she believed, stupid and dumbfounded but, still, full of belief, that her father had returned in her absence, had returned to restore her mother's happiness, her bright laughter, her life. To keep her from being entirely alone.

A ridiculous plan, she knew, even as she got up in the cold room and dressed and then, lying, told Mrs. Tierney she was going to see her mother at the convent. The lie itself, spoken out loud, making her ridiculous plan, her terrible plan, just that much more possible, the first step toward what she wanted to do. She told her lie and left the house, and suddenly her scheme was not merely a flight of her imagination but something possible. Something she might actually accomplish in the world: her mother's life, her mortal life and her eternal life, restored.

"Going by the convent to see my mother," she had said, lying so smoothly, leaving the house, and instead climbing the stairs to Mrs. Costello's apartment. Letting herself in. The good handful of alum in her purse, wrapped in the fragrant handkerchief.

And now here she was, standing alone with it at the edge of Mrs. Costello's bed.

She skimmed a mouthful of the tea and slowly moved it toward the woman's lips. Mrs. Costello took it easily, swallowed, touched her lips together. But then shook her head. She coughed, put her whole body into the cough and said, "No more."

"A few more," Sally said. She felt a fever flush, that unnatural heat, rise up into her collar, over her face. Mrs. Costello took another, listless sip. Her lips were dry, mean, and thin. Pale hairs sprouted along the length of them. The bones in her face, her cheeks and her chin, had grown prominent. She was thin and pale, barely a wisp of a body. Barely there. Hardly a real presence in the room at all: no chest and narrow hips and only one good leg under the sheet and the counterpane. And yet the impediment to so many things.

Sally spooned up the mixture at the bottom of the cup.

Now Sister Jeanne came into the room again. She, too, had a teacup in her hand, and a spoon. "If you would take a bite to eat, Mrs. Costello," she was saying as she approached the bed. "Maybe a bit of applesauce."

Mrs. Costello, still coughing, delicately now, was repeating her small, piping "No." Sinking again against her pillows. "Step aside, dear," Sister Jeanne said to Sally. She placed herself between the two.

Sally turned to the dresser and caught her own reflection in the mirror. She looked pale and disheveled, wild-eyed, ridiculous. A kind of madness in the way she clutched the delicate cup and saucer to her chest. A kind of madness in the very notion of it: to stop a woman's throat. Stop her breath. To brush aside her thin and useless life, burdensome as it was, in order to get what she was seeking for the mother she loved above all else.

She looked at the young faces in the wedding photo.

Mrs. Costello's two good feet were in satin shoes just under the lace hem of her dress. Mr. Costello's black hair was thick and wavy, glistening with pomade.

Weren't they wild-eyed, too, looking out from the past?

Mrs. Costello was coughing again. Sally glanced over her shoulder, and then, in the time it took her to turn fully, the cough seemed to change register. The woman had sunk lower still in the bed, but now, suddenly, her spine arched as she coughed and her head fell back. She lifted her face from the pillow like a swimmer breaking water. Blotches of red appeared on her cheeks and her neck—they had the scattered and arbitrary shapes of shattered pottery. Mrs. Costello pressed her palms against the mattress, as if to rise, and then the coughing took hold of her completely, her shortened leg flailing with it. Sally moved toward her and felt the tea rise up over the rim of the cup, wetting her blouse. She spun around to put the teacup down, and when she turned once again, it was into Sister Jeanne's dark back. Sister had stepped away from the bed, although her white bonnet was still aimed toward Mrs. Costello. She still held in her hands the cup of applesauce and the poised spoon. The woman's coughing changed register once more, no longer a battling out of air—a sound like the beating of laundry—but of sucking air in, deep and wounded and gulping. Her small mouth was open, and now so were her pale eyes, full of more expression than Sally had ever seen: panic, fear, pain, astonishment.

Sally heard herself cry out. She took hold of the nun's sleeve. "Help her, Sister. She's choking."

Without turning her head, Sister Jeanne moved her arm, held it across Sally's waist, the spoon still in her hand, showing the girl that she should keep her distance. Sister Jeanne held her arm steady, her eyes on Mrs. Costello. She was steadfast and calm.

Sally apprehended only vaguely that Sister Jeanne knew it was better to wait, to stand back, to let the fit, the nonsense, pass.

Mrs. Costello's face was deeply purple now. The sound coming from her was like a braying, a tearing. Sally could see the woman's tongue in her wet mouth, between her blue lips. Her chest was heaving, seeming to turn the wisp of her body inside out. Mrs. Costello curled herself against the racket her lungs were making, against the struggle to breathe, bringing her good leg up to her middle, bowing her head down as if to meet it. And then her coughing changed register again, falling off, suddenly subsiding. Sally could once again hear the rain rattling down the gutters of the building.

And then Sister Lucy was in the room like night descending. She was still in her dark cloak, which seemed to be sailing, her black veil sailing, too. Both sparkled with drops of rain. Briefly, the room was infused with the smell of rain. Sister Lucy was on the bed, hovering over the bed, Mrs. Costello, light as a feather, in her arms, so easily and familiarly it seemed the woman moved of her own accord, gave herself over to Sister Lucy's embrace. And now Sister Jeanne was at the edge of the bed as well, holding the woman's shoulders as both nuns swiftly sat her up, slapped her wrists, and pounded her back. And then, gently, like a mother with a small child, Sister Lucy cradled Mrs. Costello's head in the crook of her dark sleeve. Time passed. The woman seemed soothed. The two Sisters eased her down again. Sally saw Mrs. Costello's long braid, neatly done, swing forward. She was limp, her mouth was gaping, and then Sister Lucy's cloak covered her face as the nun brushed her forehead with her thumb, brushing away some perspiration or a tear. Sally saw Sister Jeanne bless herself. Sister Lucy did the same.

And then a strange silence, barely broken by the rain at the window. The two nuns began to move about the bed with such grace and assurance that Sally imagined they were enacting a long-established routine. Sister Lucy cupped the woman's head in her hand, lifting her skull to adjust the pillows underneath. Then she gently placed it down again. Sister Jeanne had pushed back the sheet and blanket and was arranging her nightgown over her legs, gently moving the good one, which had become bent in her ordeal, to a straighter, more comfortable position, moving the pliable shortened one into alignment. Then she pulled the skirt of her nightgown down to her ankle.

Without a word, the two nuns lifted the twisted bed linens, up into the air and then down again, refreshed and smoothed. They tucked her in neatly. Sister Lucy moved the thin rope of Mrs. Costello's braid to her shoulder and then, with a handkerchief from her deep pocket, wiped the scattered spittle of applesauce, the smooth part, from her lips. She returned the handkerchief to her pocket while Sister Jeanne went to the window to let in some cool air.

It wasn't until they both knelt, side by side in the lamp-lit room, that Sally understood Mrs. Costello was dead.

On the dresser was the teacup with the concoction she had stirred together, it seemed hours and hours ago now. The tea had splattered when she placed it down. Threw it down. There was the smell of whiskey. Beside it, too, was the cup and spoon Sister Jeanne had brought in to feed the woman. Sally had not seen her put it down. Inside the cup, Mrs. Odette's applesauce, with its lumps and bits of peel.

It all struck her as senseless now: food and drink carried in just a moment ago, carried in to feed a body now lifeless. An absurdity.

Slowly, with nothing to hold on to, Sally sank to her knees behind the two nuns. Behind their dark veils and skirts and the worn, upturned soles of their black shoes. They were saying the Hail Mary. Sally sat back on her heels. The rug here was a worn Persian, not unlike the rug in Sister Illuminata's laundry, where she had played as a child. It was clean enough, Sally thought, but perhaps threaded here and there with street sand or mud. Whatever Mr. Costello brought in on his big farmer's feet. It was February. No doubt the rug had been swept often in these last few months, but not taken out for a beating since spring.

Now Sister Lucy was standing, slowly, leaning on Mrs.

Costello's bed to get to her feet. Mrs. Costello's body moved slightly in response to the pressure on the mattress. Sister Jeanne knelt still, her head bent. Sister Lucy, towering over them all now, looked down at Sally and tilted her head to indicate that she should leave the room. "Pick up those cups," Sister Lucy said, her voice weary. Sally had never before heard weariness in Sister Lucy's voice. Obediently, she picked up the cup and saucer with the poisoned tea and ran her finger through the ring of the cup of applesauce. She held both close to her chest. On her way out, Sister Lucy stopped at the dresser, opened a drawer, and removed one of Mrs. Costello's neatly folded nightgowns, the one Sister Jeanne had put away just minutes ago. She put it on the top of the dresser and went out.

Sally followed the nun into the kitchen. Sister Lucy lifted the teakettle and then filled it at the sink and put a flame under it on the stove. She went to the kitchen cupboard and found a tin washbasin. She poured the warmed water into the basin and then, as if just remembering something—she let out a "tut" and shook her head—she went back into the living room. And quickly returned with her cloak taken off and her apron over her habit, her veil tied back with a black ribbon. She poured the rest of the water into the basin, took a bar of soap from the milk box beside the draped tub, placed it in the water. She lifted the basin and walked out. Pausing as she did to look Sally up and down, the two cups and the saucer still clutched to her chest. She saw Sister Lucy's eyes look into the cup of applesauce, saw her eyebrow rise. But Sister Lucy only said, "Clean up, won't you?"

Sally poured the tea and the pale dregs of sugar and alum into the sink. She scraped the applesauce into the sink as well and saw the large pieces of apple and apple peel hesitate at the mouth of the drain. She pushed them through with the spoon, running the water until all of it was washed away. She could not think of the future. She could not think of the next hour. And all of the recent past seemed faded and unreal. She could barely recall her ridiculous plan. What had she wanted, exactly? Why was she here?

She took the dust rag and the broom from the corner and returned to the living room, where she ran the rag along the two faded lampshades, then across the mantel of the sealed fireplace. Over the statue of St. Joseph with his hammer in his fist, his hand to his heart. From the bedroom, she could hear the two nuns moving about; there was the swish of the water in the basin, the clean scent of the soap, the occasional exchange of brief words, "Another towel, Sister," "Thank you, Sister," "If you'll just hold her there . . ."

Sister Jeanne emerged from the room with the basin full of soapy water, but her head was bent and Sally could not see her face. She heard her empty the water and put a few things away. And then she passed through the room again. She touched Sally's arm and looked up at her. Sally could see that her eyes were bloodshot and her face was drained of color, gray against her white coif and the white brim of her bonnet. Her small mouth was drawn. "Come in for a prayer," she whispered.

Reluctantly, Sally leaned the broom against the mantel, placed the dust rag beside it. She ran her damp palms over her skirt. Sister Jeanne waited for her at the door of the bedroom, and then put her arm out as Sally approached, to indicate that the girl should go ahead of her. Sally recalled the way Sister Jeanne had put out her arm as she'd tried to near Mrs. Costello's bed, blocking her way.

The room held a new light. At first Sally thought the day outside had cleared, sunlight breaking through the clouds and the window shades, but then she saw that two candles were lit on the dresser. The smell of the new flame mixed pleasantly with the fresh linen on the bed and the lingering scent of the soap they had used to bathe her. Mrs. Costello was as she had been. Her body still and narrow under the counterpane, the slope of her knee, the space of her missing leg. Her hands were now crossed over the breast of her fresh nightgown, small wisps of damp hair prettily framing her face. Her face was as pale as ever, but there was a new grayness to her lips, and her features had grown sharper, more finely honed.

The china-faced dolls on the dresser were terrible.

Sally began to cry. She lowered her head. She gave herself over to it freely. She thought of nothing at all, not the last hour or days or weeks, nothing of the hours ahead. Sister Jeanne put an arm around her waist. Sally felt the nun's small hand press itself into her side, clutching and letting go. Everything she had planned, imagined, hoped for, all her fraught negotiations with herself, with God, with the future and the past, were nothing before this stillness. She could not trace, for the moment, what had brought her here, could not parse, for a moment, what it meant. She simply cried. The scent of candle flame and soap and Sister Jeanne's habit, the fresh handkerchief the little nun placed gently into her hands. Sister Lucy. The sound of rain on the windows, rattling in the gutters. The still figure on the bed and the scent, too, of death, animal death, a dead mouse behind the wall, encroaching on the room.

Sister Lucy said, whispering—Sally had never heard her whisper before—"Mr. Costello will be home shortly." Which meant Sally should go.

She returned to the living room with Sister Jeanne, still drying her tears. She put on her hat and her coat—it seemed a lifetime since she had taken them off—and then had to return to the kitchen for her purse. Sister Jeanne followed her. She said, "Take a drink of water before you go. Put a little cold water on your face," and Sally went to the sink to obey. And then as she turned, Sister Jeanne handed her the pocketbook. The clasp was open. Sister held on to the strap for just the extra second it took for her to raise her head, to meet Sally's eyes. Sister Jeanne said, "You did no harm, dear. Whatever you'd thought to do." She said, "God is fair. He knows the truth."

SALLY WENT DOWN THE NARROW STAIRS of Mrs. Costello's building and walked the sixteen blocks to the hotel. The streets crackled with the sound of rain, and voices, and cars and trucks. Someone shouted, some girls in a shop doorway laughed, a procession of solemn faces under raised umbrellas passed her by, some looking at her, some looking away, and all unaware—she believed, briefly—of the stillness that would overtake them. Overtake their features, their gesturing arms and hands, their moving mouths and chests. She reached the hotel and saw the hurrying figures, coming in and out, making the glass doors flash, Mr. Tierney himself in his beige uniform, a whistle to his lips, his hand in the air, the black street shining like patent leather at his feet. His laughing mouth and thick mustache—as a coin was slipped into his hand, slipped into his pocket—all unaware of the paralysis that would come to them, the sudden stillness, final, irrevocable. She went inside, down the elevator to the employees' room. She imagined as she changed each of the girls who chatted around her with her head limp, caught in the gentle crook of a dark arm, eased down to a pillow, still. She saw in the tearoom, the calm hush of the place—gentle rattle of cups and saucers and spoons, soft mouthing of cakes and sandwiches, murmured conversation—the dumb oblivion of the human race. A terrible stillness would overtake them all, come what may. A terrible silence would stop their breaths, one way or another, and yet they spooned sugar into their cups or leaned back to take a watch from a waistband or pressed a linen napkin to their pink lips.

She walked home after work, in the cold darkness, under streetlamps encircled with fog. How would she live, having seen what she had seen? It had been one thing to refuse the convent, to say, "I've thought better of it," after the long train ride showed her the truth of the dirty world, showed her that her own impulse was to meet its filthy citizens not with a consoling cloth, but with a curse, a punch in the face. But now it was life itself she wanted to refuse, for how could she live knowing that stillness, that inconsequence, that feral smell of death, was what her days were aiming her toward?

Each church she passed was faintly lit at this odd hour of the day. Lent had begun. She knew the statues inside were covered in purple shrouds. Something familiar in their wet stone and shadow as she passed them. Dampness and cold rock. Familiar but comfortless. She walked to the convent. Here the lamplight at the windows seemed dim as well. The nuns would be praying at the weary end of their hard day. She walked to her own apartment—her mother's apartment—and saw the light was on in the bedroom window. Was her mother in there entirely alone, or was it Mr. Costello returned to her? She had not thought of him all afternoon. Or of her mother's life ahead. Lilac, lily of the valley. June weather. Now they were free to wed. She tried to let the notion, something about happiness, about the brightness of the coming days, flood her bones, her nerves—the way prayer could sometimes relieve that electric itch to move. But no thoughts of summer could soothe her recollection of Mrs. Costello gone still.

The violet handkerchief with the remnant of the alum was still in her purse.

Her intentions, her murderous, ridiculous scheme, struck her as childish now, naïve and innocent. She had wanted to save her mother's soul even if it meant the death of her own. But she hadn't known, childish, naïve as she was, what any of it meant.

Her father knew. Had known it all along, lying in his hollowed-out place underground: a stillness no prayer, no wish, no imagining, no sacrifice could overcome. Of course he would never return to them.

She let herself into the Tierney kitchen. She had been walking for hours. Tom and Patrick were at the kitchen table under a single bulb, books and papers spread before them. They were both taking night classes. They looked up with sibling indifference when she came in. "We were wondering what happened to you," Tom said. "Ma thought you'd gone back to your mother's."

Once more she slipped out of her hat and her coat, which were now heavy with rain, and hung them on the hooks by the door. She put her purse on the floor and came into the dim light of the kitchen.

"You look like a drowned rat," Patrick said blithely, and then, without standing, pulled out the chair beside him. "Take a load off," he said. "Have a glass of milk." He leaned back to get a glass from the drain board and filled it from the bottle already on the table. He put it before her as she sat, and then, in the way of siblings, the two ignored her completely as they went back to their studies. She had never in her life been so weary, not even after her two sleepless nights on the train.

Patrick was explaining some diagram to Tom, something he

had already drawn on notebook paper. Tom was running his hand through his hair, making it stand on end, resisting the explanation.

"Water seeks its own level," Patrick said. "Don't you get it?"

Tom said impatiently, "No, I don't get it. And saying it over and over again isn't going to make any difference. What does it mean? Are you telling me water has a brain, a pair of eyes? Does it go about with its arms stuck out like a blind man? It's nonsense."

Patrick leaned over the page. "What it means is . . . ," he said, and moved his finger across the paper. "Just try to follow. Here's the aqueduct. Here's the water tower. There's the conduit. There's the valve. Are you following?"

"I'm listening," Tom said. "But I'm not following." In the dim kitchen light, his features were shadowed. He was taller than his brother, and heavier as well. There was a hooded look about his eyes. He was slow-witted and Patrick was quick. This was a given in the family. The source of many jokes, the brunt of which was equally divided between them: Tom for the mistakes he made out of ignorance, Patrick for the mistakes he made out of arrogance.

"Well, then," Patrick went on, "water seeks its own level," and before he could continue, Tom was on his feet. "That's it," he said. "I'm through." He turned to Sally. "You can talk to this parrot if you like. What I seek is some sleep." He stabbed a hand at the wide kitchen sink. "Turn on the tap if you want to find out what the water is seeking."

He walked out of the kitchen, and then they heard his footsteps on the stairs. Patrick shrugged, took back his diagram, and slipped it into one of his books. He began to straighten his papers. Awkward in the sudden silence. "Would you like some more milk?" he asked her. She hadn't touched the glass he'd poured.

"No, thank you," she said. He emptied the bottle into his own glass and then looked at it unhappily, shook his head, annoyed, as if someone else had poured it. As if, with his glass now full, he was forced to remain at the table with her. He lifted it and drank.

"My mother thought you'd gone back to your own place tonight," he said, putting it down again and wiping his lip. "When you didn't come in."

Sally said, "No."

Cautiously, he added, "She says you're going back to your mother's, though."

Sally said, "I don't know." She was uncertain what Patrick understood about her mother's situation. She imagined very little. It was hardly something Mrs. Tierney would discuss with a grown son. Hardly something a young man like Patrick would have any interest in. For the past few months, the family merely pretended, by some unspoken agreement, that Sally had taken their spare room in order to be closer to the hotel, although Mr. Tierney had gotten her the job in the tearoom only after Sister Lucy had brought her here, not before.

She put her hand on the tall glass of milk on the table. She said, "The lady I sometimes visit in the morning, Mrs. Costello," and paused, "she passed away today while I was there."

Patrick slumped in his chair, as if he had absorbed a soft blow. He blessed himself. "Sorry to hear that," he said. "Was she ill?"

"She had pneumonia," Sally said. And then added, "She was a one-legged woman. They had to take off her leg when a dog bite became infected. This was years ago. It made her somewhat touched." And she touched her temple so he would understand.

Patrick drank from his glass again, and then lowered it reluctantly. He searched his memory for something, alighted on it, and then asked her, "Is this the milkman's wife?" as if he had just put two and two together. He gestured toward the bottle on the drain board. It was clear from his expression that he was immediately uncertain if this was the proper question to ask.

Sally said, "That's right."

He nodded again. Resolved to set the conversation on a better track. Said, "My mother mentioned how nice you were to go sit with her. It couldn't have been easy. One-legged and touched in the head, like you said." And was pleased with himself.

Sally said, "No, it was not. Not always."

Then they sat in silence. Two flights up, his father was snoring. Mr. Tierney could raise the roof on some nights. She saw Patrick glance at her, gauging her appreciation for the sound, embarrassed by it. It occurred to Sally that he was incapable of keeping anything out of his face, his eyes—clever as he was, you could read his every thought if you watched him carefully.

It was difficult to think of such a face gone still.

He said, "Did you ever hear my father's story about Red Whelan? I mean, speaking of the one-legged among us."

She said no, and so he told it.

He took the long way round with the tale, adding, as was his wont in those days when he was the brighter son, everything he knew about the history of the Civil War, the charms of the doorman's trade, his parent's storied romance, and that spring evening—dinnertime, the lilac bush at the dining room window not yet in bloom—when Red Whelan, his grandfather's substitute in the war, knocked at the door.

And he ended it all with a flourish, indicating with a sweep of his right hand the tin ceiling of the kitchen and the fine five-bedroom house above it, as if the house, the brick and stone of it, proved the validity of all he had told her. As if the tale itself, only talk, only breath on air, had nevertheless brought them both to this solid and irrefutable present where they were alone together in the middle of the night, alone and awake and—true for him, at least—in love.

He gestured widely with his right hand at the end of all his talking, because in his left he held Sally's thin fingers. They had, at long last, grown warm in his grip and he was reluctant to let them go.

Grace

OUR FATHER SAID, "After that, your mother's life went from black-and-white to color. In my humble opinion."

Her mother's wedding in June. Although it was a brief weekday ceremony in the empty church, still there was lilac and lily of the valley. And then the shedding of those two apartments—one thick with paint and repaint, the other as sparse as a monk's cell. They bought a brownstone in Liz Tierney's neighborhood. Mr. Tierney himself providing a generous loan out of his "reparations." Then—"just under the wire," our father said, "all kinds of wires"—Annie, at forty-eight, giving birth to another daughter on a bright morning. Grace, they called her.

Sally pushed the child in the perambulator when Annie

went back to the convent laundry to help out—there had been another young widow hired while Annie was in confinement, another young widow with a child who played on the floor.

Patrick Tierney joined her in these walks whenever he could—reminiscing, even then, about the charmed lives they had led as children, taken out every morning by their two mothers. The two empresses, he called them. Sally told him those days, her days as a convent child, were a pale dream when compared to the life she now lived: in a tall house with a baby sister and a mother who knew some leisure. And a father of sorts. Mr. Costello never could look her straight in the eye, but the apology he seemed always on the verge of offering made him both tongue-tied and tender in her presence. He grew dear to her.

The courtship that began on the long night that Patrick Tierney had talked and talked in his mother's kitchen didn't end until Grace headed off to school, and he finally found the courage to propose.

Sally was mourning the loss of the little girl's steady presence in her days when he asked her, "How about some babies of your own?"

As inelegant a proposal, our father said, as any man has ever made.

WHEN OUR FATHER WAS VERY OLD—we were growing old ourselves—he told again the story he had told her that wet night, the story of his grandfather's funeral, the train ride, the Irish maid behind the screen.

If your mother hadn't come back from the nuns, our father said, that's probably the girl I'd have married.

He remembered once more his father's chestnut mustache

and his trim suit, his flask of whiskey. And then his father's tears in the dark hours of that dreadful night. Love's a tonic, his mother had said, not a cure.

Old Red Whelan.

We were gathered in our father's room. His own lifetime across a dozen different tenements, a fine house with five bedrooms, the tumbledown site of our own happy childhoods, now compressed into a bedroom and a bath and a small kitchenette, his days now confined to the high-rise facility he had selected for himself after our mother died, selected with a bachelor's care: something simple and sparse and his alone.

He had begun to remind us, without the least prompting, that he'd had a good life, repeating the tales of his crowded childhood, his elegant father, his mother, who was as sharp as a knife.

Our mother, who thought to be a nun, but then thought better of it. "St. Saviour, you know, was her baptismal name."

A fatherless girl, a convent child in white wool. The girl he always knew he would marry.

Growing old ourselves, we indulged him. We listened to the same stories told again and kept silent about the truth: that our mother's midlife melancholy was clinical depression, unspoken of in those days.

That Great-aunt Rose's happy tremor as we guided her up the stairs was surely the Parkinson's that had visited us as well.

That the holy nuns who sailed through the house when we were young were a dying breed even then. The Bishop with his eye on their rich man's mansion even then. The call to sanctity and self-sacrifice, the delusion and superstition it required, fading from the world even then.

We asked, And how much would they have paid him—Red

Whelan—because it was history we were talking about so comfortably, here at the end of our father's days and the new waning of our own. History was easy: the past with all loss burned out of it, all sorrow worn out of it—all that was merely personal comfortably removed.

How much would it have cost his grandfather to hire a substitute during the Civil War?

We did a search. From the computer on our father's desk we read out: *The Conscription Act of 1863* . . . we read out, *three hundred dollars . . . an option available only to the well-off.*

And Lincoln, too, had a substitute, we discovered. Who knew? A young man recruited to serve in Lincoln's stead. Brought to the White House, given the Commander's blessing. Given a short war, it turned out. An article in an old *New York Times* about a statue proposed to honor the young man in his own hometown, the young man who had agreed to serve as Lincoln's substitute in the Civil War.

Although not at Ford's Theatre, we said, laughing about it. We said he'd have done the President more good if he'd served as his substitute at Ford's Theatre.

Our father said, "My father told his old man, 'One life's already been given to save your skin.' And never forgave himself for the cruelty of it."

He said, "It was all a very long time ago."

Scrolling down—the black newsprint quaintly askew—we saw on the same page: SUICIDE ENDANGERS OTHERS.

"That would be the man," our father said when we read it to him. "That would be Jim, your mother's father. A suicide then," he said sadly. "A suicide in the family."

He said, "Thank God your mother never knew."

We thought of the hushed afternoons of our childhood, our

mother sleeping off her melancholy, the nuns sailing in—standing in for She Who Could Not Be Replaced—keeping her in the world. Keeping her for us.

We marveled to think of it: how much went unspoken in those days. How much they believed was at stake.

"Well, the truth's out now," our father said.

Endless Length of Days

SISTER JEANNE asked us, "Have you ever worn an itchy old coat? The wool's too rough and it's tight in the sleeves. And you can't run in it too well because it binds here and there, across your hips. You've outgrown it, see? Maybe you put it on in the morning cause it's all you've got, and maybe it's a dark morning and cold, but then the sun goes up in the sky—even on a cold and cloudy day, the sun goes up, doesn't it, day after day—so by three o'clock, when you're walking home from school, there's sunlight hitting you on the head, feeling like a big hand pressing down, or maybe a sledgehammer. It's heating up your shoulders and your back, and you're starting to feel prickly inside that stiff old coat. You're feeling all perspiry, see, and prickly hot."

She hunched her shoulders in their dark serge to demonstrate our discomfort. Inside her bonnet she was smiling at us. Behind her in the frame of the dining room window, the long shadows of a golden afternoon or a descending dusk, a snow squall or spring blossoms, maybe a gray rain.

"And what will you do the minute you come through that door?" She pointed over our heads to the kitchen door, and we turned as if we would see ourselves, evoked by her words, coming into the house as we always did: hand to the glass knob, shoulder to the peeling paint.

"Don't I know what you'll do? Didn't I do it myself as a girl? You'll shimmy and shake and fight and jiggle until you get that old coat off. You'll pull the sleeves inside out."

Inside the white bonnet she closed her deep-set eyes. She raised her clasped hands to her chin—a round, protruding chin, brushed with rosacea, like the sun blush of a laborer from the field—and touched the steeple of her two index fingers to her small mouth. She said, her eyes closed, "When you finally get the old thing off, the air in this house will feel as cool and as sweet as silk on your skin, won't it? It will feel like cool water on the back of your neck and on your wrists." She opened her eyes again and we saw that they were bright with tears. "It will be like when your mother's sheets are out on the line, maybe on an afternoon in the fall or in the spring, and you walk through them when nobody's watching. You let those sheets brush over your face and slide over your head and then fall down your back, don't you? And then you turn around to do it again. I've seen you. Sweet-smelling, they are. And clean."

She laughed, her eyes shining. "That's how good the air feels when you've shucked off that old coat, isn't it?"

She said, "That's how you'll feel when you get to heaven, see? A long time from now for you, please God. Very soon for your old aunty."

And then a shadow passed across her face, although her back was to the bright window, although there was no telling its source. Her skin looked gray, her eyes lost their laughter. "But it's not for me," she said, "that relief. Never for me. That beauty."

She said, "I lost heaven a long time ago." She put her hand on the chain that held the crucifix around her neck, gripped it against her white bib. "Back when your mother was still a girl. All of eighteen, I think." She paused, thoughtful. "Out of love, I lost it. Which sounds funny, doesn't it? You'd think you could only lose heaven out of hate." She shrugged, always girlish. "But I lost it all the same."

Above us, our mother was sleeping off the melancholy that claimed her, even in the midst of our bright and happy childhoods. Old Aunt Rose, already a figure from a long ago past, was dusted with dust in our attic room.

Sister Jeanne touched her fist to her breast. Behind her, a swarm of blossoms, of yellowing leaves, of snow or frozen rain. "I gave up my place in heaven a long time ago," she said. "Out of love for my friends."

Inside her white bonnet, her small eyes, an old woman's fading eyes, were moving over us. Briefly, something affectionate, even joyful, overcame the sorrow in them, but only briefly. When that gray shadow returned, we recognized it not as a passing light, no more than the blink of an eye, but as a grief that had always been there in her dear old face. "God knows my heart," she said. "So I don't ask for His forgiveness, see?"

The fist that held the chain that held her crucifix opened itself out until her fingers were splayed over her heart.

She said, "I'll never shed this old coat. And that will be my torment."

Once more her eyes went around the table, touched each of our faces. "But you'll pray for me, won't you?" she asked. "You'll pray for this lost soul?"

We said we would, understanding none of it. Or believing, perhaps, that it was only her great humility, her holiness, that made her say she was unworthy of heaven.

And then, in her familiar way, the grin in her voice gave over to laughter. We saw her fragile shoulders move against her dark veil. We felt her delight in us, which was familiar as well, delight in our presence, our living and breathing selves—a tonic for all sorrow.

She whispered, "God has hidden these things from the wise and prudent, see? He's revealed them only to the little ones."